Toño the Infa...

Evelio Rosero

Toño the Infallible
a novel

translated from the Spanish
by Victor Meadowcroft
& Anne McLean

**A NEW DIRECTIONS
PAPERBOOK ORIGINAL**

Manufactured in the United States of America
First published as a New Directions Paperbook (NDP1539) in 2022
Design by Erik Rieselbach

Library of Congress Cataloging-in-Publication Data
Names: Rosero, Evelio, 1958– author. | Meadowcroft, Victor, translator. |
McLean, Anne, 1962– translator.
Title: Toño the infallible / Evelio Rosero ; translated from the Spanish
by Victor Meadowcroft & Anne McLean.
Other titles: Toño Ciruelo. English
Description: First edition. | New York, NY : New Directions Publishing
Corporation, 2022.
Identifiers: LCCN 2022018817 | ISBN 9780811228817 (paperback ; acid-free paper) |
ISBN 9780811234535 (ebook)
Subjects: LCGFT: Novels.
Classification: LCC PQ8180.28.O7 T6613 2022 | DDC 863/.64—dc23/eng/20220426
LC record available at https://lccn.loc.gov/2022018817

2 4 6 8 10 9 7 5 3 1

New Directions Books are published for James Laughlin
by New Directions Publishing Corporation
80 Eighth Avenue, New York 10011

to that fish

Contents

Book One

1

Confession

I WAS ALONE WHEN SOMEONE POUNDED ON MY DOOR. WHO could it be? Nobody had called at this house for a century, and certainly not like that. I stayed where I was, sitting in the living room, the open book like a hat on my knee. I asked who it was.

"Open up, hombre, I'm about to shit myself!"

The gruff voice loomed like a lightning flash in my memory, leaped toward me from the other side of an abyss of twenty years. It was Antonio Ciruelo; it couldn't be. It was Toño. Toño the Infallible, Crack-of-Dawn Toño, Toño the Ubiquitous, sickeningly, Toño.

"Just open this door!"

I opened up, and Toño Ciruelo raced past me like a wildfire; he tossed his Arhuaca shoulder bag into a corner, and I heard him yell: Bathroom?

I indicated with a glance.

Toño locked himself in.

Then came furious panting.

The entangling of clothes.

And then the most harrowing sounds could be heard: the bowels of Toño Ciruelo, my acquaintance (I could never call him a friend), emptied out over the ceiling and the walls, they flooded the foundations, breached the windows, laid claim to this old Bogotá neighborhood, shook it, until the entire city collapsed in on itself: these were the sounds of Toño's flesh, an earthquake made all the more terrifying for being so intimate; his insides were rebelling, his intestinal world exploded, and the air was overwhelmed by the horrible smell of his human shit, far more abominable than that of the noble ass or dog or hummingbird.

With my hand over my nose I ran to open the windows, returning to the living room where you could hear—and hear infinitely—the most seismic expression of the humanized Toño becoming dehumanized, his flesh in its absolute essence, when it opens up to eject what is rotten from itself, the smell crawled down my throat, transforming into a rancid flavor that mingled with the air and took hold of each and every cell, the flavor of the smell, even more invincible than those insides that roared and emptied out, the flavor of the smell, dark, viscous, transforming into a poison that affronted my very soul. Why? I asked myself, and then cried out: because it comes from the most hateful and perfidious large intestine of the even more hateful and perfidious Toño Ciruelo, yes, and I remembered him just as he'd been at school. I know that the evil that passed over Ciruelo's features when he was fourteen years old was passing over me in that instant, at the age of fifty.

And I hated him all the more.

Only once before had something like this happened to me: I was nine years old; I was traveling with my mother to Popayán, and we were waiting at the bus terminal. I needed to use the bathroom. I'll wait for you here, said mamá, and I ran off in search of the bathroom—the sole disputed altar, a single bathroom for hundreds of men and women, the public bathroom that then, in Bogotá, was something akin to a putrid tomb, but the inside of a tomb; that bathroom was all of Bogotá.

There was nobody waiting, the door was closed.

As I approached, the door opened, and out came a black nun in a white habit, who passed by my nose like an excremental blast, a deadly blast, funereal, that made me falter and give up my soul. Still, in my nine-year-old innocence, I tried to pee, although—

once inside with the door shut—the smell, like a bludgeon to my senses, overwhelmed me: I began to vomit, uncontrollably, not just the contents of my stomach, but my soul, I lost my soul. I told mamá about the nun, and she put her nose to my head and sniffed: It's nothing, she said, it's just that the nun is dying.

Ciruelo is dying, I thought, and this seemed to be the case, because the toilet flush sounded three times, and only after the third did the drain unclog, the door open, and the sepulchral Toño Ciruelo emerge. How many pounds of his filth had he gifted Bogotá? He emerged, taller than the ceiling, greenish, sweating, an extraterrestrial newly arrived from the abyss of time: if I screwed up my eyes while looking at him, I might believe that this was still the same adolescent Toño, stretched like a wire, his eternal face of a treacherous clown smiling tenderly, but with a shadowy tenderness that lurked about his moist lips, a soulless expression; a lethal being awaiting your slightest mistake.

His long, muscular arm held itself up in the nothingness, his unbuttoned shirt, his hunched bull-neck head.

"I don't know what they gave me," he said, "all I know is that I ate a chicken."

And he rubbed his head; I saw he was missing a digit, the index finger on his right hand. He began to cry, silently.

Him, crying!

Then, stretched out on the couch—it's impossible to write *just how long* he was, because he was even longer—his broad sailor's chest rose and fell rapidly, the goatish hair stuck out through his open shirt, stood up on his sickly white skin, on the tops of his ears, he was a hedgehog, the lowlife I had always known, with an angel's smirk, but the dark perfidiousness imposed itself in the end, it was evil, a distant glimmer crept into his eyes when he said: That's a lie, I never ate a chicken, I just wanted to embitter your well-being.

He licked his lips. Ah, his ruminant's tongue, his yellow canines, those bloodshot eyes!

"I began to eat," he said deliriously, "and eat some more. I threw up worse than Nero. I ate a cow and a hog and half a partridge and here I am. I came here to die in your home, poisoned, and let's hope our astute police force declares you the poisoner."

At this point he lowered his eyelids as if he were pleading—or was he hopelessly drunk? Drunk is one thing I've never seen him.

"But I came above all because before I die I want to confess, just like cowards when they're about to die, when they go looking for peace on the threshold of nothingness, once it's no longer possible to be punished or made to listen to recriminations …"

Thus spoke Toño Ciruelo, a first-rate actor, the one who delivers the final speech of the final act—or had he decided at fifty to start telling the truth at last? But which truth?

He fell silent so a grimace of pain could creep up from his lips to his eyes, his forehead creased. His pain was real; had he really been fed a deadly chicken, a contaminated cow, a fermented hog, half a partridge? Did he really have food poisoning?

Once the pain had vanished, he looked up at the ceiling, or at nothing, or he simply returned from an old and painful recollection, but was Ciruelo capable of feeling the pain of remembering? Stomach pain, yes. But the other pain? I heard his ominous voice, never able to tell if mocking or crying:

"Do you remember La Indígena?"

"La Indígena?" I asked, as if I couldn't recall.

"La Indígena, asshole: La Oscurana, the Shadowy One. Why play dumb? You did her in my own home. I was asleep, you screwed her while I was snoring, and it was the best thing that could have happened to you, Eri, because otherwise you'd be dead."

"La Indígena," I said again, nodding my head, "La Oscurana."

Toño Ciruelo, who was still reclining as if floating, suddenly half rose and his big green face wound up an inch from mine; I was sitting in an armchair, before him, a long-suffering doctor with his patient, but what a patient, my God, the Ubiquitous One, in my home. Where else might he be at that hour? In five places at once? On the hunt for another victim? Among the faithful at a church in Bogotá? At a café in Paris, a hotel terrace in Riohacha, a cinema in New York? Within the most hidden recesses of your mind, hounding you worse than madness?

"Eri," he continued, "you really are a dickhead."

And his big left hand, which still had all its fingers, wrapped itself around my neck. Two of his large fingers were asphyxiating me. I simulated a calm that I was far from feeling. The hand kept squeezing. The face behind the hand questioned me, invaded me:

"How can you not remember La Oscurana?" And he squeezed even more tightly.

Was he going to strangle me? But I didn't take my eyes from those eyes that were crushing me; his mouth moved soundlessly; he told me, contorting his lips, without ever pronouncing the words, he told me, only ever tracing those words with his lips: *I-kill-der.*

Perhaps all that could be heard was his breathing.

With a great effort I managed to ask—as if nothing could be simpler, as if we were talking over cigarettes—though I was on the verge of asphyxiation: "Why?"

"Because it had to be done, *cabrón*," he replied.

And he let go of my neck.

2

Repulsion

BUT I WILL ATTEST TO WHO TOÑO WAS, AND WHO I WAS, OF course. And I discover, on beginning to remember who we were, that it has been years since I laughed, yet I am laughing now, but laughing more from pure panic, a tightening of the stomach, a shadowy contamination of the spirit: bitter saliva floods the mouth, a wish to no longer inhabit my body, never to inhabit myself again.

I first met Toño at school, when I was fourteen years old (the last time I saw him we were both approaching thirty, twenty years ago). I met him at the start of my sophomore year of high school. He was a "new" student. The first time I noticed him was in Spanish class after listening to a piece of his creative writing, which we were made to read aloud in class every Friday: Toño read his composition as if mesmerized—mesmerized by himself? By his own voice?—but Mr. Tovar reprimanded him:

"This is plagiarism, Master Antonio Ciruelo. You have copied a fragment from *Marianela*, by Don Benito Pérez Galdós, and you had the insolence to copy it exactly. You did not even show the decency of all good plagiarists, who will make one or two alterations of their own with the aim of going unnoticed and achieving a piece of plagiarism that is ... respectable. You have earned yourself a zero, young man, and not only our contempt, but also God's."

Ciruelo tried to say something, but, knifelike, the teacher's voice cut him off:

"Now sit down, young man, unless you want me to inform Father Berrío. In a school run by Augustinian friars, scandals like this are cause for expulsion."

Though Ciruelo was merely a stranger, I felt sorry for him. I saw him go red as embers, stammer some justification, and collapse back into his desk. And then it was my turn to read. I had been struggling diligently over my composition for nights. I have enjoyed writing ever since, it was my fate. I remember I came up with a short story about a stray dog. Was it "Conversation with a Dog?"—I can't recall the exact title, something banal, but I was buoyed by the ebb and flow of admiration coming from my classmates. I can recall only one sentence, because after I read it, I was interrupted by Mr. Tovar. The sentence read: *He was a dog, and that yard smelled of bitch.*

"Where did you copy that from?" interjected the teacher.

I didn't answer immediately, perplexed by his question; but that same question filled me with even more pride.

"I didn't copy it, Sir."

"Where did it come from?"

"Nowhere, Sir."

"Where is it from?"

"From my head."

"A zero, Master Heriberto Salgado, for refusing to reveal where your story was copied from."

Here I should clarify that I am burdened with the horrible name Heriberto, but also that, thanks to the grace of the gods and people's laziness, I have been called *Eri* since I was a child.

After class, during recess, when the imbeciles, lean and battle-hardened, would run off to play soccer, I went to the library: a bookworm from the moment I learned to read. I was walking along the cold corridor when I noticed a shadow beside me: Antonio Ciruelo, it couldn't be! He wasn't yet stretched out like a wire; we were the same age, and both the tallest in our class. I stopped, impatient. Ciruelo's eyes sought mine in the cold darkness.

"So?" he asked.

"What?"

"Where did you copy it from?"

To be asked this by Mr. Tovar had made me proud. To be asked by this brute annoyed me.

"From the Bible," I said, and continued walking.

Ciruelo followed; he would never stop following me, worse than a shadow.

"Really?" he asked. "Where in the Bible?"

"Oh, it's a parable, a kind of story Jesus tells the children during the wedding at Cana. It's called 'Conversation with a Dog, or The Parable of Charity.'"

"I don't believe you, quit fooling around. I like writing too."

"Then don't believe me."

I set about reading *The Odyssey* at the farthest table. Ciruelo, standing behind me, grazing me like a cold wing, peeked at the title of the book, looked for an identical copy, and sat down beside me to read, in concentrated silence, for the whole recess.

Ciruelo wasn't drawn to writing, of course, only copying, as he had demonstrated that afternoon in Spanish class (and copying none other than the great Benito Pérez Galdós), but, to compensate, Antonio Ciruelo talked.

He *talked*.

He would tell … these … stories—about himself, about his family—that soon captivated me, to my regret, for my entire life. I accepted his devious company, accepted his coldness, or got used to it, because—and this was an extraordinary discovery—while I established that Ciruelo's presence gave off coldness, that sensation (it was repulsive) disappeared as soon as I became aware of it. Or else Ciruelo's next words must have been enough to make me forget the cold and, in its place, hear his voice descending from everywhere like fire.

Today, I recall two of these "stellar moments" from my life with Ciruelo at fourteen years old.

The first took place one day during afternoon recess: Toño proposed that, instead of *The Odyssey*, we should head to the Strawberry Garden (the priests cultivated strawberries, which nobody dared steal because it was a crime punished by eternal damnation); it was a strange part of the school grounds: truly beautiful, with willows, elderberries, and eucalyptus trees, and a number of wooden benches here and there, perhaps so boys might sit and dream of savoring the temptation of the forbidden fruit—such was the subtlety of the Augustinian education. But the beautiful garden had its blemishes: plump black birds, sisters of the crow, with a name I can no longer remember—*mirlas?*— would sometimes raid the nests of other birds, pecking sparrows to pieces, lunging at smaller birds, pursuing them unfailingly through the air, to the morbid delight of some boys, and the horror and outrage of others. The pip-squeaks in primary school used to prowl these parts eagerly; they would go to the garden simply for the temptation of stealing one of those plump red strawberries and then make the sudden and terrifying discovery that even God's winged creatures tore each other apart worse than predators did. The shade of the trees was refreshing in the midday heat, and, if it rained, the large leafy boughs served as an awning. That vision of the black executioner birds, I assumed, of the fratricidal birds, winged assassins, feathery murderers, with cold watchful orange eyes, must amount to another subtle Augustinian lesson. In any case, the delicate, vegetable aroma of the strawberry garden prevailed in the end. Toño and I hadn't yet sat down; we stood motionless, on one side of the garden; I suddenly remember the voice, the words of Ciruelo: he said that … the strawberries … resembled red and fragrant women's lips strewn across the furrows of the black earth. But by that point I was no longer paying attention: within the frozen silence of the trees you would forget for a minute that you were at school, inside that hellhole, that sewer, that prison.

Finally, we sat down. That's when some very troubled sighs began coming from Toño, who was only just starting to become Toño and not yet even a shadow of the Ubiquitous, the Infallible, the Dawn Cracker he would become. I thought I was wasting my time, grew bored, and, nevertheless, Toño astonished me: he disclosed painfully—or perhaps somewhat amused?—that his father dressed as a woman.

This is how he told me:

"Now you must listen to me, Eri, and swear to God you won't tell anybody."

"I swear," I resigned myself.

"My papá dresses as a woman.

"It all started," he proceeded breathlessly, "during a party, for mamá's birthday. Papá surprised the guests by greeting them dressed up as a woman, and mamá laughed at this, she nearly split her sides; papá was wearing her own silk clothes, and everyone applauded the transfiguration"—that's what Ciruelo said: *transfiguration*—"as if it were the best joke in the world; but our problems began, Eri, when we discovered that papá was continuing to dress as a woman."

For me, at fourteen years old, a reader of *The Odyssey*, Edgar Allan Poe, and Robert Louis Stevenson, for me, who could not even have dreamed up the tale of a family man who dresses as a woman, this revelation turned my soul to a block of ice, it left me feeling as if I'd been sullied.

I listened in disbelief:

"Now they're going to split up, Eri, and I'm their only child, what am I going to do?"

Then, after a stunned silence:

"What do you think?"

I was no longer able to think. I had never suspected such a

confession; I had never supposed such a story could take place: for an instant, I imagined my own father like this and preferred to imagine no more.

"Is it true, are you really telling me he dresses as a woman?" I asked for the first time, floored.

"Of course it is," said Ciruelo. And his eyes welled up. Then, as in the tale of the ugly duckling, "a tear rolled down his little beak." I gathered strength:

"And does your papá allow you to see him dressed like this?"

"Every morning he comes into the kitchen with his arm stretched out, his hand hanging limply, lips painted, asking in mamá's voice, does anyone fancy a cup of coffee? Some buttered toast? Who would like a soft-boiled egg? Once, I passed by his bedroom and he was putting on mamá's pantyhose, wiggling his backside so he could fit into them, just like mamá when she pulls them on, you know, identical."

No, I thought, shocked, I've never seen my mamá put on pantyhose. I couldn't imagine it, I was unable to. I mustn't.

The only thing I understood was that, all told, Antonio Ciruelo was centuries ahead of me.

"And are they getting a divorce?" I asked, expectantly.

"Yes. Mamá spends all day crying. I heard her on the phone telling a friend, I can't do it anymore, either he goes or I do, oh that massive son of a bitch! Can you imagine, Eri, what it feels like when your mother calls your father that? Who will I end up living with? I don't know if I'll stay with mamá or with the massive son of a bitch."

I allowed this last remark to slip by unnoticed, its intimate irony. Many things about Ciruelo would pass by me unheeded, although, sometime later, with the sad insight gained over years, I would recall and decipher them: ah, that horrible Ciruelo was a villain from the start.

That afternoon all I wanted was to listen to him, to spur him on:

"And are they separating?"

"It's done."

Toño Ciruelo interlocked his fingers, as if he were praying. Another tear. His voice was fading:

"I've seen the lawyers come by, they made them sign. The shocking thing is that papá receives them dressed as a woman, and he's bought golden wigs and embroidered blouses and tight black skirts, and, let me tell you, he dresses better than mamá and even looks ... prettier, his voice is ... it's hard to recognize him, Eri, I've seen papá in the swimming pool, and he's a man with hair everywhere, he looms above you like the sun, muscles like Superman, and yet, there he is, dressed as a woman, it's difficult, and now he's broken the big news that he's planning to shave his legs, I'll end up smooth-skinned, he said, just like Eve, I'm so happy, he told us."

How weird, I thought, how incredibly weird that a strong hairy guy could become a sissy.

"And he told us something even worse, Eri, he wants to have a child, and not just that, he actually said he wants to get pregnant. And you'll have another little brother or sister, he told me."

I was unable to breathe amid all the suspense; Toño Ciruelo was a weeping shadow.

"I don't know how to explain this, Eri. When he goes around dressed as a woman and makes up his face, it's as if he's a taller, slimmer woman than mamá, and he's prettier, I swear."

"That's what makes her so furious," I said at last, the discoverer.

"This morning, mamá told me, of course you'll keep living here with me, Toñito. We were in the kitchen, me all ready for school, and papá walked in, having overheard. Heavens no, he said, as if complaining in a voice that was ... how can I explain it? Syrupy sweet. Let's put it to the boy, he said, and asked me: Who would you like to live with, Toñín? It was a voice far more pleasant than mamá's, a singsong voice, and he ran his fingers through my hair and grazed my ear, giving me gooseflesh. He had on a silk robe—indisputably feminine—and I noticed that under the silk he was wearing a white, pointy bra, pink lace panties, with a pattern resembling tiny yellow roses, and a perfume like crushed flowers. It's not healthy for the boy to see you like that, squealed mamá, the psychiatrist explained that to us, don't drag the boy through your filth, you swine! When are you leaving? I'm leaving right now, darling, said papá, don't make a scene in front of the little one, I'll leave him with you, I'll fulfill all my responsibilities..."

"Did he say all of them?"

"That's what he said, and he added: When Toñín is older I'm sure he'll understand, isn't that right, sweet pea? Yes, papá, I said, and mamá let out another squeal and started screaming, oh I can't stand you, monster! And she grabbed the carving knife and said, I'll kill myself or I'll kill you; and papá said: Off to school, Toñín, she's becoming melodramatic, I'll give her some valerian tea and we'll calm her down; and I ran out of there and luckily didn't arrive late for school."

Toño sank into silence, only to add, as though it were his principal confession, his voice quivering as authentic tears dampened his face:

"That's not what matters, Eri, all that matters is that I want to go with papá, understand? How am I going to tell that to mamá?"

Sitting on the bench, but bolt upright, his hands open as if receiving waves of inspiration, his face turned skyward, his mouth open as if on the point of a scream, or as if screaming the deepest scream, his tears like dew droplets on his eyelashes, he resembled a marble statue—then suddenly Toño Ciruelo's eyes regarded me with hair-raising malice.

I felt cold.

"It's a lie!" I cried.

And Ciruelo let out the most dreadful roar of laughter I'd heard in my life.

It was the first time I had peered into his corrupted mind. Where had that story come from? A story that was terrible even if it was a lie; more terrible, more dazzling than any Stevenson, and, envying him, I thought: the fact that Toño Ciruelo was unable to write in no way detracted from his greatness; it made him greater still. This wasn't a suspicion, it was a certainty I formed then about his depraved mind, his jumble of ideas and flesh and feelings and lust, like the personality of a Mephisto. Though I hated him for the first time, I feigned calmness:

"Good one," I said, "you should try writing it down."

Did my lame barb hit its mark? What mattered to me was that Ciruelo shouldn't discover my defenselessness. The bell had rung a minute earlier, recess was over, and we both ran back into school, for the last class. From that day forward, it was I who went in search of his company. I became his shadow.

The second moment I remember of my school life with Ciruelo at fourteen (because there was a third, and abominable, one, his vile *warning*, when we were sixteen) related to the fights. You could find yourself embroiled just for a *get your paws off me*: would you fight or not? Man or mouse? Someone would begin prowling around you from day one, his flaming eyes here and there scrutinizing your soul, almost a copulation. One afternoon, a corner would unite you with your future rival. That's where Cetina, for example, and Caicedo loitered, guys both dumb and truly ugly. Here and there, they worked hard to bring bitterness to your life. One day, I could stand it no longer and accepted the showdown with Caicedo, a favorite of Father Berrío, Obdulio Caicedo—strapping snitch in a bow tie, with slicked-back hair and a missal in his pocket—was the one who took down the names of the unworthy, the one in charge of pinning to the blackboard, like insects, the names of those who "behaved badly," those who should suffer the punishment: staying on at school, sitting rigidly for two extra hours at the end of the day in that horrible Augustinian hellhole, prison for the soul, worse than the blackest solitude, like vegetables rotting at our desks; and he had chosen that for me, had inscribed me on his blacklist for doing nothing more than just that, remaining rigid, a vegetable. We agreed to meet at the scrubby field by the side of the school, the vast yellow wasteland where things got resolved. We were surrounded by a rabble of chickens and asses. Fellow students were pushing us up against each other, the circle would begin to contract, and sooner or later we would end up face-to-face, and then let the show begin, destroy each other—but still the mob prevented us from facing each other, walking us to the exact spot on the wasteland where you could still make out traces of blood in the grass from previous fights, and as countless fingers needled me, as the boys' eyes throbbed, as fear and bravado spurred me on, from out of thin air Ciruelo's pale face emerged, his invisible voice, his shadow offering me something, it was a kind of brass knuckles, a ring of rings you wear so that your knuckles are shielded by steel spikes, I had never suspected such an implement would reach me, would graze me with its edge, the weapon, the weighty brass spikes that Ciruelo's firm hand deposited surreptitiously in mine; enraged I cast it aside, I wasn't going to wear it, but at that moment there was a cry of cheat, chickens, jackals chanting, Caicedo's treacherous head loomed over me and landed a butt against my ear, I tumbled, and, as I tumbled backwards, I noticed Ciruelo kneeling, looking for his implement in the grass, the hyenas and foxes booting my ribs, I turned as far as possible and searched for Caicedo, there he was, now more painful than ever because I loathed him, but especially because his knee was pressed down on my stomach, his face above mine like a reddened sneer, but from below, like a shocking spring, my thrust dislodged him, separating us, and within a second he rose and I rose, both magnified, our breathing inches apart, we could smell each other, it was the last time we regarded each other with any pity, I could smell the white aroma of chalk on his breath, the chalk with which he'd marked down my condemned name on the blackboard, I lunged toward his stench like a propeller, and with each blow the warm sensation of his skin resounded in my memory, the pinnacle of his bones and my bones as they clashed, both of us with bared teeth, in that swirl his swollen face was just a blur that needed to be smashed, a smirk that needed to be obliterated, and suddenly his nose—as if declaring me a hero—began to spurt blood, I aimed there, there, into his nose, and all around us the rest of the furious rabble also tussled with whomever they came across, I could no longer see, I just gave and received, only at the end did I become aware of the slaughterhouse howls, the shriek of a terrified pig: they're going to kill us, it cried, they're going to kill us all! Caicedo disappeared, and I could clearly hear the moaning and see the worst of it, face after blood-spattered face in all directions, shadows of faces in flight, broken noses, smashed eyes; tiny droplets of blood rained down heavily, it was the steel-spiked fist of Toño Ciruelo having its way, annihilating them one by one, indiscriminately, a tree launching each of its lethal branches into the faces of chickens and roosters, they fled, everyone fled, crying out for mommy, as did I, after witnessing Ciruelo, ecstatic on the battlefield, his eyes turned toward the firmament, blood spattering him, palms open as if receiving who knows what kind of perfidious offerings from the blackened sky; Ciruelo absolute, Ciruelo grandiloquent; I too fled home, while he remained there, alone, having defeated an army; it never concerned him that we would be expelled from school, it fascinated him, sealing our friendship with a blood pact. And I never discovered how he learned of the new school my family had found so I could continue my studies: from the very first hour of my arrival at St. Thomas Aquinas School, Toño Ciruelo was sitting at the desk next to mine.

3

Warning

AT SAINT TOMMY'S, WE SOON LEARNED THOMAS AQUINAS'S
Prayer Before Study off by heart. Inside the frozen classroom, the
meek voices of thirty adolescents would recite:

O ineffable Creator,
You, who are the true source of light
And the supreme origin of wisdom,
Graciously allow a ray of Your brilliance
To pierce the darkness of my understanding
And remove from me the twofold darkness
Into which I was born: sin and ignorance.
You, who make eloquent the tongues of children,
Instruct my tongue and infuse my lips with the grace
*   of Your benediction.*
Give me keenness of apprehension,
Capacity for remembering,
Method and ease in learning,
Insight in interpretation,
And copious eloquence in speech.
Instruct my beginning,
Direct my progress,
And set Your seal upon the finished work,
You, who art true God and true Man,
May You live and reign
Forever and ever.
Amen.

We were sixteen years old when the third moment in my life with Ciruelo occurred, in our junior year of high school. It had been two years already since we'd struck up our strange friendship: I had never visited his house nor he mine, and getting to know each other's families is precisely what distinguishes friends. After school, Ciruelo would say his perpetual goodbye; he didn't leave school on the bus, or on a bicycle like I did. Ciruelo was dropped off and picked up in a Mercedes; the driver was some kind of officer: so his father must be in the military (I instantly imagined a military man dressed as a woman).

Around midyear vacation, Ciruelo told me he'd be taking a trip to California with his father: the Wild West, I thought, where they kill Indians willy-nilly and quick-draw gunslingers face off in duels; I recalled those Sunday Westerns I used to go see at the cinema, long before I learned to read. It was during that vacation, while Ciruelo was off riding the wild colts of the West, that I became friends with Fito Fagua, a boy with pale eyes but an Arab-looking face who lived near my neighborhood and rode around on a bicycle, like I did. He invited me over to his house to "do homework," those thorny torments left by the Dominicans to be completed during vacation.

Fagua had a sister: Ángela.

The first time Fagua brought me over to his house, Ángela opened the door: a gilded shock, she had golden hair and eyes, was wearing her blue-checkered school uniform, and would soon be turning fifteen. They lived in a neighborhood like mine, comprised of identical houses, each with a tiny garden out front.

We made friends and would go to the cinema together, the three of us.

After that vacation, Ciruelo came back "stretched." He was already the tallest among us, and doubtless would continue growing: he'd reached 5'9", resembling a wire, a large fleshless bone, and his voice had changed; from shrill and witchy, it had become that of a very low bass, an echo from the deepest depths of the earth, and he himself would intentionally accentuate that crypt-like sound; I heard him called "Vampire" and "Tombstone" behind his back, but neither nickname took hold: the fear of jeeringly chanting them was too great; everyone feared him, except for me.

Except for me?

During recess one morning, when Fito Fagua invited me over to study for the geography exam, Ciruelo, that second shadow of mine, asked if he could study with us. Fagua blanched: "It's at my house," he clarified, his one lame act of rebellion.

"Well, I'm coming, I'll make you laugh," Ciruelo reassured him.

Fagua looked to me, as though pleading for help: he didn't dare not invite him. I said, Why not? And Ciruelo, as if from high up in the sky, requested the address of the house: an order. Fagua dictated the address as if it were his own death sentence. Ciruelo wrote it down in his notebook, nodding his head gently, in agreement, his lips forming a contemptuous smile: I shuddered as I realized that I too was included in his contempt.

We agreed to meet at four in the afternoon, at Fito Fagua's house.

Fagua's sister traveled to school on the bus. One evening, she sat down with us at the table. We had already established a bond of trust, and suddenly, I noticed the princess was sad. What could be the matter with the princess? Fagua's sister asked us for a revolver, just like that. "Can you guys get me a revolver? It's for self-defense, I'm fed up," she said. From one moment to the next in her life, overnight, men had begun looking at her as if they wanted to devour her. They'd say, "You're all woman, *mamacita*," "Oh, I'd hit that," "That ass is flying," "You can see her little slit," "Tits like a bitch," "Want dick?," "So young to be hunting cock," "Want me to introduce you to my Mickey Mouse?" A street kid had put his hand up her skirt and brushed her ass, and then the kid ran off, wreathed in laughter. She'd been waiting for the bus, and when the bus arrived and she got on, the same street kid appeared behind her, inserting his whirling hand, except this time it reached under and forward, rubbing her.

By the time she told us this, Fagua's sister was in tears. And Fagua appeared on the verge.

Only I listened enraptured.

Because Ángela seemed to be telling her story not to her brother, but to me, and only me. Her golden eyes sought me out. And her flushed cheeks inflamed me. What's more, I was intrigued at how she had memorized every filthy catcall hurled at her in such detail. On that same bus, she continued agonizingly, on that dirty bus (crammed with seething bodies, I thought, with eyes looking but not meeting, improbable faces, some sleeping on their feet, others as if crazed, senseless, stupefied, some saintly, nearly transparent, and others simply simple), a man was standing, *pressed against my side ...* he had attracted her attention by tapping her on the shoulder and indicating downwards: she discovered *something sort of like a fatter, redder finger, pointy, slimy, extended pointing toward me*, and then she felt *something like an arm embracing me from below, but it was* that thing *trying to pry me open, he had my skirt hiked up.* The packed crowd of bodies pressed against them, nobody knew, nobody saw: at first she didn't understand what it was, but then she did and fled terror-stricken between the seething bodies, being smothered by armpits, jawbones dropping down on her like guillotines; from many dark corners, other hands grabbed hold of her, other male faces surrounded her, licking her with their gazes. She rang the bell for the bus to stop, and when she got off, the guy on the bus continued to scrutinize her from the window, blissfully: as if he were sounding her out, I thought. *He had a mustache like a broom, was bloated and sweaty*, she said, *and his eyes stuck to me*, but she didn't say this to her brother, nor was she looking at me when she spoke. The bus dropped her some way from home, and she was forced to walk through the evening, harassed: by the workmen at a building site, the lottery ticket vendor, by the eyes within the shadow of a hat on a street corner, which adhered shamelessly, for all eternity, to the middle of her sex; my sex is an open mouth (I thought she must have thought); she remembered the hand of the street kid chiseling her, the finger that reached, that rubbed her *there*, that stirred disgust inside her—or pleasure?—a burning, unfamiliar stupefaction (this, Ángela didn't tell us, this is what I, Eri Salgado, tell myself now).

So Fagua's sister asked us for a revolver.

Fagua was unable even to reply. I said: We'll go find one, and Fagua's sister left, as though sealing the promise of a revolver with her absence. I couldn't believe what was happening.

Ángela's ventures through the streets of Bogotá weren't exactly adventures: they were like monstrous ocean crossings, the pain of a spirit anticipating and wanting not to suffer violence.

Feeling terror, she hated.

And she wanted a revolver.

It was already five o'clock at Fagua's house, and Ciruelo still hadn't arrived. This didn't bother us, we soon forgot about him. Fagua was a virtuoso: he painted watercolors of Bogotá's sunsets that he showed me with a curious timidity, ashamed of exhibiting his own work. Fagua was one of the school's *oddballs*, in the best sense of the word: he was reading Pushkin's *Collected Poems*. He confessed to having first approached me after seeing me go by with Dostoyevsky under my arm; curiously: at the time, Ciruelo was devouring a *Life and Death of Rasputin*; so all three of us were freezing on the Russian steppe.

We were united by the fact that we were readers; we were the only readers at the school, brought together by fate at the same age and in the same classroom. But, of course, daily reading, its pleasures, its pain, its deadly virus—that of immortality—was not one of the great disciplines enshrined in the school curriculum. Even in those days, the beginning of the 1970s, it was already considered an extravagance for students to read, and that is precisely why reading bound us together, like a stigma. Our fellow students, and even the teachers themselves, were worshippers of the television: not a morning went by without one of our "professors" beginning class by commenting on the latest developments in the evening telenovela. I believed it wouldn't be long before we, the last readers on earth, formed a secret brotherhood that would be persecuted to the last; one fast-approaching morning, all of the books, the real books, would disappear, would be deemed dangerous and go up in smoke irretrievably, for instilling within souls that gravest form of rebellion: liberty; this is what I thought—following paths as fantastical as they were tragic—books would disappear, readers and all, and the final battle would begin, the final inquisition.

In any case, if, during those years, the school couch potatoes masturbated contemplating the legs of some actress, we too offered up prayers to Onan as we reread that passage about a pink-cheeked Madame Bovary on her sweating mare, Madame Voluptuous, brimming with lust beside her first admirer, the rugged horseman who summoned her to the first kiss of infidelity, or that passage in *One Thousand and One Nights* when a beauty emerges naked from the river and, glowing with surprise upon discovering an admiring stranger, raises her hands to her breasts and mouth, forgetting to cover, down below, "her delicate treasure with the perfume of the jungle."

And here I should reveal that Ciruelo was the only one of us who didn't limit himself to reading novels; he certainly read far more besides: apart from the books on magic and sleight of hand I knew of, I also saw him cradling books on science, on geology, on languages—including Greek and Latin—journals from the British Royal Geographical Society, *The Art of War*, a genuine document from the Colombian National Archive: *Proceedings against Black Herbalists and Sorceresses, 1565*; there was also a *Handbook of Electrical Engineering*, a *Dictionary of Maritime and Shipbuilding Terminology*, other books on sociology, on music, on philosophy, Morse code, hypnotism, *The Art of Ventriloquism*, and *Alchemy: The Salt of Gold, The Dodecahedron and the Quintessence, Thrice Great*, but above all I remember a strange *Encyclopedia of Meat*, by Don Cesáreo Sanz Egaña, which I asked to borrow, succumbing to my curiosity about this tome crammed full of meticulous instructions for the slaughter of livestock in every era, describing everything from the altars used for pagan sacrifices of pigs, sheep, and oxen, to the Spanish butchers of the middle ages and the modern slaughterhouses of Madrid, the anatomies of ruminants, bovines, ovines, caprines, and porcines, elaborating on zootechnics, birds and game, sausage-making, the organ-meat market, edible entrails, salting and curing, tallow-making, variety meats, hooves, horns, and pelts, butchery, slaughter, draining, skinning, blood, brains and tongue, feet, udders, ovaries, craniotomy, death by asphyxiation, peeling and emptying, neck-snapping, the bull-ring puntilla, clubbing over the head, electrical stunning, and there was even a chapter dedicated to the ethical concerns of the slaughterman.

And yet, a few months later, it was Ciruelo himself who suggested we read the Bible, in a group, and we had read almost the entirety of the Old Testament before he made his strange proposal: he said we should experiment with hair shirts, that we should flay ourselves like hermits. "I do it sometimes," he told us, "it feels …" He said nothing more, but it was as though he had. Neither Fagua nor I wanted to continue to endure those highly original recesses filled with confessions in the library. We didn't go back. How many afternoons had we spent there, submerged in the mysticism of the religious library, enlivened with paintings of martyrs, depictions of the temptations all around, terrifyingly beautiful women, their lips and tongues in the monastic windows, their eyes floating in the stained glass in which beetle-browed saints with raised quills, surrounded by tapers and sacred parchments, waged battle using the ink of blood. Ah, I remember only too well how—in fact, during one of those recesses, while in conversation ... the sort that bares the soul—all three of us confessed that we wanted to be priests.

A year later we would laugh over this.

And still Fagua and I were forgetting about Toño Ciruelo. Now we were discussing *The Narrative of Arthur Gordon Pym*: ah, if one day we could escape, *fly* to the ends of the earth on a ship! Time splintered, it was getting dark, it must have been almost seven when the doorbell rang. "It's Toño," I thought, crushed. Did I despise him too? Why did I hang around with him? We went reluctantly to the door: there we would find Tombstone, meet the Vampire, swifter and more perverse than either of us.

But it was Ángela Fagua.

She was supposed to be visiting her friend Rocío Pachón. She said nothing, she didn't greet us. Suddenly she burst into tears in front of us, worse than a somber mask. We asked her what happened, why are you crying? At that hour we were there alone, with no parents around. We sat down at the table and Ángela cried some more.

But she told us.

She'd been walking three streets over from the house, she said, on the block where the twins live; the streetlamps hadn't come on yet, and then, from out of the night, or from nothing, from the darkness, she heard someone running toward her, she didn't even have time to turn and look, something like a shudder fell on top of her, embracing her, binding her, it was the enormous weight of a body pinning her facedown on the grass by the edge of the sidewalk, squarely in the shadow of a parked truck; she couldn't move her arms, sour breath burned her cheek, *he was biting my ear*, an enormous knee was being wedged between her calves, separating them, *a hand was tearing off my clothes from within, I couldn't scream, I was mute*, and then she heard the door of the twins' house open and the voice of the twins' father: Who's there? The burning body released her, leaped up like a raging wing and hurried on its way; the voice of the twins' father came again: Beat it, thief; he hadn't even noticed her lying there, facedown in the grass, her skirt pulled up to her neck, the cold on her backside; she couldn't scream, or move her tongue: by the time she was able to, the twins' father had already shut the door, and she began to repeat *Horrible horrible* in an inaudible voice, almost breathless, her heart had stopped beating from beating so hard, and her legs were trembling, she'd barely been able to make it back to the house and she broke down in front of us at the table.

It was at that moment the doorbell rang: Toño Ciruelo this time.

Fito opened the door and, agitated as he was, started telling Toño everything we'd just heard.

"I can't believe it," I heard Ciruelo's husky voice, his bristly voice, "what a fucked-up country."

Then his long shadow appeared (we still hadn't turned on the light). Ciruelo went ahead and introduced himself to Ángela: I'm a friend, he said. She raised her tearstained face and stared at him in astonishment. Who was this giant? But Toño just acknowledged her with a nod, a brief filmic bow: Let's go back out on the street, he continued, there's a chance we could still catch the bastard.

His words, his swear words, the power that emanated from them, their energy, infected all of us. We went straight out of the house, with Ángela in tow. With livid eyes, Ciruelo scanned both ends of the street, just as the bulbs of the streetlamps came on; he had his fists clenched for all to see. "Where was it?" and a magnetized Ángela led us straight to the place, and still Ciruelo asked her to go over what had happened. At this, they looked at each other, searchingly: she was fascinated, contemplating the fascinated face that contemplated her, and a sort of strength emanating from Ciruelo settled it for her; enraged and terrified, she retold the events. We didn't want to hear any more, but what could we do? We listened; petrified, we listened. "So the pervert knocked you over here," said Ciruelo, "facedown?" She nodded. All that was missing, I thought, was for Ángela to throw herself facedown on the lawn and demonstrate in detail how everything had taken place, and for Ciruelo to hurl himself on top of her, to corroborate her story. "It's obvious," said Ciruelo, "the fucking prick chose this spot so the truck would shield him from view," and he let out a sigh as long as he was, a sigh of legitimate fury, of impotence; "but nothing happened," he said, "God is not dead, or even sick," and he asked, still sighing, "nothing happened, did it, Ángela?" "Nothing," she replied, her voice barely a whisper. There was a painful silence. Were we going to start crying? Ciruelo took us to the corner store and bought sodas and empanadas that we took back to the house to eat, exchanging more silences than words, and, occasionally, a belated tear from soul-stricken Ángela, from devastated Ángela, from dumbfounded Ángela, would dampen the tablecloth.

The Faguas' mother came home, and Toño and I immediately said our goodbyes, both stricken (I thought then), like Ángela, to our souls.

Both of us?

This is what I asked myself years later, lying in bed with Ángela. We were smoking in the room of a seedy hotel in Villa de Leyva. They were holding the Convention of Latin American Thinkers, and we recognized each other the night of the university party: there was no hesitation over ending up in bed.

And now without sex on the brain, without its torrid caress, the real Ángela emerged, her golden gaze appearing in the cigarette smoke (perhaps she had begun to remember the same thing I had). Because once I acknowledged that I had just lain with, and laid, none other than Ángela Fagua, I couldn't help but recognize, overcome, that there I was, in actual fact, with Ángela Fagua, the harassed victim of a near rape. Do you remember Toño Ciruelo? I asked her. How could I not ask?

"Of course I do," she said.

We smoked for another minute, her silence expectant, as if saying *ask me, I'm waiting*. The puffs of gray came and went, the room seemingly made of mist: through the green window, crickets could be heard.

Finally, I made up my mind:

"Was he the one who tried to rape you?"

There was no hint of the surprise I'd expected. She replied instantly:

"I don't know."

"But you've thought about it, Ángela."

"I thought that much later."

"And today? Do you still think that today?"

"Yes, today, here, now."

We continued to smoke. I ventured:

"I knew it had to be him, ever since that night, but it's only now that I fully realize; how strange, it was him."

"Who knows," said Ángela. And for the first time, some annoyance crept into her voice: "Who can know that?"

"Were you attracted to him?"

"He dazzled me."

"He dazzled you."

"In the beginning, when we first went out, then ... he repulsed me ..."

"He repulsed you."

"He ... he did this ..."

She raised her hand, opened it, wiggled it—what was she describing? Finally, she gave up with a look of irritation.

"Tell me," I encouraged her.

She didn't answer.

"Why did you decide to go out with him?"

"One afternoon, he came up to me in the street, and ... on many more afternoons. On the last one, he invited me to a movie, one of *those* ... and he bribed the ticket vendor, because we weren't old enough; then we had a beer, the first of my life; I didn't enjoy it, I preferred something ... sweeter; me, at fifteen, Eri ... Which university did you say you were studying at, and ... what are you studying? Do you get extra credits for attending this convention? I do."

I didn't know how to respond.

Ángela was already up. She was searching for her clothes, getting dressed. Soon she was covered by her black blouse and short yellow skirt. She balanced as she put on her green shoes, resembling a bird, but a terrified bird.

"I should get back to my hotel," she said, "I'm sharing a room with Lucía Fandiño." She ran her fingers through her hair. "If I don't show, everyone will say I was with Dr. Sepulcher."

"Dr. Sepulcher?"

"The professor of Colombian history. A Bolívar fanatic, he's after me."

"After you?"

"Those of us who fail his course get told there's a way he can help us, you can probably imagine."

"And what else happened, Ángela?"

"Happened?"

"What else happened with Toño Ciruelo?"

She didn't want to talk. Ángela Fagua didn't want to remember. The mere hint of that memory split her, disassociated her, she didn't want to recall. Her face contracted in readiness for flight. She glanced around before departing, as if to avoid leaving her soul behind. And abruptly she asked, unsettled, as though she couldn't accept it, as though reproaching me:

"Do you still see Toño Ciruelo?"

She didn't wait for my reply.

She disappeared forever.

4

Lair

YES. I STILL SAW CIRUELO.

And we would continue to see each other from time to time until we were almost thirty. Because then twenty years would elapse (Ciruelo's twenty invisible years) before this day: Ciruelo at fifty years old, Ciruelo lying on the couch, seemingly sick and defeated, an actor awaiting applause after confessing to having killed La Oscurana.

There is so much to talk about—where to start?—but it is necessary to talk, and as soon as possible, even if to do so I may need to dwell upon adventures and misadventures which, at first glance, might appear meaningless: that wedding in Barranquilla, for example, or the miraculous grotto, or the freedom ranch; they are not meaningless, however, as the ending will have to demonstrate.

When Toño Ciruelo, now in the final year of high school, asked me over to his house, invited me, I couldn't believe it; we'd grown apart since the previous year, after our trip to Barranquilla, and now, at the school gate, we were climbing into a Mercedes. The driver greeted Toño militarily: Good afternoon, Sir. A detour on the way home? Which way would you like to go?

"Past the lakes," said Ciruelo.

And the Mercedes took us across poverty-stricken neighborhoods, around boggy wetlands, through the black smoke of factories, Bogotá at its most discolored. All of this was observed distractedly by Ciruelo. The sun was setting: the moldy glass of windows flushed blood red, as did the roof tiles of dilapidated churches and schools, emaciated faces, toothless expressions of ragged boys and girls out playing, their recumbent bodies tracing indecipherable symbols in the dust; around them stalked scrawny, hunched shadows, recyclers of cardboard and newspaper, of scrap iron, of bottles, purveyors of pots and shoes, the hungry and unemployed. Parasites? Thieves? They were beggars, men and women as though abandoned to chance, forsaken by God or by their country—a strange detour.

Toño was huffing as if the mere decision to take me back to his house annoyed him. Listen, I said, I don't have to come back to yours if you don't want me to, just drop me on Avenida Caracas and we'll call it a day. Don't get worked up, he replied, that's your problem, you're a temperamental jerk.

Twenty minutes passed. The traffic was easing: we would soon be arriving at Ciruelo's house, on the other side of Bogotá, with its pure air, gated community, oak doors and double garage; there were pine trees and two soldiers on either side of the doors. Ciruelo's father wasn't a military man but a Colombian senator. All the same, he was protected by soldiers. An important senator, said Ciruelo, because there are senators who aren't. Does he dress as a woman? I thought I should ask him. Ciruelo cautioned: my father has enemies both great and small.

We went in.

There was no one in the spacious living room, or so it appeared.

There were thick blue walls (with no paintings, only a crucifix) smelling—how can I explain it?—of a hospital, a battered upright piano. Who played it? Toño? How many siblings did he have? I didn't know. Was he really an only child, as he'd told me at the Augustinian school? Did his father actually dress as a woman? I was unable to forget about that, even though on that distant day he'd clarified that it had been a lie.

It was six in the afternoon: a cuckoo clock alerted us to the time.

"It's a German cuckoo," said Ciruelo.

"From the Black Forest?" I asked. I'd read something about a cuckoo clock chirping in the Black Forest.

He didn't answer.

Then we heard something like two groans in the darkest part of the room.

He led me over and introduced me to his mother.

She was a woman in her sixties, dressed for a party, her glittering outfit studded with sequins, her hair in two silver buns, and she was sitting at a black table moaning, her cheek resting in her hand, her eyes way off in the distance.

"This is my mother," said Ciruelo.

She was in another world, gone.

And, when she looked at me without looking at me (as if she might have just begun to acknowledge my presence), Ciruelo put an impatient hand on my shoulder and said: Come on. And then, pressingly: We're going to my room.

The woman was left behind us like a whimper; it even seemed she had begun to tell me something, and I turned to listen to her, but Ciruelo tugged forcefully at my sleeve: We're going, dammit. The spiral staircase in that enormous house called out to me worse than a premonition: the thick red carpet, the reddish sheen of the bronze handrail; up we went. I heard the distant barking of dogs and then a whistle, far away, very far away, but still inside the house. Then, before reaching the top of the staircase, with two or three steps to go, a woman's figure appeared on the landing: I must already have known this was Ciruelo's thirty-five-year-old sister; to me, at nineteen, she seemed like an old woman.

"What are you doing, Toño?" she yelled. "Have you even stopped to think about what you're doing? Why can't you give us some warning? You just show up with your little friends, haven't you heard of a thing called privacy? Aren't you aware it should be respected? Get him out of here, send him away!"

"You go away!" came the immeasurable, bristly voice of Ciruelo. "Vanish!" he shouted.

She stepped back. I remember a pair of white arms, extended. Her long hands in the air were open, as if conjuring up a tempest. Her dark eyes sparked. She wore a black dress, and her straight black hair reached below her scrawny backside. A nervous spirit that gasped—radiantly? Wretchedly?

I was about to say something: it's fine, I'll go, when I saw Ciruelo bound straight to the top, with her letting out a joyful squeal (or at least that's how it seemed, like acceptance, delight), and scampering inward, down the endless hall of that endless house, they both ran off and disappeared.

One after the other.

And, within the echo, something like a slap exploded; then, rolling bodies; a shriek of laughter—a cry?—it was their clothes, their clothes tearing.

I froze, near the top. Where was I going? I had to wait.

And that's how I stayed. Listening.

Suddenly, the protestations of flesh, something like muffled blows, and then an *Oh*, a faint, drawn-out *Oh*.

What were they doing?

Was Toño *with* his sister?

Then I heard their mother's tragic voice, from below: "What's going on?"

And then:

"The sin of it, the sins."

An unspeakable silence took hold, as if the siblings upstairs had heard their mother from below, and an icy silence, the most fearsome kind, fell over all of them.

How much time passed? From out of that eternal minute emerged Toño: Damn it, can't I even bring a friend over?

What had he done with his sister? What had happened? How had he overwhelmed her, shut her up?

The silence warned of a senseless danger, the kind to make you laugh and flee, leave for good. But Toño's shadow was already leading me down the hall.

Inside his room, which was the size of half my house, I went over to Ciruelo's books. Aside from the ones I already recognized, I was attracted to his colorful childhood books, his "firsts," in a discreet corner: *Sleight of Hand, Hypnotism at Home, Mesmer for Kids, Good Spirits, Clairvoyance and Telepathy, Who Wants to Be a Medium?, Merlin's Magic Formulas, The Power of Suggestion: How to Influence Others, The Case of X, Personal Magnetism, Your Box of Magic, How to Pull a Rabbit out of a Hat*, and many others. I was admiring the covers of these books, young girls slumbering under a magician's spell, astrological charts, crystal balls, playing cards swirling around a nose, gypsies reading tarot cards, when Ciruelo appeared before me, shirtless.

He was naked from the waist up, in front of me.

"Look," he said, "my tattoo."

A year before, when we'd traveled with Fagua to the then crystalline Atlantic coast, on the beach, I hadn't noticed a tattoo.

Inside the gigantic room I couldn't avoid smelling his naked skin. It was like in gym class when we took our clothes off inside the locker room to put on our white shorts, T-shirts, and shoes: schoolboy doves who jogged into the fields, with our armpits and slick inner thighs hot and sweaty, a kind of voice of the flesh marking us out. But this time it repulsed me. It was similar to that smell from a few moments ago, of hospitals, in the big empty living room, with his mother about to speak.

"I've come to show you my tattoo." Ciruelo turned around, displaying his back.

It was Alice in Wonderland, one of those illustrations from

the first editions; Alice sitting in a garden, but a shameless Alice; although wearing the pinafore of a young English girl from her century, she had her legs open, and a sort of eager anthropomorphized rabbit was making for her sex as though to its warren. The tattoo was enormous, in shades of gray and blue, and it covered his entire back, pore by pore. I was left open-mouthed contemplating it, and afterward I let out a laugh.

"I didn't know they did tattoos like that," I spluttered.

Triumphant, vainglorious, Ciruelo put his shirt back on:

"A tattoo that will be difficult to reproduce," he said, "I took the drawing in myself. It's my work. My withering critique of that simpleton Lewis Carroll, who lacked the courage to reveal even Alice's knees."

And, losing his temper, he yelled:

"Not even the first sprouting hair, for crying out loud!"

"His name was Charles Dodgson," I said. "He was a deacon, and he wrote what's called a children's story."

"All the more reason," he fumed. "Children have peckers, don't they?"

He passed me a cigarette: You can smoke in here, he said. And we smoked—a truce? He launched his offensive:

"The same happened with Nabokov and his Lolita. He was unable to devour her. That was a terribly sentimental novel, he got scared; he approached his damsel partridge like the good hunter he appeared to be, but he was unable to swallow her alive, one feather at a time. When did he really show her to us? When did he ingest her, bones and all? Never, never!" he cried.

"I disagree," I replied.

"That's because you're a dickhead, Eri."

"You're talking about what you would've liked to have read."

"A dickhead, or even more naive than a dickhead—in any case, an asshole."

I had already given up on insisting Ciruelo not use this kind of language toward me. Cursing and swearing was his answer to anything that came near him—man, dog, or book. Of his father the senator, he would say: He's a sanctified ass-licker, an illustrious imbecile, stupidity at the service of stupidity.

Ciruelo watched me attentively:

"Don't get worked up," he said.

And he produced a silver platter, one of those that small towns present to politicians as awards. In large Gothic letters, it said: *Presented to Senator Dr. Don Pablo Antonio Ciruelo, distinguished defender of San José.*

We stubbed our cigarettes out on the platter.

"By the time I was five years old," said Ciruelo, propping up his assault on Carroll and Nabokov, "I was already getting stiff, Eri: blood hardened, a baseball bat, and a pain you can't fucking imagine. I would go to girls' wardrobes and search through their clothes for their undies, sniff them; it was me who put on that silky underwear, Eri, not papá. At seven, I became even harder when I found my cousin Carmencita wearing one of those little skirts, like from a dollhouse, it was hot at the farm and ... there she was, glowing, on all fours, studying the tiny ants on the ground, each one carrying a small leaf, those exemplary ants ... I clambered onto her from behind: 'Can you see?' I asked her, 'that tiny ant is waving to us ...,' and I lifted up her skirt and slid her bird-print underpants down below her thighs. Did she notice? Who knows, I think so, she adjusted her position, leaned forward, parted herself slightly, tainted, her voice, either placid or frightened, asked me: Which of them is waving to us? I would have buried it in her if she hadn't started wailing; my aunt Hortensia appeared, gave me a wallop and yelled, 'So small and already doing filthy things!' ..."

We sat looking at each other.

Suddenly, he said: "Do you want to leave?"

And just as suddenly, I answered: "Yes."

"All right," he said, "everyone who comes here wants to leave."
And he sighed, happily.

"Hold on," he said, "I'm going to make us some tea, then you can go."

Tea, I brooded, why not black coffee? Who are you supposed to be, the Marquis de Carabas? But off he went.

I could hear his voice, in the distance: "It's a tea made from seeds, he said, hold on."

Seeds? What seeds? He wasn't coming back. I started to leave the room: one step, two, three, trembling; I slipped into the hall, and there was an absolute calm; the light was twilight. I took my first steps on the red carpet, like a toddler: I was going to leave without saying goodbye, I wanted to flee. And I was already approaching the red top of the staircase, where I would descend and sneak away from that house, from that smell, from that woman who continued to babble, from my friend with his tattooed Alice, from that Alice who aroused me, who seduced me, how can I deny it, it was precisely *this* that had embarrassed me most, that remote excitement—carnal and spiritual, intertwined—I was almost at the landing, where I might roll down, incorporeal now, when the door to one of the rooms opened, the last along that hall reddened by the carpet, it opened like an exhalation, a burning hand grabbed me by the scruff of the neck and snatched me inside; Ciruelo's sister was taller than me, frail and slender, but also fearsome, she had a hooked nose that made her even more of a woman, straight black hair down below her waist, thin red lips, a voice like a feminine roar: "But what a lovely boy they've brought me today."

And she kissed me, long and deeply.

Ciruelo's voice rang out in the immense silence:

"Eri. Tea's ready!"

Still that tongue overwhelmed me. The sweet, sinuous tongue

of Ciruelo's sister, and, all of a sudden, her burning hand on the zipper of my pants: "When are you going to become a man, *papito*?" she asked me. As if she were asking the wind. I fled from her, and from the house, without a thought for Ciruelo's cries.

I fled from her, or she let me go, to my shame.

I dreamed of Ciruelo's sister every night, her question, her breathless kiss. But, one day, Ciruelo came into school dressed in black. In mourning, for the first time. He told me: My sister fell into an abyss.

What kind of family was his?

Did they die off just like that?

I went to Ciruelo's sister's wake and then her cremation. I learned her name. I learned, at that age, that this corpse they were about to turn into a cup of ashes had one day made me live. Ciruelo's father, the impassive senator, said a few words: "Today we bid farewell to Laura, a much-loved daughter. When did she …? Why? How could she …?"

And he seemed to sway. The senator was going to collapse. Three men surrounded him. He wept, held up by the arms of strangers. He was tall, with a steely, wrathful gaze, just like his son.

And then he left us.

My second and final visit was worse. It took place some months after the death of his sister.

In the most silent depths of the house, Ciruelo opened a door and peered in: Papá, this is Eri, my friend from school.

His father, who was bald and taller than Ciruelo, emerged from the darkness. Eri, he said, I've heard about you, you were at our Laura's funeral. Do you want some whiskey? He embraced me and led me inside. Ciruelo came in behind me.

Inside his study, we encountered some men who it would be impossible to imagine, three or four of them, I remember no more; guys who made you want to run for the hills: *composite sketches*, what can only be dreamed up by fear. They made no objection to my presence, but, nevertheless, I was an inconvenience; doubtless they expected my visit to be brief, a brief inconvenience. I set about greeting them, one by one. I shook their hard, calloused hands. I saw a face like stone, a hand by a waist, as if ready to produce a whip or a gun, another pair of bleary, embittered eyes, a homicidal mouth that appeared to scream *kill*, narrow foreheads, stubby fingers, broad fingernails, square palms, bloody lips, just as Sherlock Holmes and Dupin affirmed in my books: murderers in the flesh in the home of Toño Ciruelo.

"He deserves a shot," said one of them, and extended a glass of neat whiskey toward me.

Ciruelo's father was killed along with his wife when their Mercedes was blown to pieces with dynamite on the Avenida Circunvalar, one night in December of that year—it was Christmas. There was nothing the bodyguards could do. An important senator. Two uncles, brothers of the senator, would take responsibility for Antonio Ciruelo. They were his only family, except for Hortensia, his maternal aunt, lost in the jungle of New York with her daughter Carmencita. "My uncles are two Bogotá bachelors who dabble in the stock market," Ciruelo told me, "good guys, good brothers to papá, one a lawyer, the other even worse—an ex-priest, a deserter from God."

Thus spoke the surprising Ciruelo, dressed in black, receiving condolences, master of ceremonies.

His uncles got straight down to brass tacks: the house and farm were sold.

They bought him a small apartment in the center of Bogotá, on Calle 19, and they granted him a monthly allowance. Ciruelo demanded a car, they gave him one. Which meant that Ciruelo was the only one of us who was independent, with his own car and apartment, as well as an allowance.

By then we were looking at universities. I would be studying philosophy, Toño chemistry.

5

Airport

STUDYING AT DIFFERENT UNIVERSITIES DISTANCED US. BE-
sides, I didn't want to continue my friendship with Ciruelo: he
exasperated me, it was an aversion that stemmed from instinct—
yet his living word still won me over, that subterranean world
he projected, able to corrupt you at any moment, intimately, fe-
rociously: the abyss of an evil that was elemental but overpow-
ering; it involved animosity toward the world, an inescapable
bitterness, sex, and rebellion—which I shared, who knows why,
it was our age, I suppose.

I discovered, during my fifth semester at the university, that
Toño Ciruelo was traveling around the world for a year with his
uncles. He dropped out of his course in chemistry, happily ir-
responsible—him or his uncles?—sending me three large postcards dated at intervals, one from Japan, another from Egypt, the
last from Singapore; on them he talked of Beirut, Doha, Durban,
Kuala Lumpur, of elephants and lions, of mosques, the ancient
ruins of Tyre, the mysterious Hamra neighborhood, the Persian
Gulf, futuristic cities, camel rides, the Gombak and Klang Rivers,
the Batu Caves Temple. In the final postcard, exactly a year after
the start of his travels, he provided me with the date of his return
to Colombia, so I could meet him at El Dorado Airport, no less.
And I thought: I'm all he has. Because Toño Ciruelo's life, what he
was going through at that time, stirred in me nothing but compassion, atonement rather than the loyalty of friendship; his sister, his parents, his entire family, had vanished from one day to
the next, and Toño was all alone—more so than a stone, I thought.

I went to meet him on a Friday night.

On the flickering international arrivals screen, I saw that Ciruelo's plane was delayed: it would be a couple of hours; God, I should have brought a book. It surprised me to find myself face-to-face with Fito Fagua, who had just noticed the same update on the screen.

"Fito," I greeted him, almost laughing, "you too?"

"Apparently he has two friends," he said, and there was something in his greeting that disconcerted me: irritation? It had been ages since I'd seen Fagua. He too was studying at a different university—visual arts—and, since that final year of high school, he too wanted nothing more to do with Ciruelo. We shook hands but did not embrace (I thought we might). Fagua had put on weight; I noticed the beginnings of a receding hairline, at such a young age, poor Fagua, I thought. I began to remember Ángela, through Fagua's pale eyes, his sultry sister—my best memory of Fagua—but his impatient voice brought me back to earth.

"Come on," he said, "let's have a beer, or six, it's a long wait."

Fito Fagua had remained our friend after what happened to Ángela that night. But he was careful about inviting us over to his house: was he trying to keep us away from his sister? Could he have imagined that Ciruelo was already asking her to the cinema, as Ángela herself would later tell me?

The most remarkable thing: after that night with Ángela, Fagua became addicted to Ciruelo, a suffering addict, a little admiring servant, never disagreeing with him, Ciruelo's words constituting the oracle; Ciruelo referred to him as his "amanuensis," because it was to Fagua he dictated his "notable phrases," phrases loftier than their author, sentences that Fagua, in rounded, feminine letters, scrupulously transcribed in a notebook titled: *Reflections of Antonio Ciruelo upon himself, and upon schools and convents and their secret relationship to Colombia's prisons.*

Needless to say, the title itself was another of Ciruelo's notable phrases. I remember, vividly, other phrases: *There's one thing I would like the world to be sure of: Antonio Ciruelo. Death will always come as a surprise. Solitude is mostly silence. The world is made by imbeciles—and for imbeciles. I am one of those who only recall the heavens when it rains. I, conspicuously unknown. My imagination takes the place of friends. At your service, world, so long as we agree. Every forest has its Little Red Riding Hoods. Fetid waters run deep. If you're over there, I'm over here. The world is wary of me, I inhabit it from the great within. You'll be old when you look in the mirror and ask yourself, but who are you, what are you doing here with me? Laugh, laugh, your time to cry will come. Caution: your photo does not speak the truth. If you should come across me dead, let no one observe my nakedness. Nothing like a bit of tittle-tattle to bring you back to reality. The Bible is the book that most unites us, through terror. The past has passed. The cows bear witness. Even stupidity creates its own music. Writers like Eri are vultures that pick through trash: I am the ideal trash.*

All of this unsettled me, without overlooking his Latin, that thousand-times-repeated cry: *Dentibus fremebant!* Or that phrase reiterated at the slightest provocation: *May this ignominious country excuse my ignominy.* And another, as famous as it was feeble: *Search for anything you desire, but find it,* phrases that whinnied almost to the memorable heights of Gongsun Long when he asserted: *White horses are not horses.* And I was even more unsettled—to begin with, because later I became resigned to it—by Fagua's servitude; I had thought of him as an upstanding guy, a watercolor artist, knowledgeable about Pushkin, and I was unsettled by the arrogant authority Ciruelo wielded over him. Ciruelo wasn't like that with me: I can certify that Ciruelo respected me, though I too found myself at his mercy: I was subjugated by his schemes, his *public spectacles*, his "extraordinary narratives," the never-ending catastrophes that would befall us by his side.

My few female friends—those who met Ciruelo during our school years—were immediately attracted to him; yet a short while later they would despise him. Why? None of them could or would explain it to me. Only one, "Gringa" Katy, a sassy hairdresser at the mall who was not really a gringa but from Santander, eighteen at the time just like us, blonde, willowy, and whom I never managed to sleep with, was able to shed some light on it, saying: "He just walked into the salon and stood at a distance from me, a real distance, but he laid his eyes on me and it felt like a tongue was licking me, there, and it burned so much that I put my hand between my legs as if to protect myself from something deep inside, it was him, and he continued to pierce me, he repulsed me, and, when I looked up, he was no longer there, he'd vanished."

Now I can remember the time I was walking with Toño along Carrera Séptima, near the Planetarium: we were behind three girls—we used to pursue strangers without any grand intentions, giving up before uttering a word to them. I recall that, as we followed them, Ciruelo was talking about Catherine of Siena, one of his favorite coprophagous saints, he said, who used to lash herself with an ox sinew, an instance of rapture, he proclaimed. But when we moved even closer to the girls, I heard that he was murmuring, this time to himself, incessantly, almost in a rage: Snatch them as if I were a tiger, carry them skewered on my fangs, whimpering, struggling. Noticing I was listening, he collected himself; he took my arm, pulled me toward him, and said, as if believing I were Fagua and willing to record another of his notable phrases, he said, hunched forward in this thinking pose, frowning, his arms behind his back: Women are always in the act of seducing, Eri: it makes no difference whether it's an old man, a boy, a dog, or a donkey, all females know that every male is looking at their ass: many lives are built and destroyed upon this knowledge of seduction.

How to respond to Ciruelo?

The climax, that time by the Planetarium, occurred when he performed some showy magician's hand gestures at the necks of the girls, who were walking a couple of feet ahead of us, swaying provocatively, intimidatingly, entirely unaware of our pursuit. Ciruelo's eyes blazed, I watched them seemingly bury themselves in those nubile napes: suddenly, all three girls turned to look at us with a single cry, their arms raised as if shielding themselves from something or someone that was invisible, yet far more powerful than they were, as if an enormous wing had grazed the hairs on the napes of their necks, prickling them, coloring their faces (their mouths hung open), I'll never forget those faces, terrified but breathless with glee—actual glee? Today, I ask myself: telepathy? Only today do I take into account Ciruelo's books on hypnosis; the girls scampered off like deer, a predator on their trail, they flew across the street, now appearing to lift almost off the ground, propelled by fear. To Ciruelo, I said only: How did you do that? And he replied, haughtily, though trembling, like someone after an unimaginable physical strain: It would take you two hundred years to learn, Eri.

What a blowhard, I thought.

But then I remembered his ridiculous ventriloquism exercises, when he made the walls talk, when he made cats talk, when he placed three rude words on the lips of a poor old lady passing by, doing so in the voice of an old lady: *Life's a bitch*; and I became convinced. His exercises might seem ridiculous, but they were effective, demonstrating his magnetic powers—in the case of the three Planetarium girls—or his skills as a ventriloquist: Ciruelo would imitate Fagua's voice and my own to perfection, and, even more impressive, without moving his lips, seemingly able to make his voice come out of us. Once, he made me say: *I think I'll kill myself today*. And Fagua: *What a cute little tush I've got.*

6

Road Trip

FAGUA, CIRUELO, AND I WENT ON A LONG TRIP, OUR ONLY one, in the penultimate year of high school, when we still believed we were friends, as happens with kids. That trip would signal our separation, the certainty we could no longer carry on, or didn't want to—excluding Ciruelo, who would rely on us whenever it suited him.

These are recollections I should linger on. Only by doing so will the irrefutable face of Ciruelo emerge, incontrovertibly.

We took advantage of the midyear vacation. We weren't even sure where to go: It doesn't matter, said Ciruelo, to the north or south, Colombia's vulva awaits. Saliva moistened his lips, he was the happiest among us, and why not, being the only one with cold hard cash: he was sponsored by his father, the Colombian senator. Thanks to his support, Fagua and I were able to afford our fares.

In those days, the train still existed, the country's pitiful, juddering train, soon to die off like the last elephant on Earth. Whichever way we traveled, we would have to end up at the coast, so we set off for the sea early one morning.

The journey took hours, amid the sleep-inducing rocking of the train. We were awakened twice because twice, like a groan, the train derailed: there were hours of waiting. The crew would get to work and we could hear their wisecracking. The evening advanced across the fields, the high mountains darkened, the dense jungle came out to meet us, and the train tunneled into it, solemnly, moving astonishingly slowly; we'll never get there, I thought. I can't recall all the details of that journey, let alone our conversations, only one dark event, and I'm sure Fagua remembers it too, but you don't want to remember, do you Fagua?

"Right, I don't want to remember, why are you dredging that up?"

Night passed; you could feel the arrival, like a gaping maw, of the sticky white breath of heat. At nine in the morning, the train came to a clattering halt: breakfast. Sweaty, yelling vendors clambered onto the train selling warm *bollos* and *arepas de huevo*, or dispensing coffee spiked with aguardiente. Drowsily, a number of passengers got off the train, with new passengers occupying their places, bustling cheerfully, roaring with laughter; a long stretch of expanding hours lay ahead, with no horizon; the mountains and cold disappeared, and the salty breeze alerted us to the sea. I sat by the window, behind Ciruelo and Fagua, Ciruelo near the window, his profile absorbed by the landscape, Fagua happily beside him. The burning air and swaying of the carriage made everyone drowsy. I pulled down the window so the wind could save me from asphyxiating; but it was worse: a puff of hell reminded me I was no longer breathing the pure cold of the Andes.

Then I saw Ciruelo's head turn toward me, over the back of his seat: his enormous pale face winked an eye at me. He pointed at the opposite row of passengers. Across from us, diagonally, there was a corpulent woman, asleep, a string of blue rosary beads hanging from her hand. Farther down, a black couple, their skin glistening, dozing with their heads together, then three motionless children dreaming on top of each other like sheets, and a big guy, with a boxer's neck, a straw hat, his head tilted forward onto his chest.

I understood nothing except that the whole world was asleep. Ciruelo goaded me on; he was murmuring something, was he suffering? I surveyed the carriage again: the big guy had a pistol at his waist, like some movie cowboy, a black pistol in a leather holster poking out from under his yellow waistcoat. I noticed that Fagua had already cottoned on and could not stop staring at Ciruelo. I listened to Ciruelo's voice, in disbelief: Fito, bring us that pistol. God damn it, I said to Ciruelo, but he didn't hear me, or chose not to. I didn't believe Fagua would dare, but I saw him stand and advance down the aisle, zigzagging like the train, and, almost kneeling to one side of the cowboy, I watched him remove the pistol cleanly from its holster and bring it to Ciruelo.

Fagua sat back down without even looking at me. What have you done? I yelled under my breath.

Ciruelo was observing me with a mute smile, beaming. He showed me the black gun, holding it up like a trophy. Give it back, I told him, you know what'll happen if they find out. And I turned to face Fagua, who had brought the weapon. I couldn't believe this either: he appeared to be sleeping with his eyes open, contented.

Fearing the worst (I presumed the guy with the pistol must be some small-town authority who would annihilate us), I devised a scheme to defeat Ciruelo. I feigned a look of admiration, veneration: Let me see the pistol, I said, and he instantly handed it over to me. Without hesitating, I tossed it through the open window, not believing myself capable of returning it to its rightful place. I heard something resembling a wail come from Ciruelo, and then an imprecation, his face pushed right up against mine: Eri, he snarled in protest, you aways screw up. And he climbed over Fagua and came down on top of me, grabbing me by the shoulders and shaking me against my seat. He was about to pulverize me, but I defended myself, warning him: You'll wake the cowboy. He froze. And then, as if by design, the train began screeching to a halt. It was stopping at some nameless town, one that was before the town we were heading for, where the sea began. In that nameless town the world was also sleeping: nobody was waiting at the station; nobody got on, nobody got off. Right, Ciruelo ordered us, let's get out of here.

We threw our packs down on the ground and leaped into the still, searing air, the smothering climate. The train abandoned us: it chugged off, swaying slowly, carrying its noises with it.

There was silence everywhere.

Eleven in the morning and the entire world was sleeping; skeletal dogs lay as if dead on the sidewalks. Beneath the droning of insects, zinc roofs, doors and windows roasted. The road to the sea awaited us, another long journey of many miles. I set out in the direction of that road, but not without first rebuking Fagua: Why did you obey him?

"Relax, nothing happened."

"Nothing? Something still could."

Our adventure was beginning.

Ciruelo yelled for us to follow him. He was moving off with great strides, hunched over, down one side of the railroad tracks, he was moving in the opposite direction to our train. Fagua scampered after him, and I followed Fagua. What was going on with the world? Ciruelo had a huge lead on us. Though he wasn't running, Ciruelo's gait made him fly. His dark silhouette steamed against the rugged horizon. He was examining one side of the track, among the weeds, here, there. He was searching for the pistol: I understood this, dumbfounded.

When we caught up with him, he said: I think it was around here that asshole Eri lost the pistol.

But we didn't find it.

I recall thinking: If we find it, I'm leaving, I didn't come here to play at being a gunslinger. But now I must admit that the situation perplexed me: a pistol, what for? Were we going to rob banks, like in the movies?

I was excited, deeply excited to be searching for this pistol among the foliage, the shaggy grass, my fingers under the sand, in the roots, the gaps between rails, among prickly shrubs, in the staggering solitude of that nameless region, around midday, beneath a lethal sun.

I imagined that instead of a pistol, I was searching the thickets for a naked woman: I felt my sex awaken and begin to throb. I loathed myself for feeling this, but if I'd been alone, I would have started masturbating right there.

We gave up.

In withdrawn silence, we followed the route to the sea under that blazing sun; we had no hats: faces to the flame. Our packs dug into our shoulders. From the top of a sand dune with huge jagged rocks, we caught our last glimpse of that fading town submerged in slumber. I wondered whether it had ever really existed, because we'd seen no one, only dead-looking dogs. Ciruelo walked ten feet ahead, in the center, with us behind, at either tip, panting: I thought of a human triangle, melting in the honeyed air. And we didn't stop at the store that appeared by the side of the road, that sole abandoned shack on the savanna, far from the sun and the moon, with a pale beer sign nailed like a tombstone to the door; we didn't stop at this oasis, and our thirst was devastating—as if we were atoning for who knows what sin. Hours went by. As we arrived at the peaceful village by the sea, as we ran toward the illusion of the waves, toward their very real din, as we began undressing for a swim, Ciruelo's voice slid into my ear, his bristly voice:

"This time I'll forgive you."

7

Hunger

HUNGER WAS DEVOURING US ALL, BY THE WILL OF CIRUELO. Why did we come on this trip? We knew Ciruelo had money, so why just a coffee in the morning, with no lunch or dinner? We'd spent six days like this, why expose ourselves to his impulses? We didn't eat, but neither did he, that had to be recognized. We wasted away in that village for six days. Not one lentil or grain of rice. The moment we swam, we began wasting away. What was Ciruelo playing at? Was this his revenge for the missing pistol? We needed to get back to Bogotá.

I consulted with Fagua. In spite of his servitude, he was suffering from a hunger greater than his devotion. Sitting on top of a rock on that sixth noon without eating, the Caribbean Sea at our backs and the sun-bleached village before us, we deliberated, cheerlessly.

In the distance, Ciruelo was conversing with the fishermen, laughing and making them laugh. What a knack he had for gaining people's confidence; we would witness this over the course of our journey: whether a teacher, a pastor, a boxer, a musician, a butcher, Ciruelo would rekindle friendships that seemed to go back years; but it was simply an aptitude, not a genuine desire to establish bonds; I never saw him display an interest in any human condition, apart from his own; his sociability was born of self-interest, always on the lookout for an opportunity, to use and use.

The settlers in that part of the world, the first we came to, would only acknowledge *him*: as if we didn't exist; they appeared to feel contempt toward us; young and old watched over the two of us with barely concealed irony. Had Ciruelo turned them against us? Fagua and I wandered in the background. On the fourth day of our starvation (Ciruelo had gone off with the fishermen, not bothering to invite us), an old woman selling fried fish discovered us alone on the beach around lunchtime, exhausted from swimming, and came over to us. From her claw-like hand dangled a string of fish with an aroma that was a balm worse than heartache. And in her other claw, she carried a basket from which boiled cassava poked out. She stiffened, a short distance from us, her eyes on ours: "To travel with little money is for kids," she said, "but to travel with no money is for morons." "You're right," I replied, feigning disinterest, but I could smell the fish on the air; for the first time in my life I would have eaten a whole fish head, eyes and all, and licked the bones clean. Fagua astonished me: "Beat it, grandma," he said, "if you know we aren't carrying cash, why are you here?" It seemed hunger had re-awakened his spirit. The old woman stood there, undaunted. I was hatching a survival plan that was spoiled by Fagua: I wanted to beguile the old woman, woo her, to the point that she would offer us each a fish, biblical manna. I wanted to recite her a poem, who knows which one, a love story, I would surely seduce her, but Fagua ruined all my plans: "Beat it, grandma," he repeated.

She was an old woman in a black tattered dress, with a toothless grin, her head half-bald, furry ears, she was tiny but magnified, like death itself watching over us; she left, walking slowly along the beach, turning back to stare at us after doing a dance step, raising the string of fish as if delivering it to the wind; her grin was twisted and triumphant. Had she been sent by Ciruelo?

There, from the top of the rock, Fagua and I caught sight of him; it was easy to make him out, glorified, an antenna in the midst of the huddle of fishermen, a naked Christ, he could be mistaken for another fisherman, the strong, fortunate one. Young women, black- and olive-skinned, married and single, couldn't help staring distractedly at him. When Ciruelo walked past (I sensed this on the first day) the women's aromas intensified, the air became intoxicated with their emanations—at what moment would they begin to detest him?—they hung on his every word, smiling when he passed like hens obedient to the rooster, I thought, sitting on the rock with Fito; and such a comparison warned already of my weakness, not so much physical as mental; I hallucinated, and it wouldn't be long before I began levitating from pure hunger, like Saint Francis; for God's sake, I said to Fito, we can't go on like this, we've got just enough for the return journey, we'll make it as long as the train doesn't derail, let's escape.

We would have to face Ciruelo and say our goodbyes.

It was noon on our sixth day.

We picked up our packs, debilitated by the effort, or by the senseless pleasure of swimming hungry for six days out to sea. Our bodies trembled.

We found Toño, alone, on a small soccer pitch that was almost pearlescent, more sand than grass, the posts and crossbar just three rotten reeds.

"We're leaving," I said. "We aren't going to die of nothing but morning coffee."

His enormous jaws yawned open; he was releasing an invisible howl of laughter.

"You lasted until today?" he asked, eyes skyward.

He gave the ground a sweeping kick: we heard the sand fall like the lash of a whip.

"Why don't we fish?" he cried. "Why don't we hunt monkeys in the jungle?"

I had no response. Fagua and I had tried fishing, without any results. The silence engulfed us. There was no one around, only us. But we knew that the whole village could hear: men and women were listening to us, or listening *to him*, in suspense.

"There are people who eat snakes," he came back at us, "insects or mice. Will you allow yourselves to die just like that, running home to mommy? Didn't you read Defoe and his sexless castaway, that faggot Crusoe, that zoophile? And what about *Moby-Dick*, Long John Silver? Sinbad and Tarzan and Jonah? Didn't Gilligan survive on his island?"

"You can fish if you want to," I told him, "or go off and hunt monkeys, let's hope that keeps you fed. We're leaving."

Without uttering another word, I made for the road. Relieved, I noticed Fagua was following me. Hunger was no laughing matter. But deep down I admired Ciruelo, his strength to fool around with such hunger on his shoulders, with his Defoes and his Stevensons and his Melvilles. So then he'd read them? Unless, I considered, he'd been eating in secret. The suspicion flashed through my mind like lightning and it stayed there. I seethed, I quivered. I repeated, disbelievingly: Unless the big sneak has been eating while enjoying watching us suffer.

Because on three occasions, when the drowsiness and fatigue were heavier and for that very reason I'd been unable to sleep, I had seen Ciruelo leave our cabin, surreptitiously. I presumed he was going out for a pee. But just peeing? This is what I wondered in that diabolical moment; what if he'd been going out to gorge himself on the village nightlife? Every night you could hear the accordion, women howling like an invocation, sweaty cumbias, the murmur of the dance to which we were never invited.

"You know full well we haven't got any money," said Fagua reluctantly, dragging his feet. At least he was backing me up. Ciruelo didn't respond, he never took any notice of Fagua—unless he needed him to steal a pistol. He came after me, as I walked resolutely away.

"Take it easy, old Eri. Don't get worked up."

I carried on walking. Inside, I cursed him.

"Hold on, hombre," he insisted. "Even an insect would understand."

I pulled up, stupefied, and listened to him:

"I was conducting an experiment … Survival. We should make slaves of our hunger, understand? We have to be resilient. If I forget about hunger, I no longer feel hungry, can't you get that into your head?"

"Sure," I said. "I die of hunger and so no longer feel hungry."

"You're still worked up, Eri, you're not thinking about what I'm telling you. Think, for example, of the fakirs."

"All well and good in India," I replied, "but I won't be the first one in this country."

"It's okay, Eri; you passed the test."

He opened his arms like Christ:

"We're going for lunch right now."

Fagua and I exchanged a glance. Dumbfounded, we listened to him:

"I hear they're baking this fish, a nine-foot grouper, for the feast of San Andrés. It's the saint's day of Andrés Melchor, the ship's cook. Come on, I'll introduce you."

A fish. A grouper. Nine feet long.

Fagua awaited my decision, I saw his face as a hungry stomach, and heard the loud rumble of a belly. Whose? Fagua's or mine? Or was it both our stomachs, rejoicing in unison? Ciruelo was laughing, now truly magnificent. He squeezed in between us, grasped us by the arms, and led us to the only restaurant in the village, *Melchor, the Ship's Cook*, where we'd never set foot before.

"We'll have ourselves an orgy of fish," he said.

8

The Wedding

AND WE DIDN'T LACK FOR FOOD AGAIN. HE GAVE EACH OF US
money: "Buy souls," he said. What was he proposing? I'm still
unsure.

We had wanted to go to Santa Marta and Cartagena, but only
got as far as Barranquilla. We went to a few towns scattered along
the Caribbean coast, traveling to Martillo, Sabanalarga, down to
Las Caras, up to Tocaguas, Bocas de Ceniza, and plowing across
the Magdalena River. Do you remember that wedding in Barranquilla, Fagua? *Yes, I remember, we had to hightail it out of there.*

At the Hotel Sirio in Barranquilla's historical center, a dilapidated building from the century before last, wreathed in street
music and rowdy voices, with no potable water, no electric fans,
we became aware of Ciruelo's nightly absences: he abandoned us,
perhaps unworthy of his escapades. He snuck out.

"Where do you think he goes?" Fagua asked me from his distant cot, in the appalling heat of that room.

To hell, I told him.

"He goes to the brothel," replied Fagua. "He goes every night.
I keep hoping he'll treat us. We aren't invited because he doesn't
think we're up to it; tell him we are, Eri, that I am." Thus spoke
Fagua, yearningly, idolizing Ciruelo.

It was as though we'd arrived in another country: the blistering
heat, the lethargic eyes and gestures, the indifference of time,
the still air, occasionally a thick, burning breeze, another world
for those of us arriving from the frigid mountains. We would go

swimming in Puerto Colombia, beside the orange-hued Salgar Castle. There, amid a phosphorescent wind, black women with shining eyes walked past, women who maintained the most indecipherable distance, just like the sea. With them we drank rum and coconut water, listened to the thundering of music in our bones, and nothing more; we would trek for miles under the sun and return to the hotel ravenous; Ciruelo would chomp down a suckling pig; one day, he dictated another notable phrase to Fagua: *All like to devour, precious few dare hunt.*

So passed our days until the afternoon of our escape arrived, the final afternoon.

We had come across a park like an oasis, a green enclosure that would no longer be possible in this country today: there was a duck pond, a colossal ceiba at its center, and all around gigantic coconut trees, almonds with extravagant leaves, nameless shrubs, oaks, bougainvillea, showering golden petals, the trees were in blossom, loquats, bamboos, totumos; there were orchids bursting with color, this was a jungle from another century in the heart of the city, its large dark leaves refreshing us; we lay down in a corner of monstrous creepers that hid us from the world; the park lingered behind a small church, and we stretched out with our backs to this church, buried in the undergrowth. However, before lying down in the grass, we had noticed the church and the lively crowd outside its door; I observed that the white-gowned bride was waiting for her betrothed. I deduced from her suffering *mestiza* face that she was trying to find out whether or not the groom had arrived, and this was confirmed by the voices flying about: He must have got lost, He's such a daydreamer, He never knows where he is, He'll have forgotten.

"Hear that?" I asked Fagua and Ciruelo.

They hadn't heard, they'd carried on straight to paradise, which is where we remained, within its abundant jungle, lying back, perched on our elbows, heads raised as if inspecting our shoes. All around, and inside of us, a dense jungle of chirping crickets, the green water in which ducks traced rainbows, the near-pink sun of three o'clock in the afternoon, the strange atmosphere, the church behind us, all aflutter. A bell tolled.

"They're calling for the groom," I said.

Neither Toño nor Fagua were paying attention.

I looked back at the church: its burnt-brick rear, some black birds flying over its peak. The bell tolled again: an anxious priest was also waiting.

Paradise reasserted itself, verdant.

There, for the first time, Toño Ciruelo offered us some high-grade marijuana; it's Punto Rojo, he said, Colombian, home-grown; he had it stashed away, ground up inside a matchbox, and, proudly, he showed us a small bible printed on rice paper, already half-mutilated, using three pages to dexterously roll the joints; three pages of Ecclesiastes for smoking. Fagua and I exchanged glances as though caught transgressing, genuinely frightened; for the first time, we would smoke the sacrilege.

"Here?" Fagua managed to ask. "Beside the church?"

Ciruelo pulled a face. No talking, he said.

We smoked.

The sharp, sickly sweet smell imposed itself for a few moments on the pure essence of the air. Time came to a standstill. I think I spotted purple caimans emerging from under the foliage: they were coming to sniff my shoes. But the sky was calling to me, Eri, Eri, Eri ... the clouds, the earth, coming and going, Adam and Eve, the tree of imagination, rotten red apples, I started to laugh worse than an accordion, Fagua and Ciruelo joining in emphatically, then we became silent as stones, transformed into grass, I think a bird crossed the sky, signaling the way—what way? and how much time passed?—I think I was still contemplating the groomless bride when I suddenly heard Ciruelo's voice, his bristly but now whispering voice: Don't move, don't make a sound.

... We began to see what resembled great pale birds descending from the sky and coming to rest like enormous petals behind the church where we lay; these weren't birds, they were women, and they were peeing. One, with long frizzy hair, standing with her back to us in the tall grass, cheerfully hiked up her violet skirt, bearing a white fullness that was beyond naked, a brief dark center, before squatting down and beginning to pee; we listened to her as though we could hear the warmth, sprinkling everything with vapor, truly a human bird, then she wiped herself with a handful of leaves and stood up, dazzlingly naked, squeezed her roundness back into the tight skirt, wiggling as if about to break into dance, and walked off, fluttering with relief, whispering something to other shadows that were arriving and beginning to pee, simply, steadily, for us, the invisible ones; some sauntered in the vicinity of those who were peeing, speaking of the groom who was yet to arrive, smiling surreptitiously, while others kept a prudent silence; there was one who came close to peeing on my shoes, but changed her mind and hopped off delicately like a bird, before unbuttoning her pants and sliding them down to her knees, revealing, as though it were bursting into the open, her other immensity; we blinked, enraptured, a gentle watery murmur rose from the ground to the sky like an offering, rivulets snaking like ribbons over the moss; there was an impossible number of nameless, ageless women, and it had occurred to all of them to pee at exactly the same time, surely to allow for more time, allow the groom time, for him to make it to the wedding, let the devil not take him, this is what the visions prayed for, selecting a nest and hitching up, and, for a breath, displaying the delights of their souls to the world, their gazes flying off into the distance as though absorbed in who knows what dreams while they sowed their outpourings into the grass; some, circumspect, reserved, looked around as though fearing being spied on; others helpfully assisted in the rearranging of dresses; the majority squeezed until the last drop, though still others were already rolling down their dresses before having finished; we heard what sounded like squawks in the clouds, something tipped us from the sky down toward the earth, toward the skin of those who floated, toward the murmur that flowed from them, peeing flowers, truly terrifying flowers, who raised their petticoats to reveal the origin of nightmares, their hairy lines of triumph, those mysteries akin to pink mouths, cries summoning us; all the while, smooth, slender hands curled up as if caressing invisible gnomes, the squatting legs opening or closing, repositioning themselves, some examining their more intimate halves with inordinate attention, all appearing to exchange secret messages with just a glance, a language understood by them alone, because they would nod or shake their heads or smile, and many sang after they had finished peeing, or during; from a corner of the jungle a little girl's diaphanous voice could be heard asking her neighbors in the universe, what's older: a one-year-old elephant or a one-year-old cat, and the voice of a wise old woman replied that it was the cat, of course, but only by a whisker, and the clear sound of the peeing women's laughter swirled amid the roar of the vapor, the haw-haw of that laughter almost resembling the quack-quack of the ducks; I felt I was inside a biblical manger, I believed I could distinguish the calls of birds, a cock-a-doodle-doo, a cooing of pigeons, a warbling of fowl, and then something like celestial braying.

Incredibly, the bride arrived: she was passing by ten paces from us, turned white in her white dress, for her skin was almost black, her expression seeming sadder by the second, advancing through the green thickets, her tiny feet appearing sporadically from beneath her dress like the strange faces of two mollusks;

wearing her silk gown and veil at one hundred degrees in the shade; she was waited on by her three bridesmaids, who very carefully lifted the ends of the dress so the exquisite bride, the disconsolate bride, could pee; but she peed just like the Queen of Spain upon her treasure from the Indies, long, lengthily, and how white and how black she was, a *mestiza*, the black, almost pious eyes, a somewhat Arab nose, Greek cheeks, a Japanese neck, a singsong Italian voice and the protestations of a German, and then something volcanic, because this bride on the verge of her wedding let out a fart that was like a blessing upon us, for we heard it, that's how close we were; I turned to look at Fagua, at Ciruelo, they were dying, the afternoon turned blue, the bride peed, the three bridesmaids raising her dress were chatting: He'll be here soon, He likes to keep everyone waiting, He's very shy, He's playing games, It's a ploy, My grandfather did the same to my grandmother: when he finally arrived she said, you'll get yours. The clouds were calling to me, Eri, Eri, Eri … all of a sudden I could no longer see Toño. Where are you, Toño Ciruelo, where have you got to, you son-of-this-nation? I was answered by a thin muffled scream, the voices of the bridesmaids as they ran after the bride, no longer holding up her dress. Finally, the bride came to a halt, not far away, panting.

"He had his face under my ass," she cried out, repeating it under her breath as though still unable to believe it, under her breath, but even the stones could hear her, and already the men were making their way into the jungle, having detected the bride's scream, and now they swooped, their gruff voices carrying; and the fact is, moments before the bride took flight, followed by her bridesmaids, I had glimpsed—or was it an illusion?—Toño Ciruelo, the whole length of him, lying beneath the bride's dress, staring up brazenly, as though he were sniffing her, him, snake or insect or alien, him, beneath her, and when the bride discovered him, Ciruelo stood up solemnly and came over to us, as if nothing had happened: I think he was running his fingers through his hair, his expression distant, his beanpole figure seemingly drunk, brushing the powder of love from his face, the nuptial waters that had bathed him, before lying down beside me as though after an extraordinary journey; Fagua hadn't even noticed, his eyes were shut, he was sleeping, or meditating; Ciruelo sighed noisily, unconcerned by the bride who had discovered us, as surprised and flattered as she was offended. Wouldn't it be better to run? But Ciruelo had already started to captivate me: Do you want to see what I saw? he asked. Could they hear him? Could the bride hear him? He didn't care, Ciruelo the hero, though I noticed his hands were trembling, for the first time I heard him stutter, him, Toño Ciruelo, author of notable phrases: I was frozen, he said, by those perfect ivory curves—that's what he said—and the dark opening just above my nose, my eyes submerged in its abyss, my ears immersed in its sound, that trilling, warm, yellow voice, from her, and that scent mixing with the grass, which became moist and produced another scent, Eri, like a damp animal, think of a steaming hide, black smoke pouring into your lungs, filtering into your blood, the pink pinprick of the anus like a sun with many rays, and surrounding it the rain; you're crazy, I said, let's get out of here, but he insisted: The forested region of her nuptial sex released its warmth powerfully, the chalice of her flesh scalding me, her polyglot anus, Eri, I spoke to it, my mouth pressed to her wound, as though I were speaking to that wound; what are you talking about? I asked him, what did you say you spoke to? ah, Eri, enthused Ciruelo, as if moaning, what have I done to deserve this world, such intoxication. I looked closely at Toño Ciruelo, who appeared immersed in pain, trembling painfully; and?, I asked, and he, rapt: She discovered me. Her?, I asked, and him: Yes, the bride; I said: She discovered you, and he: She discovered me and said *What are you doing* and burst out laughing, Eri, but as if she regretted laughing, as if she too were committing a sin. Ciruelo looked up at the sky. Was he going to die? No. Let's get out of here, I said, but he paid no attention, he was smiling impudently, waiting, indifferent to that world of deliberating women; everything happened in seconds, we heard Fagua snoring, and I couldn't help confessing to Ciruelo: I saw some, too, God, I never thought I'd see them, and Ciruelo's voice, very close beside me: Eri, you're like me. The women's eyes were closing in on us, but Ciruelo continued: That's why I like you, Eri, you're identical to me, my soul mate. And he laid one of his huge hands on top of my head, which I shrugged off. In that moment, what he said didn't matter, but it does now, watching over him as he sleeps, sick, lying on the couch inside my home: No, I say out loud, I'm nothing like you, we're not identical.

Fagua awoke with a groan, "What's going on?"

Someone had chucked sand in his face.

It was too late to run.

"Quit screwing around," we heard, "trio of faggots, shameless Peeping Toms, it had to be kids, they've never seen a woman's ass in their lives, what's the matter with you, shall we rough 'em up?"

The men were surrounding us.

The bloodshot eyes. The bull-like necks. What arms. What hands. We thought we were dead.

But then they began to laugh, all together.

That laughter was worse than a blow from a machete. The fright they'd given us was enough for them.

We must have looked very pale, must have been quaking in defeat, but their complacency restored our spirits, providing us with the perfect opportunity to make our escape: the groom had arrived, but he was a peaceful guy, though a giant, and master of the situation; he'd already been brought up to speed and seemed willing to pardon us, magnanimous on the day of his wedding; as good-looking as the bride, he commiserated with us; he was a black man dressed in black, eyes of a kind Othello, full of mockery. Ciruelo sprang to his feet, his height equal to that of the groom. They regarded each other, admiringly, each astonished by their respective heights, their inquisitive faces, their massive fists, ready to do battle at any moment. But the groom wasn't stupid. This was his wedding day. He even winked, laughed. Ciruelo arched his brow, equally splendid, in his own way: I had the impression he was silently expressing his gratitude. Each forgave the other. And, nevertheless, there was another pair of eyes blazing, behind the crowd of eyes, and I wanted to warn Ciruelo: a pair of eyes belonging to an eighty-year-old body, a pale-faced old man dressed head-to-foot in a pale pink suit, with a sky-blue tie and a yellow explorer's hat (just like the English rhinoceros hunters, a *gentleman* of Barranquilla), tall, gaunt, weather-beaten, oh you goddamn sons of bitches, he said.

He produced a revolver.

He pointed it at us, trembling.

We beat a disorganized retreat. A chorus of laughter accompanied us on our way, men and women, who continued to laugh and laugh and laugh.

We fled.

On the most peaceful corner in Barranquilla, we sat to eat ice cream. The memory was fading, it was just the embers of some peeing women, the jungle of peeing women, and that *other jungle* of each squatting woman, such were our daydreams when we discovered him: he appeared on the corner, wheezing through his toothless mouth, his raised arm holding the gleaming revolver, seemingly scenting us. Again, we ran, what a stubborn old man; he's following us, still following, he'll follow us until the last night on earth. We eventually lost him, but not thirty minutes had gone by when, on a crowded fishmongers' street, we turned to look by sheer luck—as though something or someone were compelling us—and there he was, trailing us, inquiring loudly about us, sniffing us out all over Barranquilla.

Suddenly his eyes met mine.

Lifeless eyes really do exist.

We began to flee seriously, to save our souls. It would be impossible for him to catch up with us. Yet, presiding over the old customhouse, standing upright on the flagstones, there we found him again, the silhouette of a vengeful hunter, the promise of his weapon. Then he showed up limping at Montoya Station, yet still advancing.

In Plaza Bolívar, and all along the Paseo Bolívar, ever-present, like the air.

Inside the San Nicolás church, where we had planned to lose him, he appeared again, unconcerned about brandishing his weapon beneath the crucifix.

A bus dropped us outside the zoo: there, surrounded by lottery-ticket peddlers, all apprised of the news, he awaited us; what a stone-carved face, impossible to forget; what eyes, determined to cleanse this affront; what words, catapulted on exclamations; we heard them: There's no ethics in this country! Such shamelessness, we should remember Heraclitus: all men have a claim to self-knowledge! The eyes and ears are poor witnesses to those with barbarian souls! Pigs rejoice in filth more than in pure water! Lightning steers the universe, fire will judge and condemn all things! ..."

And he shook the weapon like an index finger pointed at the sky: Oh soulless youngsters, oh rats, oh louses, retribution will come, I shall watch your mothers pee, said Seneca in his *Moral Letters*, Athenodorus in his precepts on wisdom ...

Was he crazy? Who was he?

Things were getting serious.

From his hell, we fled.

And, just when everything appeared to be over, after we had done justice to a spit-roasted baby goat and it was growing dark, as we lit our cigarettes on the patio of a beer garden (on the outskirts of Barranquilla), the old man appeared—again, the old man—waving his revolver, pointing at us, from the other side of the street.

"You aren't even the groom!" Ciruelo yelled at him, getting to his feet: was he about to start the chase, the perpetual race of Achilles? Would he tear him to pieces?

The old man licked his lips:

"No," he cried, "I'm just the bride's grandfather!"

Time seemed to sharpen.

"Leave us alone, you've scared us already, we didn't do anything," squealed Fagua.

His pleading shocked me more than it did the old man.

"Sickos," shouted the old-timer, and it was as if he took pride in his discovery.

"Who are you?" I called out.

"For you guys, I am death," he replied, continuing to aim and tremble. He was about twenty paces away, on the other side of the street. Surely, he took no further steps only because his body would no longer obey him. He could die, keel over at any moment, but not without shooting us first.

We watched him, frozen.

"An envious old man," Ciruelo whispered to me, unperturbed, "nothing more."

Fagua broke down:

"He's going to kill us," he screamed.

"Don't say that," I told him, "it's what he wants to hear—so he *can* kill us."

The old man wavered, imposingly; the hand of justice; he removed his hunting hat with a single swipe, mopped the sweat from his brow with the back of his trembling hand, then smiled, smiled triumphantly, squinting one eye and aiming at us. Just the flutter of an eyelash and he would begin shooting, but the sun began to sink, it was setting, it set, it was nighttime; a weak bulb beamed yellow onto the street; two waiters from the beer garden, the girl behind the counter, the three or four customers, a few passersby, the entire world stood to one side, watching us as if they were at the cinema, as if they'd found themselves seated inside a cinema with us up on the screen: nobody was going to help us, nobody was going to call emergency services, the whole world was looking on, cautious, an astonished witness: another carnival was drawing near.

And then a bus drove past fortuitously; exhausted, it was driving along the road: a discolored bus, with its big, old-fashioned, round headlights on.

Ciruelo waved his hand, the bus slowed, an elephant sinking to its knees; we ran over to the door, electrified, bullets whistling by us, I'll never forget the howl of those bullets in my eardrums, he was trying to kill us: This is my country, I laughed deliriously beneath each boom, thank God he's an awful shot; he's crazy! cried Fagua, terrified, and all three of us leaped onto the step, and the driver accelerated. What did you do to him? beamed the driver, a cheerful guy from La Guajira, that's Abel Cisneros, he said, *the Versifier*, an old man with a terrible temper, what did you do to him?; and he accelerated even more, with us bouncing up and down, the wheels screeching, the other passengers seemingly captivated, eager for news; the Guajiro raced onwards as if in a carnival, the night closing in on us. Where were we going? The driver's plump dark hands steered the bus like a ship through a squall, his big round face calm, small eyes adrift in the void: he told us he'd saved us from certain death; I'm charging you double, he said.

9

The Miraculous Grotto of Our Dancing Lord

ON THAT HOT, OPPRESSIVE NIGHT, THE BUS ARRIVED AT A
town that was like square shadows around the skeleton of a
church: in the dusty central plaza, the entire town slept, or so
it appeared. This town used to be called Pedro Mártir, the Guajiro informed us for some unknown reason, I won't tell you its
name now.

"You aren't going to tell us its name?"

"This is where I leave you, and this is where I stay. Tomorrow
I'll take you back to Barranquilla, if you like."

"And the town, what's it called now?"

"That's for you to find out."

But in the end he made a gesture of resignation and, as if apol-
ogizing for having to reveal the name, or as if it were an ominous
responsibility that did not concern him, he whispered, like a secret, that the town "bore" the secret name *Secreto*, that's what he
said, or what we understood; we didn't know if this was some
kind of joke, and we didn't care: a tiredness in our souls, more
than in our bones, seemed to be draining us; we would have to
spend the night in Secreto and then return the next day to Barranquilla, recover our packs, retrace our steps, and escape to Bogotá, far, far away from the Versifier.

The Guajiro charged us the same as everybody else.

On the bus, just seconds before getting off, we were startled
by a sound as if we were still under attack from the Versifier's
gunfire: in the darkness, the passengers stood up with a bang, as

though they were all armed with clubs and pounding them furiously. We leaped off in a single bound, believing the nightmare to be upon us again. However, once on firm ground, we turned to discover that it was people on crutches, mostly men, mostly old, who were climbing awkwardly down from the bus. The Guajiro assisted the worst-impaired, lifted them gently—I thought of porcelain dolls—and set them down, or emptied them out, into the sweltering air, onto the scorching earth, delivering them like a secret, entrusting them to the town.

Like us, the passengers would be staying at the Hotel Oasis, the only one in Secreto.

Inside, we formed a sweaty line in front of reception. From the ceiling, like monstrous spiders, hung six fans, all motionless. In the wooden-floored lobby—a floor that would have groaned under the weight of a cricket's feet—we came across still more guests on crutches, as well as a few being pushed along in wheelchairs. As a result of the new arrivals, the lobby began to vibrate as though with unearthly drums. Crutches, wheelchairs, and footsteps as if from beyond the grave came and went like a terrifying refrain—worse than a raucous party. Our exhaustion doubled. I was startled by a fly buzzing around Ciruelo's ears, around his thick-boned skull, his biblical jawbone, his egg-like eyelids, his inexhaustible eyes, his colossal nose, but Ciruelo appeared not to notice—neither the fly nor me. Suddenly, the fly dropped dead at his feet, scorched and wriggling on the grubby wooden floor—as though zapped by a bolt of lightning.

Ciruelo merely looked at me and smiled. His sinister smile, as if he had triumphed over me. Over me—not the fly.

I assumed this was a coincidence, that it hadn't been Toño who roasted the insect, that he would never have been able to incinerate it with a flash of thought, but he would take advantage of any opportunity to play the miracle worker. And then I forgot about the incident.

Now in the room, naked on our beds, our voices continued to travel through the pitch-black night; there must be some famous hospital for paralytics in Secreto, Fagua and I suggested.

"For cripples," Ciruelo corrected us, "for the lame, the muti-lated."

He continued:

"I've never come across a more bitter group of people.

"It's as if what's happening to them were our fault. As if we owed them something.

"While the Good Samaritan assists them, or spontaneous do-gooders push them along in their chairs, or carry them, they spend the time paring their nails, or brushing their hair.

"They're superior, in their terrible way.

"They're filled with a hard resentment against the world, and take advantage of any opportunity to let you know it; they're vile."

"Some limping devil must have given you a good kicking," I told him.

"Not yet, Eri, and likely never."

His voice came toward me in the night and turned into a knife:

"You can go to hell with your *Limping Devil*, which I'm never going to read."

"Unfortunate souls," interrupted Fagua. "I imagine myself in their position."

"Then give them your legs, dipshit," said Ciruelo.

We could hear him breathing vehemently. The minutes passed. He became meditative: at least, that's how his voice sounded to us.

"I knew one, as a kid," he said. "Wicked, really wicked; the fingers on each of his hands were stiff, like birds' claws, and he swore to us that when he was younger he'd been a pianist; on top of that, he had a bum leg, and used to wear an enormous shoe to even out his step, and he swore to us that, before the 'accident,' he'd won the San Silvestre marathon; he was a sweeper, a mopper, a duster, a jack-of-all-trades; he was short, a dwarf, and, during vacations, at the farm in Tocaima, they had him take care of the kids, his name was Martín Montaña, the steward, but mamá and her guests called him 'Martincito,' and he would put on an angelic little face, with the eyes of a slaughtered calf, he'd stretch out his neck like a kitten, his twisted little hands resting on his belly, he must have been around seventy, but so wicked, truly wicked; he taught us how to jack off, boys and girls, he'd play 'doctor,' we'd take off our clothes so he could 'examine us,' he'd say I'm going to show you where tickles are born, he'd half bury his stiff grubby finger inside the girls and pull it out, and he'd take us in his hand—why not his mouth?—ha, he *took care of us.* Papá: you never imagined who you were leaving us with."

I wanted Ciruelo to remember further details, further deceptions of this steward I'd never heard him speak of. That didn't happen. Only silence answered. It was minutes before we again heard his venomous voice in the darkness; he was spewing out word after word as though competing with himself:

"Asymmetrical," he said, "uneven, distorted, misshapen, wrong, oh, wayward, oh, deformed, uncoordinated, lame, weird, pug-nosed, defective, maladjusted, clumsy, oh, out of sync, oh, rigid, paralyzed, dismembered, oh, invalid, broken, crippled, disoriented, oh, treacherous, stunted, truncated, shattered, chopped up, and aborted, destroyed, destroyed, destroyed …"

He was spewing out the most acerbic terms—with the amusement and sass of a healthy young man.

This was the game Toño Ciruelo played before sleep.

Or that's how painful the memory of the steward was.

There was no hospital in Secreto: the following morning, during breakfast, we learned this was the site of the renowned miraculous Grotto of Our Dancing Lord. "Have you come here to pray too?" asked the cook, as she served our portions of rice and fried eggs. She was a young woman who could have been old, or a young old-woman, mannish, with a wispy mustache; she swaggered, showing off her treelike arms, before waggling a wooden spoon and pointing down below her navel: "You don't seem to be missing any legs," she said, and she returned to her corner, limping, and wouldn't stop laughing, wheezing to herself, watching over us as we ate.

"You boys are too white," she said.

It was thanks to her that we made the fateful decision to go explore the miraculous Grotto of Our Dancing Lord, rather than return to Barranquilla.

It wasn't hard to find: a crowd of sufferers, arriving from all four corners of the earth, was advancing single file; they moved forward however they could: a few were carried lying on makeshift litters, a number pushed along in wheelchairs, but the majority hobbled, while still others leaned stubbornly on their crutches, all praying noisily, ascending with difficulty, but as though delighted, up the dusty path to the hill where a great wooden cross—casting its shadow over the summit—signaled the entrance to the Grotto. The dragging steps, the sharp hammering of crutches, the jamming axles of wheelchairs, the heels, the footsteps, all kicked up a hot gray dust that clung to our eyelashes. The invalids shook their heads, but within a minute were gray-haired once again; the dust lay heavy in the air: no wind was needed for that dust to rise up through your pores, suffocating you.

Secreto was a town to be referred to in that manner, *in secret*, lest anyone should learn of its existence; it was as if not only the sufferers who labored onwards, but the dust, the stones, the dilapidated dwellings all strove to avoid discovery. Out of simple respect, I wouldn't allow us to walk quickly; Ciruelo didn't oppose this; we overtook nobody, progressing slowly behind someone helping himself along on crutches.

Fagua told us he'd heard of Our Dancing Lord from his grandfather, but had thought it just a tall tale. I said that, as a kid, I'd traveled with mamá to visit the Lord of Canchala, experiencing an identical pilgrimage, the lame and wounded dragging themselves painfully along a dirt road, and also sellers of scapulars, of colorful little saints, tiny crosses, toy-sized Bibles, all noticeably absent here; no one's pouring liquor, no bells are tolling, nobody sings. Well look, said Fagua, here we are, let's pray we're never afflicted by similar misfortune. Speak up, said Ciruelo, so all these weaklings can hear you. The one walking ahead of us on crutches stopped and turned to look at us; his deep-set little eyes inspected us loathingly: If you haven't got faith, then don't go in, he said, don't call upon Our Dancing Lord, don't pray to Him, because your miracle will be twisted.

We listened to him dumbfounded.

He was as young as we were, his bare arms wielded the crutches energetically, his blond hair was cropped, and he was sweating. He came across as quick-tempered, but mystical:

"The sacred image of Our Dancing Lord appeared miraculously on a rock, seventy years ago, in case you didn't know. It was a large slab, with a bare surface; it was dug up by children playing at finding treasure. And they found it."

Here the invalid raised his hand and slowly traced the sign of the cross.

"On that rock, right before the children's eyes, the divine image of Our Dancing Lord and his apostles appeared. Children do not lie. Those children are now old; well, one already rests in the peace of Our Lord, but the others can attest to the miracle, they live here."

"They live in Secreto?" Ciruelo asked, with affected surprise.

"They will attest to the miracle if you ask them. Asdrúbal

Granados and Ramón Valle, a pair of saints, go find them. The old do not lie either."

"By the sound of it, no one around here lies," said Ciruelo. "Not even the saints."

The invalid seemed to ignore what he was hearing. His lips twisted into a look of disdain, but also pity, resignation. With his final shred of patience, he continued to listen to Ciruelo:

"I'd like to meet these survivors," Ciruelo said. "Asdrúbal and Ramón, do they suffer from paralysis too?"

"Not them. Us. That's why we visit Our Dancing Lord."

"I'd do the same," said Ciruelo.

"If God intended us to be this way," replied the invalid, "it is because He planned this act of penance for us. Only through our disability do we draw near to Him; we speak to Him, and He responds. If we were healthy, none of this would have happened, we would not have received His Light, would live without His Grace, like all of you."

"He must have another plan for us," said Ciruelo. Oh, how insolent, how inopportune. By this point, he was becoming irritating.

"You can be sure of that," said the invalid, "He has another plan for you."

"I don't doubt it. For me, at least, He must have a different plan."

I, like Fagua, wanted this absurd discussion to end.

The invalid reproached Ciruelo, waving a powerful hand:

"If faith can move mountains," he said, "why not a paralytic?"

Ciruelo managed a laugh:

"It looks to me like you're moving now."

"I'm half moving—have some respect."

"Half the faith."

"That's why I'm visiting Our Dancing Lord."

And he stood staring at Ciruelo, studying him, feeling him out:

all at once, it was as if he suffered a wave of panic; he turned his gaze toward the cross up top and began walking on his crutches without waiting for a response; oh, how he tried, ineffectively, to get away from us, what a pitiful shadow, how his suffering crutches hammered against the stone. I wheeled indignantly on Ciruelo; he looked abominable to me. And this time Ciruelo did set off with long strides: he began overtaking the invalids one by one, and we followed him—when did we ever not follow him?—reaching the front of the line and leaving everyone behind, swallowed up by the dust; we ran, and ran, and ran, euphoric, proud colts under the sun, Ciruelo triumphant, Fagua and I ashamed, do you remember, Fagua?

"I remember."

At the top, we peered into the Grotto.

"An opening in the earth, do you see? A cleft, a slit," said Ciruelo, standing before it. "I'm its phallus." And he grabbed his crotch as if in defiance. Beneath the great wooden cross, Fagua and I imagined the implausible female sex, thirty feet wide and sixty feet deep, the shadowy gap through which you could make out the beginning of a stairway carved in stone, leading downwards; we did our best to shake off Ciruelo's extraordinary invocation, and in the mystery of the fissure, were able to make out the weak glow of candles flickering from within.

Surrounding the breach was a stone wall lined with crutches that hung like pendulums, slings and orthopedic shoes already fossilized, desiccated bandages and gauzes, plastic flowers, stone plaques expressing gratitude for miracles received with improbable names above bygone dates, and all around painted saints and angels, plaster virgins; it was a vertical cemetery, with iron tears and crosses, wooden flames, ancient candelabras with melted wax, Bibles and whittled doves, and a cold odor, in spite of the heat, emanated from all of this, from the stone, from the bandages, from the plaques, from the iron; it was a bitter smell that came in waves, suffered in the stomach.

And, at the very top, a wheelchair, folded up, hanging off enormous nails like those of the Holy Cross, and beneath the chair a stark notice, warning:

> *This wheelchair was targeted by two thieves.*
> *The two thieves instantly lost their four hands.*
> *The four hands transformed into four clumps of nettles.*
> *You can see them.*
> *This is a Divine Warning to all those who steal.*
> *May Our Dancing Lord forgive them.*

Indeed, four clumps of nettles sprouted miraculously from the stone; four clumps of nettles, which, at that moment, a small boy was busy sprinkling from a jar of dark water.

We came across him unexpectedly.

Indifferent, the boy scanned the still distant column of invalids that was crawling its way to the top. We were the first to arrive, we believed, and, for the first time, the boy became aware of us. I presumed I should say something to him, a greeting, and was about to do so, when the voice of Ciruelo interposed, the bristly one, that imperious voice that mastered all:

"How often do you water these nettles?"

"Every day."

"Just you?"

"We take turns."

"Who?"

"The students from the school."

"And you believe these four clumps of nettles are the four hands of the thieves?"

"I do."

"You swear?"

"Once it rained and I saw a finger poking out."

"Honest?"

"Honest."

"You must be the pastor's *nephew*."

The boy raised his pure eyes to look at us:

"No," he said. "I'm his son."

I let out a laugh that froze on my face when the boy, seemingly in response, extended a hand as if requesting alms—or demanding payment.

"You're just *one* of his sons," Ciruelo assured him, depositing all his coins into the boy's hand; some coins spilled onto the ground.

"I've never seen so many," the boy was saying, his hands trembling as he gathered them.

"Plant them," said Ciruelo, "see what sprouts." And he couldn't resist dropping one of his notable phrases, it was as if it crashed over the boy: "You can grow the hand that hangs you."

We began our descent into the Grotto amid the fragrance of the burning candles; we made three turns down the spiral stairway, arriving at a circular temple cloaked in shadow: was this Grotto natural or man-made? We were not the first to present ourselves before the Lord: on long wooden benches rested sufferers waiting for their miracle, immersed in their faith. A remote silence, encircled by flickering candles, by dauntless saints watching from their stone niches, by incense fumes, a silence that grew from within the murmur of prayer itself, overwhelmed us for a few minutes, before we dared go any further.

The temple was spacious; it could accommodate at least a hundred sufferers; some prayed standing upright, clinging to their crutches, others, in spite of the benches, prayed lying faceup in the dirt: these were the armless, the legless; they had their heads raised, their expressions abstracted before a large flat slab at the center of the blackness. It was toward this that Ciruelo strode resolutely, and we followed him.

It was a vertical slab embedded in the stone, illuminated by candles; at its center, the image appeared; faded red, framed by shafts of purple, gazing at us, there was a blurry Jesus, upright and laughing; he had one knee raised under his tunic, and this sharp knee looked to be at the point of kicking out; to either side, his disciples danced more explicitly, some hunched over, others with their scrawny hands raised to the sky; some of the faces smiled beatifically, others were buried in their chests; I wondered which of them was Judas. It was a tribe of twelve who danced around the Lord, in a ring: this seemed remarkable to me, for I had no recollection of Jesus ever having danced in any of the gospels, or laughed; only Buddha, who was fat and jolly, as fat men tend to be.

"What the fuck," said Ciruelo, drawing me out of myself. "This is acrylic."

He scratched his irreverent nail against the miraculous slab, and rubbed it with his scientific finger.

"Hey, what's the matter with you," said a deep voice from among those praying.

And another:

"Stop that. Don't meddle with Our Dancing Lord."

Ciruelo behaved as if he hadn't heard:

"This must have been repainted not seventy years ago, but yesterday."

"Toño," I said, "you're heading for another scrape."

"Let's go back to Barranquilla," Fagua chimed in.

But the volume in the temple had already risen because of us.

"What are you laughing at? Who let these assholes in? Excommunicate them! Why are they profaning the temple? Today's the day Our Dancing Lord will make *them* dance!"

The loud noise of crutches seemed to shatter everything; the cave contracted. And, on top of this, the first invalids from the pilgrimage were beginning to arrive, the ones we'd left behind, who doubtless already knew about us.

"Not even the pastor can save us now," said Fagua.

Ciruelo regarded us tenderly.

"Our Dancing Lord will save us," he said. "We can run."

Run? The invalids came toward us, all twisted, with Ciruelo their trophy, not just for blaspheming when he had scratched the Lord's slab, but also because, at the moment of truth, you should always aim for the tallest, strongest, most insolent one. Ciruelo's decisiveness had them beaten in seconds: he charged forward, knocking them over as he went, sending them flying at first, then falling down, muffled rag dolls; I heard bags of flesh, I'll never forget the sound of bodies and crutches crashing down. He took pleasure in thumping the jaw of more than one of them, lifting them up into the air, and tossing others aside like sacks, dumping them into the sacred niches; he must have believed himself Samson, but none of his rivals were Philistines, just Catholics devoted to their miracle. Why had he offended them? What could he hope to gain from it? Depraved, jubilant, he flung them into the miraculous slab itself, and was carrying on like a child kicking toys around when someone on crutches—the blond young man—rested his body on a single crutch and landed the other like a dull bludgeon above Ciruelo's ear: he stumbled, stunned, a toppled Goliath, and then a murmur of wicked delight revived the fallen, compelled them to attack us, coming at us as one. I found it incredible that I was really about to enter into a kicking match with invalids missing arms and legs; our hesitation was our downfall, do you remember, Fagua? Those invalids presented us with the most perfectly formed guard, we barely made it out of that grotto, crutch-beaten, my ribs still ache today. Run? We staggered away, spurred on by a multitude of blows to our hamstrings; they battered us, it was a tunnel of stinking bodies we groaned our way through, the horrible voices cursing us, a confusion of snarls, bellows, howls, their toothless mouths spitting at us, lacerating every one of our bones with the full force of their bitterness, we surfaced and still some welcomed us with hurtling stones, they tried very hard to take their paralysis out on us, and that's how we made our way down to the town—beneath a sun that burned like another volley of stones.

There was no respite.

Upon reaching the third street beside the plaza, we heard Fagua whimper as though he'd stumbled across a specter. We followed his gaze: on the opposite corner of the plaza waited the Guajiro's bus, and, beside it, a green jeep: a group of men in hats had surrounded the Guajiro himself, their backs turned to us. And then we discovered the Versifier, recognizing him by his bearing of an octogenarian gentleman, except now he was dressed in black and seemed even worse, sepulchral; he wasn't waving a revolver, but he sent a shiver up my spine. He was engaged in a solemn discussion with the Guajiro, probably interrogating him, and those who accompanied him were making anxious gestures, impatient; one of them turned his indignant face and attentively scanned the plaza, his gaze circling. He sported bushy Mexican mustachios, and rested one hand at his bulging hip.

"Fly, birds," said Ciruelo.

He showed no signs of guilt: a dignified general ordering a retreat; nor did he appear to be suffering the effects of the sticks and stones: he stood tall and unscathed, in spite of the large dried bloodstain at his temple; only Fagua and I were hunched over, still sore.

We made our escapes down different streets, heading for the main road. On the final corner, like fat, dozing boulders, shadows sitting in the shade observed us. The cries from these shadows cooed at us, hurled untold insults at us—justified, no doubt, but more painful than the stones—and it was all Toño Ciruelo's fault, isn't that right, Fagua?

"Yes, it was Toño's fault."

We had to escape through the undergrowth at the edge of the road, concealed, looking back over our shoulders—in case the Versifier's jeep appeared. As soon as we spotted it, wreathed in its large yellow dust cloud like an animal following our scent, we would dive down to the ground and lie there, stones among stones, allowing the ants to crawl over us, pebbles to dig into our cheeks, mosquitoes to feast on us; nothing mattered; anything was preferable to the Versifier, to his avenging bullets—or his envy, according to Ciruelo.

And then something extraordinary happened:

After the Versifier's death wagon had vanished from the road, the much-anticipated bus of the Guajiro appeared in the distance, a discolored elephant traveling in our direction. It was advancing so slowly, it didn't even raise the dust. Ah, we would be able to sleep all the way to Barranquilla.

We waited by the side of the road, waved our hands, smiled in greeting.

The Guajiro drove past us.

It was as if we were unworthy of him.

And from behind the windows, paralytics pulled all kinds of grotesque faces at us, baring their few yellowed teeth, their noses pressed to the glass, fingers aimed like pistols; the mockery continued, but mute, as if almost dejected, and for that very reason terrifying, a thousand times worse than the stones.

10

The Dance

FAGUA AND I DIDN'T WANT TO RETURN TO BARRANQUILLA. Why retrieve our packs from the Hotel Sirio when the Versifier was hot on our heels?

I proposed finding the highway, catching the first bus to Bogotá, and escaping as soon as possible from this sun, this drenching sweat, the persistent ants, the bloodsucking mosquitoes in our armpits; let's not risk it, I said, if that maniac is still looking for us, why go looking for him?

"We'd lose our backpacks," said Ciruelo. He said it as though passing a sentence.

"They're not worth more than our lives," Fagua backed me up.

"Aren't they, Fagua?" Ciruelo asked.

"You left money in your backpack," I speculated.

"I keep my money on me," said Ciruelo.

"Then there's no problem," I said. "We find the first passerby in the desert, ask him where we are and how to get to the highway, and we disappear."

"Passerby in the desert," mocked an unsmiling Toño Ciruelo.

"Agreed," said Fagua, preparing to leave. "We're going to Bogotá. Let's get walking."

"Hold on," came the bristly voice.

He had planted a big hand on the scruff of Fagua's neck and drew him in to a few inches from his chest. Fagua would later tell me he felt as though he were being grasped by fingers of red-hot iron, so stonelike were those fingers, the sun laughing in the sky, right, Fagua? *Right, he scorched me.*

"My notebook is at the hotel, Fagua," said Ciruelo, "don't you remember? We left my phrases there, the ones you take down, participating in my immortality, don't you remember?"

Fagua and I were stunned: Toño Ciruelo wished to recover his notable phrases at the risk of facing another hail of bullets.

And he made us return to the Sirio, in search of his immortality.

So we dragged ourselves for what remained of the morning, dissolved in the afternoon, struggled on through the night, we knew where we were going: to rescue an immortal notebook. And not one word was exchanged; we each existed far removed from the others, forever; and so the staunchest friendships and greatest love stories end, with a journey.

But, while readying our packs in our room, after showering and putting on clean clothes, always in acrimonious silence, we heard his exultant voice, that other voice. He spoke not to me, but to Fagua:

"Now, Fito, aren't you forgetting something else important?"

"I haven't forgotten anything."

Ciruelo's beaming expression alerted him, and Fagua gasped: it was his deepest desire. His eyes shone, his mouth dropped open, drooling; he would finally get to visit his brothel.

"Let's go," he said.

I protested for the final time:

"He could show up, guns blazing," I said. "He won't just kill us but a handful of prostitutes too, then he'll kill himself, he's crazy."

"Let's go," pleaded Fagua, with a whimper. But I wanted to go too, I admit.

And we left following Ciruelo, this time taking our packs, his notable phrases, the weight of his notable phrases: these were borne on the straining back of an exuberant virginal Fagua, true or false, Fagua?

True, true.

So this was Ciruelo's nightly vanishing act, I thought, the red night, the district of delight.

For just a minute, I slipped away from Fagua and Ciruelo: I went down a narrow street crammed with drunks and expectant women; on a corner, a sudden apparition, a shadow swimming in cigar smoke: slouched in a rocking chair, an old crone like a fairytale grandmother raised a bony hand, offering up a nine-year-old girl who yawned, her lips painted.

"Eri!" Ciruelo's voice called to me from another corner: I was grateful he hadn't shared my vision. I rejoined them; they were drinking rum straight from the bottle; we walked along even narrower streets—different music blaring from every doorway—and arrived, finally, at Ciruelo's door; above it was a balcony of bougainvillea and a wooden signboard: THE TRUTHFUL PARROT.

A big guy with a beard came out and embraced Ciruelo as though they were bosom buddies, and, to our surprise, Ciruelo spoke to him in *Costeño* as fluent as any Barranquilla native, though we were unsure if this was from the heart or simply mockery. The big guy stowed our packs for us. Once inside, a bright yellow light dazzled us, and the music reverberated in our hearts. A crush of dancing couples; men's shadows lurking as they drank; a perimeter of little tables: girls sitting, legs crossed, knees raised, with the scent of cosmetics, their eager eyes shining in the haze of cigars, their skirts like tiny curtains putting everything on show, their tongues moistening their lips, but in the end a monumental exhaustion on their faces, a disparaging look behind their eyes. Their exhaustion was quickly forgotten when someone turned off the jukebox; it was a woman, and she pounced on Ciruelo, to an accompaniment of clapping and whistling. Ciruelo was among family, I thought, money buys you everything: he was exchanging firm handshakes with reticent men who might be truckers or boxers, and who greeted him submissively. The girls hung around his neck, laying claim to him. Then a record began to play, his favorite record: someone must have selected it in his honor. Ciruelo and the woman raced to the dance floor; the room vibrated to a kind of hurried cha-cha-cha:

> *Cuando te veo con la blusa azul*
> *mis ojos sin querer van hacia ti . . .*

We watched him dance, do you remember? I remember that he danced in wide circles, clinging to his woman, he knew how to dance, moving backward and forward as if he were floating, spinning and catching her before sending her off into another set of revolutions, then pulling her in close, fusing with her as she allowed him to fuse, breath on breath; Fagua and I drew near to the edge, we'd never seen him happier, and the music accelerated, its echo hammering inside us, we watched him lean forward and whisper into the ear of the bewitched one—what was he saying to her?—he led her here and there and, with a flourish, spun her right toward us, and then I could see him more clearly: he appeared to be suffering, or to be suffering alongside his happiness—who was he battling against now? Why the contorted expression? Why those bloodshot eyes turned inward as if pleading?—the woman dancing with Ciruelo was a third his size and dressed like a little girl, she was a schoolgirl in a checkered skirt and a blue blouse, a *blusa azul*, with braids and the face of an angel—or was she actually a little girl?—and *cuando te veo con la blusa azul* rang out again, and this time they leaped forward into the ring of dancing couples, the entire world leaped forward, because Fito Fagua was dancing in there too, imprisoning a Marilyn-like blonde; I envied him, she was nothing but a pair of hips wiggling on the tips of her toes, wearing a long silk skirt and surely naked underneath—I suffered, looking around desperately, but there were no more girls sitting in the room, only a large white cat napping on a chair; I suppose I could dance with the cat, I thought, or with the chair, and I resigned myself, an eternal watcher at the party.

Suddenly Toño's sweaty face turned to me: Eri, he cried, spinning, Eri, he cried, and spun, Eri, why aren't you dancing, his splendid schoolgirl fastened to his chest, revolving as in a terrifying waltz, then the swirl of the orchestra set them free, they flew libidinously away, intertwined, locked in a kiss, I drank rum; this is the purest memory I have of Ciruelo, the distinct image of his happy yet unhappy face, that sort of inconvenient dual being that was tearing him apart, and the demented dance that they repeated, insatiably, for the rest of the evening. Why didn't you stop there, Ciruelo? Better to dance for the rest of your life than to kill.

And when the hour of that other truth arrived, I was the only one without a girl. The dance had paired everybody up, and I was done for. "Don't worry, honey," Fagua's blonde shouted over to me. "Head up to room thirteen, that's where Fátima lives, she'll teach you."

Fagua was staring at her deliriously, eyes glazed over, rocking back and forth.

I wanted to abduct that Marilyn; I brushed—dared to brush, assisted by the gods—against the erect tips of her nipples, and she glanced at me in surprise—grateful? But Fagua, all eyes, implored me: Stay out of it. And we climbed to the second floor, the one with the doors, Fagua and his blonde first, me behind: behind the long skirt, behind the swaying backside that was ascending; then came Toño Ciruelo, happier than happiness itself, I thought, for he appeared monstrously happy. I heard him whispering to his schoolgirl as he clasped her by the neck: Do you want to see my missing link? and he also told her, after cupping her rear with one large hand and throwing her over his shoulder as if she were a feather—a hunter's throbbing kill, a bleeding trophy: Don't cry, it's only a small incision.

The schoolgirl laughed as though possessed.

Soon, all four of them disappeared behind their doors and then, as if a gust of wind were tugging me by the ears, I arrived at door thirteen, the fatal number my grandparents had taught me to dread: *On the thirteenth of March, neither wed nor launch*. I became aware of the time: I realized, with a shudder, that on top of everything else, it was now the thirteenth of March.

And I entered room number thirteen and tumbled into the middle of a whore who was bone ugly and hungry, for she ate a pastry as I struggled to rid myself once and for all of the seething lava that condemned me. Still dripping, I dressed and fled, but not before hearing her call out, What's the hurry, *papito*, I'm just warming up and already you're flying off; oh kiddo, you'll spend the rest of your days alone—I curse you!

And she even repeated it, feigning tears though she was laughing: I curse you, goodbye.

Goodbye! I yelled.

And at first light, we set out on our way back to Bogotá. Do you remember, Fagua, we took the bus? A four-hundred-mile highway stretched out immeasurably; we were no longer the same, this was the *end*, we were fed up. But that first and final journey, Fagua: the peeing women at the wedding, the Versifier's gunshots, the cripples who battered us, the night when everyone danced except for me, the hungry woman who prophesied I'd spend the rest of my life alone, I shall never forget any of that.

"Never."

"All thanks to Ciruelo."

"Thanks to him."

And we toasted.

11

Disappearances

HE ARRIVED *EXUBERANT*—IF THAT'S A STRONG ENOUGH word; he was no longer a wire but a man, 6'5", solid, and still growing; surrounding him like an aura was the exotic scent of other shores, though this was belied by a gold watch, and hanging from his neck was a sapphire in the shape of a fish, reminding me of that gentleman from Barranquilla. "Careful," I reminded him. "They can kill you here just for being alive." I said this and, for a second, felt fear begin to take hold of me. Kill? he responded, and let out an indefinable sigh, a sigh as long as he was.

Within that El Dorado (the everlasting name of Bogotá's airport, the only everlasting thing in the city), beautiful travelers cast their veiled smiles in his path, but he didn't acknowledge them; he smiled only for himself. By his side, at 5'9", I must have seemed almost a dwarf. He told me in French that he spoke fluent English.

"Quit showing off," I replied, "you know full well I speak only Spanish, and I'm still learning."

"Don't get worked up," he repeated, like a tradition.

He was looking in all directions, searching, no doubt, for Fagua, but Fagua had fled, and, in that instant, I envied him for fleeing. I said: Fagua left, Toño, he asked me to say goodbye, to tell you it's forever. Ciruelo shrugged: That about sums him up, he said.

We were heading to his apartment on Calle 19 in a taxi. He wasn't carrying much luggage, just a green canvas backpack: I brought back a mezcal with worms from Oaxaca, he said, and absinthe from Czechoslovakia, sake from Japan; I couldn't find hemlock in Athens, and he swore under his breath. It began to drizzle. Two in the morning: two drunks were embracing in a park, holding their guitars up in the air; in the wide entrance to Las Nieves Church, a dozen street kids, and a dozen of their dogs, slept strangely in a pile, intertwined, mouth-to-muzzle, hand-to-paw, the children's cheeks lying on the dogs' scrawny bellies; I lost sight of them as the windows darkened with condensation.

Ciruelo had closed his eyes.

"And your uncles?" I asked.

"Those guys stayed on in Java, screwing the Javan women, you know how it is."

He seemed withdrawn, immersed in who knows what mistakes; his voice rang with resentment:

"Pair of crooks," he said.

We never spoke of them again.

"I'm going to ask you a favor, Eri."

Fagua contemplated me from behind his glass of beer an hour before Ciruelo's arrival; Fagua resembled a moan incarnate: he was no longer buoyed by the revelry we had shared on remembering the trip to Barranquilla. I was staring at him in bewilderment, and he woke me up.

"I'm leaving," he said. "I don't want to wait for Toño, he'll be fine with just you. Greet him on my behalf, and then say goodbye for me; tell him it's forever."

He caught me completely off guard.

"Why don't you stay, Fito, seeing as you're already here."

He drank in silence.

"We'll greet old Ciruelo together," I urged him, "it'll only take a minute, let's be there for the man with no daddy, no mom, no little sister, what do you say—in the end we all suffered through the same school."

We finished our beers. Fagua's pale eyes welled up all of a sudden; he was going to cry, I thought, disbelievingly, but he didn't cry, he asked for another round. He took the plunge:

"We expressed our thanks to Ciruelo, Eri, but actually: I'm not grateful to him, why should I be? I'm not as big a moron as I look. I've been onto Ciruelo from the start, although he always had me … suckered. Laugh if you want to, there's no need to hide your face behind your hand."

"I wasn't laughing," I laughed, "just crying like you." And we both laughed spontaneously, openly, as we had at school. Nevertheless, we finished our beers in silence. Fagua requested another round: Don't worry, Eri, I'm paying, and he ran his hand through his hair:

"I'll start at the beginning."

It was as though he were driven to despair by finally recognizing the truth:

"I'm sure …" and he went silent for another instant, before drawing a breath of courage from the air, "I'm sure it was Toño Ciruelo who knocked my sister over that night, do you remember?"

"I remember."

"I bet you didn't suspect him, Eri."

"No, never. How do you know?"

"I asked Ángela herself."

"You did? And what did she say?"

"She didn't say anything, Eri. Just an assenting silence. But that isn't what I want to talk about, it's … It's so you understand that I'm perfectly aware that I shouldn't be here, waiting for that demon."

That's what he called him, a demon.

"It's as if my eyes have been opened, Eri."

He ran his hands over his face again and again. Finally, he became motionless, as though lost in time:

"That same year, Eri, months after my sister was knocked down in the street ... Toño came looking for me at the house one night, around seven. Only now do I realize, he wasn't looking for me but for Ángela, though that doesn't matter anymore: I opened the door and there he was, like fate. He asked me where I was going, wearing a tie, dressed for a party. I was going to Ana's fifteenth birthday party, do you remember Ana?"

"You liked her, the one with the beret. Toño compared her to a toad."

"Thanks for reminding me."

"I'm sorry, Fito, it was his comparison."

"No need to apologize, Eri. Now let me remind you: he didn't compare her to a toad because she was ugly but because she wore those tight leggings ... and, whenever we bumped into her ... remember, she lived near the school ... he'd point at her and say, what a toad that girl's got, what a toad. I made friends with her beside a pay phone, we were both in line to make a call, it was casual ... I didn't want to share her with you, much less with Toño—see, Eri, I've corrected your recollection."

"You win, Fito, you've got the better memory."

"Speaking of memories, I've read some of your stories in the newspaper, Eri. You remember too. But they aren't worthwhile recollections ... I'll say this to you frankly; they're boring recollections, if it helps you to know that."

"Thanks for reminding me."

"Now don't get resentful."

"At least I remember."

"Are you going to listen to me, Eri?"

"What's wrong, I'm listening."

"'Then I'll go with you,' Ciruelo told me, 'I'll accompany you to the party, Fagüita. The way I'm dressed, I'll add a note of dissonance.' I brought him with me to Ana María Botero de la Espriella's quinceañera."

"Fate," I said.

Fagua didn't hear me, or he intentionally ignored me:

"Ana and I had already kissed, we were seeing each other in secret, do you remember what that's like? First love, sunsets, a ballad we listened to at the same time every night, each in our own home, lying in our own beds, a sublime rendezvous, and the gift of a petal concealed in a copy of Neruda's *Twenty Poems* ... and then the joy of seeing each other again, in the flesh, the next day, hands that brush and tremble and ... finally ... clasp ... for no other reason, but because that's all love is—you understand?—when the sexes no longer exist, just a glance that means life and death ..."

He sank into a painful silence, was he going to cry?

"We loved each other, Eri, if that's even something you can say these days. Anita and I were pure."

Fagua had astonished me. I remembered that he'd read Pushkin.

"No sooner did Ciruelo arrive than he conquered all, Eri.

"He became master of their souls.

"He dazzled as you well know he can dazzle.

"He dazzled the dad and dazzled the mom; children and grandparents circled him; he gave Ana's father fishing tips, invited him fishing, said he had an uncle in Cartagena who owned a schooner called *La Magallana*—can you believe it?—he told us about the adventures of Amundsen the explorer, the intrepid Norwegian who reached the South Pole, and he mocked Captain Scott, a big-eared Englishman, defeated by Amundsen, adding, to put the cherry on top, that Jules Verne had more imagination than William Shakespeare. He read Ana's mother's palm in secret and made her squeal with glee—he told me the truth, she shrieked like a parrot—and when he slipped a prediction into her ear we saw her blush with delight, you're a monster, she told him, and kissed him, Eri, devastatingly, on the mouth, in front of all the guests, who clapped, in front of the dad; he didn't lift a finger, didn't say a word, in front of Ana—who watched Toño spellbound, Eri, enamored, I would say, today, so far away from her, in time and in my heart."

Fagua's voice became melancholy. I had to lean forward to hear him:

"We went over to Ana and danced."

"She was your girlfriend after all."

"*We* danced, he and I," he corrected me, exasperated. "We took turns with her."

Now his tone became belligerent, but also hair-raising:

"And he was the better dancer, as you know ... Oh, Eri, how he thrust his leg between her legs, and how she let him, parting completely for him—can you imagine me watching them?—I suffered, Eri, I suffered. All of that pure love with Ana was vanishing, disappearing before my eyes, I didn't recognize her, this was another fifteen-year-old Ana in her most libidinous awakening, she didn't care about her grandmother, much less that boyfriend of the concealed petal, who observed her while sitting lonesome as hell, I thought she was sprouting wings from her ass; God, Eri, I wanted and did not want to watch; the music track ended, we were meant to swap, it was my turn, but they continued dancing in silence, Eri, whirling round and round, and suddenly the music kicked back in and it was he who carried on dancing with her, him, Eri, him ..."

"Ciruelo?"

"No, Napoleon."

"Sorry."

"It's the beer, Eri, you dozed off. Just forget about it."

"No, no, go on, please."

"Toño and I left Ana's house ... the final guests. It was in a neighborhood by the school, remember? Tercer Puente. We reached a park and Toño said, stop, we're going back. Where?

I asked, and he told me, we're going back to Ana's, she's waiting for us. She's waiting! That's what he said. Oh, the scumbag! As though we'd finally triumphed in battle together; he made as if he were doing me a favor, doing it out of compassion. But he knew what he was killing, Eri. Or did he? Of course he did: love, my love, my first love."

He drank feverishly, an unrecognizable Fagua:

"I'll tell you soon how I know I hate him."

He looked up, addressing a vision:

"I couldn't believe you were waiting for us, Ana. Obliterator! You had eyes for him alone as we entered your house in darkness, following you, you were a ... a nervous stranger, Eri, as if the shadow of her sex were indicating a secret path, soundlessly, so nobody in the house would find out. Where was she leading us? Where was she leading Ciruelo? ... Because it was Ciruelo you were leading: I saw how you took his hand; Eri, she guided him through the shadows of the house, with me following, Eri, me following. We reached a kind of sunroom I knew very well. There were three long sofas, with cushions, rugs, the flowers of the sunroom all around us like witnesses, like faces, Eri, they were faces; that was where Ana's parents had their intimate encounters; there was a fireplace, and ... Ana had already lit the fire, and ... on the coffee table was half a bottle of gin she'd stolen, Eri, which I finished off entirely because I didn't know what else to do; Ana, you wouldn't look at me, not one word, I didn't exist. She put on some songs by the Beatles, which sent me to sleep, or else it was the gin, or my desire to avoid seeing them so as not to suffer, I sent myself to sleep ... And when I awoke—how long had it been ...?—I saw you naked, Ana; I saw her naked for the first time, but sitting on top of Ciruelo, also naked and lying on his back, Ana rocking back and forth and biting her lips in the firelight, and I felt ... I don't know, as if I were dying, it was that vision of Ana naked for the first time, but without me, her breasts suspended like bells that tolled in mourning, oh God, they tolled for me, that was not my love, I staggered away, making for the living room, the way out, and had already begun turning the doorknob when my hand was covered by the hand of Ciruelo. He whispered to me, urging me: Run to her, Fagua, run, you can have my leftovers. And he exited the house, unscathed; I stood frozen; his leftovers! I screamed to myself, how vulgar can you get, Ciruelo! I don't know how long I stood there, listening to my heart in the darkness. I wanted to run in search of Ciruelo, find his heart and ... But most of all I wanted to look at you for the final time, Ana, to see if ... you would look at me again like yesterday, just for an instant ... suddenly that is what I wanted ... to witness the mark of my pain in her like a retribution, Eri, and I returned to the sunroom, the flowers like faces, mocking faces, I don't know why I returned, I don't know why I peered in ... I don't know if you could see me, Ana, but you were crying and looking toward me, you seemed to be crying on your knees, your arms open, your arms and body seemingly open ... but we had already been sacrificed by Ciruelo."

"These things happen," I said lamely to Fagua.
It was all I could say.
"I'm leaving, Eri, but I need to finish telling you."
Again, his eyes welled up; he was going to cry, but he didn't.
"I left that house, Eri, I don't know how. Like her, I was crying. And when I was in the avenue, waiting for the bus, the bus that ... would forever banish me ... I heard the voice behind me ... the voice you know, Eri, the voice. He greeted me as if nothing had happened, said hello, but also ... he said something unusual, he called me ... *dear. Querido*, he said, and only now do I realize he said it mockingly, *I've been waiting for you here.* He was still behind me, and gave me no time to turn: he wrapped an arm around my neck, I thought he was going to strangle me ... but

suddenly I felt he was just squeezing me tightly up against him, caressing me, he ... kissed me on the mouth, he told me, you're so handsome ... so intelligent ... and ... his hand ... Eri, you didn't suspect that either? Are you laughing?"

"No."

Again, he was overcome by a terrible silence.

"I love him, Eri, that is my tragedy. My eternal debasement. My humiliation ... It's horrible how, in an instant, our lives can change, or life changes us and ... it happens from one moment to the next ... we simply discover who we are, to our own surprise, eternal shame, unhappiness—or joy? ... Ah, I haven't worked it out yet ... but listen, Eri, to the most abhorrent part.

"We took a taxi to my house, it was still dark, just before dawn, we entered, lay on the living room carpet, he embraced me as if he were going to smother me, whispered in my ear that I should search in my own sister's room for some lingerie and ... that I should put it on, Eri.

"He told me that, ordered me.

"And that's what I did, Eri ...

"If he'd ordered me to bring him my naked sister, I would have obeyed, Eri. I would have obeyed.

"And then he ... and I ...

"That's why I'm here, because ... but that's also why I'm leaving ... because ... it's simple: he finished me, he crushed me.

"On that trip to Barranquilla, Eri, I struggled ... Not even I knew who I was, or what I was: from one day to the next I found myself transformed into ... You must have assumed my greatest desire was to visit that brothel, right? I pretended that I wanted ... I wanted him to ... to once again ... with all his strength ... to finish discovering who I was ... Eri. When I shut myself away with that blonde ... I couldn't rise to the occasion, thinking about him ... I couldn't do much, despite her efforts, she was kind to me."

Oh, my Marilyn, I thought, what a waste! I think I sighed my soul away. "And what does it matter," I told Fagua then, summoning all of my wisdom, "worse things happen, why make a tragic hero of yourself? You draw your conclusions, Fito, and go on living as you want to; you can turn this experience to your advantage if you're smart, or into a cruel joke if you're a fool, and you're no ..."

My coda disappointed him, he didn't listen to the end. He fled, resolute, and, what's more, without picking up the check.

Then the announcement came over the loudspeakers. Toño Ciruelo was landing.

12

The Exiles

"THOSE FRENCH ARE ALL SO STUCK-UP, SO FULL OF THEM-
selves, they think they're God's testicles—or tits, if God is a her-
maphrodite."

This time Ciruelo did want to talk.

We were in the living room of his apartment, long, white, devoid of paintings, and we wandered along the walls—as if *we*
were the paintings: still lifes or already dead?

Having mastered the world, he wanted to relive his world tour,
by talking about it. He set the bottles on the floor: Let's drink a
toast, he said, selecting the absinthe, and I raised my glass to his;
he contemplated me, beatifically, awaiting the moment—his moment—to speak; I was all too familiar with his expression when
he was preparing to recount, deceive, invent, or simply remember—in any case, to explore the root of his actions—consulting
only with himself, because the world before him appeared in-
iquitous, truly worthless, no matter whom he was addressing:
Ciruelo was the magician preparing to leap onto the stage, the
boxer into the ring, the bullfighter, the actor, the swimmer holding his breath underwater, the judge.

But why did I follow him? Why, after Fagua's confession, his
lamentations, his corroborations? Why, after "attending" that
quasi-deflowering, not just physical but of the spirit, that Fagua's
sister and girlfriend, and even Fagua himself, had suffered at the
hands of Ciruelo? Why had I greeted him with an embrace and
climbed into his taxi? Why did I still hang around with Toño
Ciruelo and raise a glass with him, with the devil? Was it a result

of my *writerly curiosity*, or was it just me? Had I too—I cursed myself—succumbed to his dominance? Ah, I thought, I've been corrupted worse than any whore.

"The Germans are a bunch of imbeciles," he warned, far removed from my act of contrition, convinced of my devoted attention, "as well as great sausage makers: that must be why they like war. And don't tell me there's no need to generalize, Eri.

"The Japanese have been morbidly repressed for centuries, and what more can we say about the English, pale as milk, a calflike odor, slave traders? The whole world is disgusting, Eri, the terrorists and bankers are its masters, not even the Church, what wishful thinking! None of those reprobates are to blame, they simply take part in the world, nobody knows who kills whom, and we Colombians are no exception, we don't even know who we are.

"The campesinos who sow, the fishermen who fish, embody Earth's only hope, but because they're simple, elemental as the trees, the family idiots, they'll disappear like the rhino, and ... you'll see, Eri, if you live, if you last somehow, you can't last."

Having listened to this muddle of ideas, his *elevation*, his final phrase kept running through my head: *you can't last*. It wasn't the first time he'd alluded to my demise, which at that time I considered near at hand, as though I myself had prophesied I wouldn't be able to last, that, in the words of Ciruelo, I couldn't. It wasn't the first time Ciruelo had alluded to this, abruptly, as if driving a dagger into my spirit again and again, swiftly, and without my ever having revealed a wavering purpose to anyone, as though he'd read it on my face.

Always, in the presence of his brief but piercing assertions about what he referred to as my "ineptitude" for life, I would remain silent, sometimes inflicting my bewilderment upon him, but all the same: I sensed I wouldn't be able to endure it; and, nevertheless, during those days, in the frenzy of that same extraordinary purpose to sacrifice myself, I would immediately think of the book I was writing at the time, think of a humming-bird, distract myself from the final decision, distract myself until the next morning from the increasingly firm conviction that I couldn't withstand another morning.

This is what was happening to me then, and I have been able to recall it by remembering Ciruelo's trip and his return; and today I am so far removed from that sorrowful Eri, that I can only claim that I suffered from existential candor—just like Fagua. And that night in his apartment was no exception; yet I was distracted from succumbing by his voice itself, which seconds before had demanded that I acknowledge that I could not last; Toño Ciruelo himself helped me live—with his furious understanding of the world and of himself, like someone equating cows with carrots or squirrels with coffins.

"No religion," he rhapsodized, "no political ideal or social structure truly concerns itself with the human being; they are concerned only with the interests of an organization, a society, a family, which may or may not be numerous ... but never the human being, or planet Earth as a being, and they won't ever, Eri: evil is congenital, it is some innard alongside the heart of man, if not the heart itself.

"The best we can do is enjoy this vale of tears; life is a circus: some have a good time of it, others get screwed because they can't afford the ticket.

"God is very old and no longer aware of the bullets striking his sheep; poor God, indifferent God, cretinous God."

That's how he spoke, stomping the ground and replying to himself with bursts of laughter I now remember as furious and deranged.

And we drank.

"The trip has worn me out," he said suddenly, sitting like Buddha on the carpet, spreading his arms, his palms upward, exactly like God; then he leaped up and disappeared in the direction of his room without saying good night, not the least bit concerned about abandoning me.

He went to bed.

But he came back a minute later and woke me from the torpor in which I found myself.

He came back naked, au naturel. What were his intentions? To bewitch me, rape me as he had Fagua? No. He was pacing around my armchair; his European trip had truly affected him.

"You won't believe who I met at the Barbès metro station in Paris, you'll never guess. I came across this guy who was paler than Dracula and looked half-dead, that Beto Garzón, remember him? He was at school with us."

"Yes. All alone during recess, he looked as though he barely existed from so much existing."

"I came across him blowing into a flute like a bum, a musician with no audience; I dropped a few green bills into his black hat, and he stared at me mesmerized and stopped playing. What was he playing? Those Andean songs about flying condors, weeping Indians, the sun god and the godly sun and the virgins of the sun, etcetera ... then he jumped up and embraced me, what are you doing in Paris? he asked, as if from underground. And I told him: The same as you—I have no clue what the fuck I'm doing in goddamn Paris.

"And so we got hammered in Paris.

"It's entirely different running into an acquaintance in Paris: you know in Paris, a friend is closer, laughter's better, an embrace more of an embrace, etcetera.

"I bought him drinks his throat couldn't even imagine. And, drunk but elegant, he told his stories as though he hadn't spoken for years and was afraid he'd forgotten how to talk. He'd arrived in Paris with a girlfriend from Bogotá, one of those eager to live. His girlfriend eventually found work, pampering little old deranged Parisian men. All well and good until the little Indian ran off to Tokyo with one of those incurables, who was apparently very much alive and could afford the daily wages of a Latina cock-sucker; I never heard from her again, he told me. He overcame this loss and found an Ecuadoran woman who cared for young children with Down syndrome. The Ecuadoran slipped away from him too: *that* little Indian ran off to India with the mystical father of a child who you could truly call an Indian—how about that?—she went looking for God. From then on Beto Garzón decided he was better off alone than in bad company. He told me: I have such brilliant luck that if I met an Argentine, she'd probably work in an insane asylum and run off with the biggest loon.

"He told me how he was forced to give in to poverty, like all those who prosper as exiles in Paris. How, in a supermarket, he'd discovered some biscuits they sold by weight, at an unbeatable price, and survived on those for a year; how, one day, a customer stocking up on these same biscuits asked him what breed *his* dog was, and how, because of that, he'd suffered nausea for a month. How he'd written a novel, Eri, but a novel of exile, he told me. I asked him why he didn't write instead about the girlfriends who'd abandoned him. Ninety percent of those emigrant novelists are brilliant, but they're isolated, frustrated, searching in vain for a publisher who'll deify them.

"He told me he rented a room in the apartment of a Danish woman who was mature but doable and who got drunk alone on a bottle of vodka the first Friday of every month, dancing by herself, hugging the bottle, plastered, tottering, a blonde willowy Danish woman who let out a diabolical laugh of disdain one extraordinary Friday when he proposed they dance together—how about that?—and the Scandinavian kicked him out for being an ambitious Indian.

"That moron Beto went without so much as yelling slut, without spanking those cheeks red, without saying goodbye like he should have, without forcing himself on her, without busting that ass, Eri.

"He told me he left for Marseille to work as a hired hand at a hotel run by Chileans; he came close to drowning himself in the Mediterranean; he was rescued by some black men from Senegal who happened to be bathing near the shore, they rescued him out of compassion: If you cannot swim, why are you swimming? And he responded: I wanted to talk to my fishy friends. You see, Eri? That Beto's a bit like you.

"And will he have finished his novel? Ninety percent of those exiles write the same novel for their entire lives, that final period only coming when they die. That's the way it is with geniuses. Poor geniuses.

"He told me he returned to Paris and went to live in that two-bit apartment in Barbès, with Arabs, Chinese, and all sorts for neighbors; his window there looked onto a wall; wait till you see it, he told me.

"So I fed him food his belly never could have dreamed of; he was a starving compatriot: give him bread and circuses and he'd be willing to die for you.

"And he took me to his apartment, a damp, dingy dungeon, with a yellow plastic flower and stuffed kitten in the window: the flower grew and lit up and the kitten mewed in that window that really did look out onto a concrete wall, gray like Paris, what a pretty picture, a dismal window that made Beto genuinely proud.

"He introduced me to his friends, the majority of them Latinos, and I spent a good fortnight restoring them, Eri, nourishing the stomachs of the Latino diaspora.

"The majority of them were bewildered by life, more idle than romantic. A bunch of assholes.

"There was one who worked an honest job. A joker from Antioquia who traveled around the world sponsored by Coca-Cola.

He was a wizard with a yo-yo, you know, that toy for dimwits that goes up and down, the incredible Coca-Cola yo-yo. They were right to finance his trip around the world: the guy could do trapeziums and animals with his yo-yo, insects, prisms, flowers and octahedrons, the everlasting Eiffel Tower, probably the Taj Mahal; within a second he'd set his yo-yo spinning inside your shirt pocket, you felt as though a frantic beetle were fondling your heart, the yo-yo leaped out of your pocket without ceasing to spin and rose in circles, tracing something resembling blaring trumpets, the depiction so accurate it was as though the trumpets were actually playing, and this was immediately followed by the blades of the Moulin Rouge, a Japanese pagoda, the steps of Machu Picchu, the peak of Everest, the head of Nefertiti, and, in a moment of magic from his yo-yo, the guy finally disappeared entirely, Eri, he *dis-a-ppeared* and ... reappeared; ah, with his yo-yo, that guy was as good as me, or better, Eri, I can acknowledge the genius of imbeciles."

"With them I was happy, as far as possible, although ... we were occasionally visited by a European primatologist couple who specialized in Latin American primates—she was from Marseille and he was a Berliner—in whom I must have aroused a great deal of curiosity, I don't know why, Eri, surely because of the size of my head—or both my heads? Rather than questioning them about their real interest in me—my soul, my intestines?—I made them groan one day by mentioning those colonies that throughout history have been and will be exploited by liberal France and democratic Germany, their chemical weapons and their atomic tests, you give the Earth indigestion, and I laid bare all the dirty dealings sponsored by fraternal France and carnivorous Germany, hand in hand, with the third world as a storehouse, and ... they bluntly refused to accept this reality, what primates: they argued, anyway, we aren't responsible for the decisions of our politicians;

aren't you? I replied, you elect them, I called them bastards in elegant French, like the Spanish, you sell us the weapons you manufacture, and then it's let the wars begin, *jijos de la gran chingada*, I swore, in perfect Mexican; it was beginning to rain; I thought if Paris was a movable feast I'd have to be Balzac, but no sooner had I mentioned Hitler and his hominids than the Norman and the Aryan immediately took their leave, promising never to return, *es usted un ba-rrio-ba-je-ro*, the Berliner said, branding me a lowlife in flawless Castilian; I'll walk you to the metro, I proposed cheerfully, I'm going for cigarettes; they stared at me open-mouthed but allowed me to accompany them because civilization never loses its composure, Eri.

"It was pelting down, and in the street, they unfurled their sensible umbrellas; don't you have an umbrella? they asked me, and, most considerately, each offered to shelter me under their wing; water delights me, I replied, I've been dying to bathe in pure water; you, Eri, probably assume I was just being resentful, but no: I was being genuinely me, without any constraints: I've always enjoyed getting drenched to the bone with rainwater. Then the primatologist who specialized in Latino hunter-gatherers muttered in a devious little voice that if I liked water so much, why didn't I go swim in the fountain for a bit? It was a marble fountain, Eri, the kind that can only exist in Paris, tall and round, a small basin presided over by one of those blushing Greek goddesses in the nude, gushing water from her nose, her nipples, her cunt and anus, her mouth, her eyes, her ears, a feminine spout, the frothy water that poured out sounding just like Berlioz; without a second thought I leaped into the fountain and threw myself under the goddess and her cascade, joyful, the goddess and I; I planted a kiss on her snow-white lips, sucked her tits, licked her anus, pretended to stand and penetrate her from behind before allowing myself to fall backwards with exhaustion, like a duck among the tumult of the foam; I submerged myself, emerging only to spot the primatologists racing frantically down the avenue, Eri, clearly sensing that I'd go after them, that I'd capture them, would force them to couple with me ... and that's what happened, Eri ... I frightened them ... no, no, I exterminated them.

"This absinthe is green poison, Eri.

"I spent that half month growing disenchanted, surrounded by Peruvians and Chileans and Bolivians, most of them hopeless, some toothless, others titless, all of them 'refugees,' 'political exiles'; I was king (though a sad one) for a day, and, upon waking, Eri, with those frail, flat-chested Parisians whom I paid to suck off the sons of the sun, I thought it would be preferable for us to wake up dead, whores and Latinos, flesh of one flesh, of one fart, one despair, for us to wake up torn to shreds, I don't know why ... I felt ... felt ... I began to ... At a pet store, one of those fancy ones where they sell bonsai horses and purebred cats, I said to an elegant lady's daughter, a pink-cheeked little girl clutching to her chest a very well-groomed guinea pig that was even wearing winter clothes, I told her that we bred those little creatures in my country; but what a lovely guinea pig you've got there, I said, and I touched it, tickling it; I told her in my country we roast and eat those little creatures well-done, I don't know what face I must have made as I said it, but the little girl began to howl and the lady went to get help from security—why am I telling you this?—I think, however, that I told the little girl upon departing that here in Paris they eat little creatures like you instead, I said that and I think ... upon saying it ... that something broke inside me, Eri, something inside me changed, something changed me, that's the word, *changed*, something in my brain—my cerebellum, my heart?—my tailbone, Eri, I said that in Colombia, too, and all over Disney World we also eat little creatures like you, *en tout le monde*, I said, it was something strange within the remotest part of me, a ... cannibal joy, Eri, like feeling hungry and discovering you could devour an uncooked little girl, ha! Are you falling asleep? Have some absinthe. Or would you rather we changed the subject? Or the liquor? We should've bought some aguardiente at El Dorado.''

"Then listen to me, it wasn't all cavorting in penury, Eri—pour yourself some absinthe—there was other cavorting: alongside my uncles I frequented Paris's most exquisite restaurants, with Gustave Eiffel as our witness, in the company of the loftiest figures in Colombian society, ex-colleagues of my senator father, I must admit, and you would find yourself dining beside riffraff who'd been sentenced to 'house arrest' in Colombia; one of these had swindled the nation of I don't know how many billions, an ex-governor, fiddler, white-collar crook, plunderer, he'd feathered his nest at the expense of the treasury, and yet, here he was a 'refugee,' a 'political exile,' and there were many others like him, mayors, magistrates, congressmen, who would very graciously raise a glass with you, as would prominent leaders of the national underworld, Harvard graduates, narcos, ex-generals, each possessing a 'license to kill' like Bond, extraordinary people; one, a crafty councillor, was free to walk around in the world after winning a famous ruling in his favor by demonstrating (without demonstrating) the insanity of the four campesinos testifying against him; these were four direct witnesses to his crimes, but Our Law dictated: Stark Raving Mad; another, an ex-colonel, claimed that he too was a political exile: he was under house arrest for having slaughtered more than a hundred honest indigenous Colombians during a celebration in the Cauca Department, a dark celebration of an inevitable massacre, necessary, because that's life, he said, because God willed it, because it was their turn, and what a pity, I'm sorry; and there were even common murderers, one in particular, a horse breeder and exporter, who had 'liquidated' his last three wives in fits of 'anger and intense pain,' and due to his anger and his intense pain, he was able to walk around Paris absolved of any guilt and speak wistfully of 'my dead wives' as he ate with his fingers, picked his teeth with a fish bone, and belched in your ear, and next to me, another of this universe's *capos* raised his glass, famous for having a bathtub made of pure gold installed in his house and filled with emeralds instead of water, he'd been sentenced to twenty years for aggravated homicide, conspiracy to commit a felony, and possession of illegal weapons, but in order to ensure house arrest, the judge, 'Vasquecito,' had argued that the *capo*'s mamá was sick, that she worked in domestic service and was already displaying signs of serious mental illness due to the absence of her son. We come from the land of the cunning foxes, those snakes would tell you without a hint of shame; there was another who repented belatedly, loquacious in the retelling of his deeds: there were a couple of tough guys, he told us, that we were just about to kill, and they were laughing, we were about to kill them, who knows why, probably no one could or would pay the ransom, their salvation, and I would later learn they were simple shoe salesmen, but we'd decided to execute them, we made them dig their own graves following a trial, and read them the verdict right there, by the side of the graves they'd dug—the two men, meanwhile, joked about death, the terrible stench of corpses, the advantages and disadvantages of deodorant, my body will turn into a mosquito and bite you all, the virgin awaits me in heaven, they laughed, and laughed wholeheartedly, and this incensed us, I'm sorry, but we wanted to inflict terror, not have our victims burst into laughter; and the dinner ended with a small-town politician, a welfare pilferer, who assured us very seriously that 'his dream' was to be 'replicated' at the wax museum in London; all of those happy, fat men seemed entirely different from those other 'refugees' and 'exiles' who visited the apartment of my journalist friend, bitter, suspicious, never having read a book in their lives but managing to pass themselves off as erudite, a coterie of young Dutch girls hung around with them, enthralled, organizing student collections to 'finance' the liberation forces, stamping T-shirts with revolutionary slogans in every language, they were well-endowed in ass and pocket; one night, they held a dinner in honor of the ideologist most sought after by the Colombian *intelligentsia*, the scowling little man arriving 'incognito,' surrounded by his 'muchachos,' baby-faced militants with terrible tempers; the incognito wore a Che beret emblazoned with a silver star larger than his head and, embroidered on his heavy jacket, shining yellow-blue-and-red, were the sacred and bloody colors of the flag; he became drunk in no time, opening the window facing the Arc de Triomphe and poking his bearded face out to swear aloud to the world that one day he would liberate Colombia from the yoke of imperialism—how about that?—à la Simón Bolívar; on hearing this I laughed heartily, but I was defeated by the deathly silence that followed his words ... the boys escorting him did not approve; those boys have nothing resembling political ideals, they coin some phrase or other as a motto, then grunt over it, wheeling it out on any grounds, no matter how irrelevant: in the end, they're nothing but people who kill to make a living— that absinthe has poisoned me ... Have I told you about the time I caused a stampede? ... Let's drink to the last drop, Eri, ah—they make good sausages in the Philippines, but there's none better than the ones they make here in Suta. I walked along Barcelona's beaches with a Portuguese man for the whole summer, we did our thing, he was a ... who ... and some alcoholics from Norway ... high-class beggars ... their government pays them for being unemployed ... they spend every summer enjoying the Spanish sun ... they made me ... and I ... anything can happen in Barcelona, even more than New York, in Valencia I threw my books off a train; in the Basque Country I shattered the jawbone of a guy even bigger than I am with a bottle ... I think I escaped from prison in Lisbon, but I think ... before ... I had lunch in Dublin with the son of a ... he was a ... well, there was no reason, but a ... worse ... I don't know ... who ... what I'm for ... Eri ... help me."

I heard no more; I couldn't; the absinthe had doubled me over. But I'll never forget that he asked me to help him.

I awoke at midday. I'd been covered with an alpaca throw. "Toño," I called. Had I dreamed about him? We were walking, I was behind him and could only see his back, his shoulders, and suddenly he turned to look at me and I closed my eyes, dazzled by a godlike light. There was nobody in the apartment, I went to the kitchen looking for a beer: I found a stash of them, and in the living room I discovered the mezcal from Oaxaca; I forgot about the beer, waiting the whole afternoon; I wanted to leave but couldn't. Why? I remembered Toño's Latin, his famous *Si sedes non is, si non sedes is—if you sit you do not go, if you do not sit you go*. I had questions to put to him—would I dare?—terrible questions that were like assertions: You knocked down Fagua's sister in the street, didn't you? You pushed your own sister into the abyss. You blew up your parents' Mercedes. You did away with your uncles.

Would I dare?

He never arrived.

It was getting dark by the time I left his apartment, drunk on mezcal. In my head, I repeated to myself lurchingly, zigzagging along Avenida Caracas, repeated to myself exactly as Fagua had: This is the last time I see you, Ciruelo, you'll never find me.

It was I who found him, a year later, without looking for him, on a sunny Bogotá afternoon, despite him not looking for me either—or had he been looking for me? Had he been looking for me and arranged that chance encounter? It was at the library, outside the glass entrance; an insignificant Athena statue listened in on us, impassively.

"You won the national award," he said. "Who but you could've won it. You've got the face of a winner, Eri, frightening. Don't get worked up. In any case, you're the voice of a ... disaffected generation, you're doing well, you're our champion."

I'd won a short story competition, and the story had been published the week before in *Magazin*.

"That story is a landmark," Ciruelo hailed it. "'Doubt,' what a title, it creates an appetite for doubt, Eri."

His vehement eyes gave me chills.

"I read it and thought, how good that Eri is, how magnificent, he's awesome, we can only hope one day he considers writing for real. Writing, for example, about me."

I didn't want to hang around with him and came up with some excuse. I looked up at the unusually blue Bogotá sky; the surrounding mountains shifted like a mirage, it wouldn't be long before it rained. I looked at him; he was wearing his blue overcoat; he shone, master of everything, as he'd been throughout his entire life, with his supercilious smile. He invited me for coffee, but I wanted nothing more to do with Toño Ciruelo, ever again.

"Goodbye, Toño," I said. "I'm going to write about you."

"It'll take you your whole life if you don't talk to me."

"Then I can do without a life, Toño."

He seemed unaffected by this thrust, my definitive goodbye. He shrugged with amicable disdain; it was as though he were congratulating me.

"Now I see I'll have to write about myself," he said.

And he slipped into the crowd, without once looking back, so tall, his head towered over the other bodies, a giant among this country's dwarfs. I continued to watch him until he disappeared, submerged in his staggering solitude. Where was he going? Or, rather, where had he come from?

I felt no regret, only peace, as if I had finally rescued myself from something, from someone, from him.

Book Two

1

Here, with Me

I DIDN'T BELIEVE, HOWEVER, THAT TOÑO CIRUELO HAD *PUT an end* to La Oscurana, or didn't want to believe it, didn't want to invoke that other word, murderer, here, with me, in my home. Such a confession must surely be the climax to a performance, the performance Ciruelo had prepared in order to torment me, in his own way, and yet the superhuman effort he had made in telling me—not so much physical, grasping me by the throat and asphyxiating me, but rather intimate—no longer seemed to me like a performance, it was true, it had to be.

He collapsed.

It appeared he was being humiliated by a guilty dream: sudden nightmares startled his eyelids, his swollen body; I heard him swear, spout dark phrases in who knows what language. He settled down and I decided to leave him; I took my things through to the study. I didn't last long, though, and began pacing back and forth—just like an inmate.

All on one level, my home was one quarter of an ancient mansion in La Candelaria that had been converted by its owner into four separate apartments and rented out. There was a bedroom, a living room, a bathroom, study, and kitchen. I tried to work, but this was no longer possible: his ... presence ... pulsed there; it was getting late; I went to the small utility room behind the kitchen, turned on the washing machine, began taking dry clothes off the line, rinsed some plates. In a corner near the entrance to my apartment I discovered, like a crouching animal,

Toño Ciruelo's Arhuaca shoulder bag, the fraying bag he had dropped on arriving.

Stunned, troubled in my soul, I thought that it smelled of blood and earth.

I shoved it into the umbrella stand, though not without first inspecting its contents: a pair of dark, round Lennonesque glasses, a rusty Swiss Army knife (the multipurpose kind, with a spoon, fork, can opener ...), a Toledo pocketknife with an engraved greenish handle, the blade of which I did not wish to open but imagined curved, sharp; a leather wallet, smooth, tattered, swollen, not just with pesos but postcards of Klimts and Van Goghs; another small rice-paper Bible; and there were also worn-down black pencils, a metal sharpener, a chewed cream Pelikan eraser, a set of keys (surely the keys to his home, bound by a heavy copper ring), and a large-format composition notebook with graph paper, a hundred pages, its hard covers imprinted with a photo of Charles Lindbergh standing beside his plane.

I opened the notebook: I'm not sure why I was reluctant to read even a single sentence; I merely confirmed that it was Ciruelo's handwriting, minuscule; this was surprising, for I recalled how, at school, his broad-stroke handwriting would fill a whole page within a few sentences; inside the notebook, what stood out was an insect-like smallness, square by square, as if, when writing, Ciruelo were making an effort to save paper, or to alter the style of his handwriting—or had he, perhaps, altered his personality? And he wrote only in pencil; not a trace of ink; it was noticeable that many passages had been erased and later written over. I supposed it must be some kind of diary, or a collection of letters, and that a number of these letters were addressed to me, for I glimpsed my name scattered here and there; all hundred pages had already been written on, front and back, as well as the inside covers; and, in the margins, there were sporadic drawings, inescapable miniatures, faces of women: black, white,

Asian; bodies in the most sinuous positions, with breasts and nipples and lips, feminine sexes that were brief or stretched or swollen or parted or closed or hairy or hairless, stomachs with navels like eyes, wide or narrow, and pupils like split vulvas; there were drawings of boats, moons, suns, seas, rivers, strange animals, maps, telescopes, nautical charts, compasses pointing north and south, dolphins and tridents, lighthouses, question marks, a microscopic man advancing like a defeated shadow, a three-legged dog, an upside-down piano, villages, cats, owls, stone cities, all between smudges like dirty tear stains that may have been drops of coffee. Or drops of wine. Or drops of blood. Sickened, I returned the notebook to the shoulder bag.

I organized my books in the study, then reorganized them, dusted my desk, lamp, my papers, and opened book after book, reading at random like someone consulting an oracle—an oracle that augured nothing. Hours must have passed before I returned to the living room. I found him in absolute stillness, his eyes half-shut, mouth open, his tremendous bulk as if floating in the shadows, a dark reptile patiently awaiting its victim. Was I his victim? It was cold, so I searched for a ruana and threw it over him. Just by dying in my house you'll already be making me your victim, I told him, and switched on a floor lamp, for it was getting dark, and then I leaned over his face, assessing him: it was extraordinary how someone who, in his youth, in spite of everything, had captivated so many young women, now provoked nothing but fear; Ciruelo, yesterday a perfidious angel, but an angel nonetheless, was horrible today. So? I must surely be the same, or even worse; at fifty years old, what is most grotesque in us has already started to emerge.

He was sweating feverishly, his breathing uneven. Listen, I said, do you want me to call a doctor?

"No," I heard him, faintly. The hand missing a finger searched gropingly and clasped my arm. "Don't even think about it."

He was gathering strength to speak, opened his eyes, delirious. I asked him, for the sake of asking, to revive him, why he'd plagiarized Benito Pérez Galdós at school. To mock the teacher, he replied. And, with no clear connection, I asked what had really happened to "Gringa" Katy, the neighborhood hairdresser, had he mesmerized her? And the three girls at the Planetarium, how had he touched them without touching them? On hearing me, he instantly recovered, his eyes widened, and for a moment he was once again that talkative Toño. He told me, brimming over, filled with that strange energy brought on by fever: That hypnotism thing always struck you as a sham, Eri, but it's real; it was something I learned, and is, above all, a gift. I traveled to the temples of sleep, and I achieved it, but I never contemplated performing the tricks of a common magician; my plans, my purposes, were different, very different; that must be why my powers of suggestion, my magnetism, had only a brief, fragile effect, and I discovered that the person caught in my web, man or woman, once shaken from my power, loathed me, Eri, loathed me consciously and unconsciously; and if it wasn't loathing it was terror, they ran far from me; men, children, and women fled far from me, and that wasn't what I wanted. What for? Something similar happened with my gift for ventriloquism, and I abandoned it forever; you know that since I was a child I always wanted my own ventriloquist's dummy, one that looked exactly like me, I wanted to live off that dummy, talking to it or to myself in the world's theaters, making fun of the world, shitting on the world; I imagined dialogues, amusing but macabre, and wrote them down, rewrote them, memorized them; I already had a name for that dummy, and even hoped, on my death, that I might be buried alongside it, both of us dressed identically; but never again would I project my voice using another voice, another place, never, and this was because of my dream, Eri, I dreamed I awoke to discover, sitting on the edge of my bed, a man with a suitcase on the floor;

I opened the suitcase, and inside was a ventriloquist's dummy with my own face, transfigured, I mean dummified. I turned to look at the man, about to ask who are you, what are you doing on my bed, when a voice coming from the dummy interrupted me: Are you scared? it asked me, and it was my own voice, transfigured, also dummified. Then I woke up, it was daytime already, I jumped out of bed, got dressed, and went to the bakery for breakfast; reality helped me relax, I ate a couple of fried eggs and was still drinking my coffee when a man with a suitcase came in, it was the exact same guy from my dream, Eri, and you have to believe me, when I walked past his table a voice from inside the suitcase asked me: Are you scared? It asked this in my own voice, transfigured, like a ventriloquist's dummy, that guy, that nobody, that apparition had a dummy version of me inside his suitcase, *me*. Who was he? *What* was he? My persecutor, my judge? I fled from him, I fled from them, I fled—mc, always the hunter—fled with terror ringing in my ears, because I couldn't avoid hearing that voice, my own expanding voice: *Are you scared? Are you scared?*

Ciruelo took a deep breath:

"It's true, it's the truth," he said. "This time it's the truth."

"It's the truth," I responded. "You probably dreamed it just now. Get some rest, Toño."

"I'll revive at any moment," he said. "Bring me water, it's the only favor I ask of you. Tomorrow I'll leave without saying good-bye—or tonight, if I can."

I went to get water and offered it to him, but already he was sleeping again, deeply. I put the jug and glass on a small table beside him, and stayed there, indecisive, sitting in the chair, watching him: how had he known about my apartment? How had he been able to find me? As if he were somehow listening to my thoughts—or had I spoken aloud?—I heard him, from far away: I discovered this was your home years ago, Eri, and never bothered you; so leave me alone, go write another book, find a girlfriend, bone her, run off wherever you like, but leave me be.

"Where did you come from, Toño? Where were you before?"

"Nearby. Staying with the nuns. They poisoned me, Eri. And they were unsuccessful—as you can see, it was in vain. But they're searching, they're looking for me, they and the others, they're following my scent ... and you were thinking of bringing over a doctor."

"Who did you say you were staying with?"

"Leave me in peace, Eri, for crying out loud!"

"I don't have a guest room, just my bed. Let me know if you'd rather move onto the bed."

He sighed by way of response, turned his shivering back to me, grabbed hold of the ruana and pulled it over his head. Leave me be, he pleaded, and curled up in a ball. The couch was large, though not large enough for Ciruelo; half his body hung over the edge.

"Here's the water," I said, and he replied without moving: "Thank you, thank you, stop talking," and later, when I switched out the light, when I left him alone—it was after 9:00 p.m.—I heard him cry out, in the voice of one dreaming in the grip of a fever, in ravings, I heard him cry out, "Forgive me, forgive me, forgive me for all of them, my God!" He yelled this many times and then said nothing more.

I climbed into bed with a book, though not without first locking the door: *Are you scared?* I heard inside of me—just as if I were being asked by the ventriloquist's dummy. *Yes, I answered, you're frightening, Ciruelo, you frighten people away, but that's exactly why I want to listen to you, scream by scream; what became of your life these past twenty years?*

It began to rain—it had been raining for days in Bogotá, steadily, imperceptibly.

It was impossible to read.

Lying on my back, the blankets pulled up to my neck, I turned out the lamp. Through the window, the light from the streetlamp came and went, and a dream, rising first to my eyes, crept over me, fickle, faltering: that skin stained with hieroglyphs, the painted face of La Indígena, her nervous expression, her copper body, her long, jet-black hair, but very long, so much longer, La Oscurana's dark eyes, her distant, troubled silence—it was as if she were hoarse, almost audible, with a stammer. Was it true that he'd killed her? *It's true*, I heard myself say, *it's true; he killed her.*

2

An Exhibition of Pain

AT THE EDGE OF THE UNIVERSITY, IN A QUIET PATCH OF WIL-
lows we called God's Laughter, where we would smoke marijuana or argue about the world and other worlds or simply sleep,
I heard talk of Antonio Ciruelo, and not just once. I hadn't seen
him again, but it was as if we were back in touch. Many at my
university knew of Toño Ciruelo, Mr. Crack-of-Dawn, the Infallible, the Ubiquitous; many kept track of him and spoke of him
without suspecting I'd known him since school. Any street dog
on any corner, they said, would remind you of Ciruelo, for he
had taken more than forty Bogotá mutts, the mangiest of street
dogs, to live with him in his own house (he'd sold the apartment
in the center), until one night, with no one able to guess why,
he returned them to Bogotá, plump and resplendent: Fend for
yourselves as best you can, they say he told them, go off and die!
This could be true, it's how Ciruelo spoke.

And whether you found yourself detained without an ID at
the police station, or drinking rum in a bar, a curious visitor to
the slaughterhouse in Chía, or at the stadium, concert, or theater, there would always be someone who knew of Toño Ciruelo,
the dog savior of Bogotá. In the most fortuitous ways, without
my even mentioning him, his story and his name would come
up, as if searching me out. In the most varied locations, I would
hear news of him, and always beneath the feminine scent of marijuana. And many were the voices that would chime in when
his acts were judged. Guys and girls conspired to evoke him,
supporting each other's claims, contradicting each other; they

would seem exalted at first, then become appalled and go silent, as if repentant—ashamed?—or as if the recalling of distant acts could somehow make them participants in those very acts, the abominable acts of Toño Ciruelo.

He had dropped chemistry and enrolled in sociology before starting performing arts and switching to medicine (without ever completing any of them, of course), and not even cinema studies had inspired him. I learned he'd won a music contest for performing the breakneck "Vino Tinto" and the even speedier "San Pedro en el Espinal," on his requinto guitar. I had never imagined he could also play the requinto, as well as being who he was; I had never suspected him of possessing hidden musical talents; not once had I heard him blow into a dulzaina or a flute or strum a guitar. It's possible it wasn't true, that even music had been incorporated into his legend, but I remember clearly how, inside his dead sister's room, on the wall, skeletal, stringless, yellowed, there had hung a requinto guitar.

I even heard it claimed that Antonio Ciruelo was dead, that he'd been killed in Santa Marta in a bar, "in revenge," but others said no, he'd drowned in Santa Marta, which was altogether different; nobody knew anything, and, nevertheless, Toño would reappear, alive, always alive, around the corner in any conversation.

Those who hung out in God's Laughter would recall his glorious Exhibition of Pain, about which I had received only vague news but formed an impression while listening to so many differing accounts. An exhibition that I—despite the apprehension I harbored, for I was already acquainted with Ciruelo—would have liked to have suffered in the flesh. It was Ciruelo's brainchild: he had rented an old house in the Teusaquillo neighborhood, a dark house that operated for years as a "House of Horrors" before going bust, in spite of the bats and witches bursting out, the Draculas and Frankensteins. Inside, across three floors and two courtyards, within two drawing rooms and nine bedchambers, supported by a theater group (*Magma*)—a troupe of blossoming girls, the most intrepid students of the Santa Teresita Convent School—and a company of hungry circus dwarfs (the *Reykjavík Brothers*), he put on what he called An Exhibition of Pain.

Every Saturday, from six until nine in the evening, amid fantastic scenography, there was a live performance featuring some of the most relevant—in terms of sheer gore—scenes and figures from human history. Unfurling like blood-soaked flowers before the eyes of the defenseless ticket holders, you had the Conquest and Genocide of America, the Crusades, the Holocaust, as well as the irrefutable, parading arrival—furtive, grotesque—of Hitler and Nero, Napoleon and Alexander the Great, Tiberius, Ivan the Terrible, Genghis Khan, Agrippina, Richard the Lionheart, Bokassa, Aguirre, Pizarro, Queen Ranavalona of Madagascar, Liu Pengli of China, the monk Arnaud Amalric, Simon IV de Montfort "the Pious," General Butt Naked, and so many other "beasts of nature," as the signs in the exhibition stated. With no distinction between epochs, villages, and continents, Attila, Bolívar, Caligula, and Pinochet came out to dance; Vlad the Impaler, Boniface VII, Joseph Stalin, and Abimael Guzmán congratulated themselves; Shirō Ishii, Charles Manson, Carlos the Jackal, Mary Tudor (or "Bloody Mary"), Idi Amin, and Pol Pot waved undaunted; Mad Sam, Leopold II of Belgium—misnamed His Serene Majesty of the Congo—Yellow Mao, and Torquemada the Inquisitor burped, kicked, grunted, and groaned, nuzzled about, squawked, bellowed, and howled; the St. Bartholomew's Day massacre and the Nazi extermination camps were reenacted, and also exhibited were whips, gags, racks, cages, wedges, and screws, cat's paws, ropes and pulleys, needles and garrotes, and other implements coming from the most hidden depths of man's imagination.

And there was, so they told me, a mishmash of episodes,

inexplicable events, dark incidents, from history and prehistory, jungle scenes, street scenes, not just real but mythical and even biblical: the Via Crucis, the Crucifixion, Abraham's affairs and his concubine, the rape of Tamar, Absalom's adultery, the sexual practices of Solomon, nubile Susanna and the horrible elders.

The exhibition only lasted four Saturdays.

The authorities, who had assumed this was just one more Bogotá exhibition, were alerted by the parish priest of Teusaquillo, the Reverend Father Franco. For, sprawled in his throne in the first room, there sat a lustful and naked Jesus, allowing his feet to be washed, amid moaning, by a fifteen-year-old Mary Magdalene, who appeared just as God had brought her into this world, deranged with love and calling out, like canticles, the spiritual verses of Solomon:

> … Let him kiss me with the kisses of his mouth: for thy love is better than wine. Because of the savor of thy good ointments thy name is as ointment poured forth, therefore do the virgins love thee. Draw me, we will run after thee: the king hath brought me into his chambers: we will be glad and rejoice in thee, we will remember thy love more than wine.

This was the first detonation, but also one of the apparitions most celebrated by the audience, as if, in the midst of so much pain, they were grateful in the end for the presence of another kind of pain—or so we joked in God's Laughter.

Exhibited in the second room were the hardships endured by Saint Daniel, plunged into a cage with a tiger—a real tiger?—yes, a *tigrillo*, a wildcat—where had it come from?—from the Eastern Llanos, a makeshift tiger for a makeshift circus, sick, desiccated, perishing, poorly tethered, almost a kitten, but a tiger in spite of its sadness, one that cast its most tender look toward the praying man, circling him, weighing him up, evaluating him, sniffing at him in imitation of a Roman circus, breathing him in with the urgency of a lover, tasting him, and meanwhile the saint declaimed; he was a committed actor, a good actor, a saint through and through, his faith would redeem him, and the tiger listened, and listened, and one day, as had to happen, on the final day, it broke loose and pounced and ate him: the saint?; who else?; no, the *tigrillo* was just a dwarf in costume; no, it was a skin-and-bones *tigrillo*, I watched as they gave it a meager pound of horse meat shortly before it began *its* exhibition of pain, and the saint was a flesh-and-blood actor, not some rag doll, he earned his denarii, it seems he lost a leg as one loses a lover, half his thigh, his knee; no; *yes*, we know him, a confident guy, today he goes around on just one and a half legs; and?—and the tiger was mercilessly put down; was it shot?; no, Toño Ciruelo climbed into the cage and wrung its neck.

A second detonation.

Nor could Colombia itself escape the exhibition of pain: a third detonation; with no further explanation, the massacres of the Colombian *bandoleros* were presented, bands of armed peasants killed during *the grimmest era of our history: grimmest of all eras*, according to a label that fluttered like a flag.

Liberals and Conservatives, reds and blues, did battle for the bloody palm branch of victory. In different rooms, using an abundance of makeup, crimes against the people were reenacted: the rape of young girls, beheadings, machete butchery, the "flannel cut": they would slit your throat and pull your tongue through, leaving it dangling like a red necktie; a crowd of wax dummies (life-size compadres, priests, widows, watchmakers, bakers, and vagrants) lay, sporting neckties, in one of the nine chambers of pain. The audience passed through in silence.

Dwarfs representing three-year-old children were tossed up into the air: on landing, they would be left as if skewered on machetes raised aloft by the eternal Colombian *bandoleros* in the presence of horrified mothers, and then that entire house, the entire Exhibition of Pain, would shudder with screams; there was uproarious howling; the entire neighborhood shook with the caterwauling of the impaled children, it was the climactic moment of the exhibition, its supreme victory, and would take place at eight o'clock at night: no street sounds, sirens, ambulances, or whistles could overshadow the clamor, and, while this lasted, in the adjoining room, pregnant campesinas were slit from top to bottom, their fetuses (rag dolls soaked in chickens' blood) torn out and hurled by the actors at the panic-stricken audience, so that it was not only the shrieking of the pregnant women that could be heard, but genuine shrieking from the disgusted audience, an audience that, in any event, would end up laughing (laughing nervously, but laughing), because they had paid good money for their tickets, because they embraced the pain of the exhibition, and because, whatever else, it was with good reason that this area of the house had already been dubbed *The History of Screams*.

The *bandoleros* danced in unison. These were the sounds of Colombia: a village band diligently blasted out pasillos and torbellinos, cumbias and contradanzas; you could hear bambucos, porros, the guabina rhythm, the puye, the bunde, the paseo, merengue, and mapalé; the *bandoleros*, engaging in a merciless dance, a fiesta from the other side of memory, invited the curious with their dancing to join in with the dance; these were the valiant *chulavitas*, the valiant *cachiporros*, our Homeric heroes, our legends, and labels fluttered like banners announcing their noms de guerre: Black Blood, Leaping Pedro, Revenge, Sparks, Captain Poison, Captain Vengeance, Black Soul, Claw, Mariachi,

Danger, General Winner, Revolution, Scissors, Blue Bird, Green Bird, Black Bird.

The chambers howl; each one resembles an enormous vault: the body of a small boy is found in the hollow of a tree; beggars sleep under bridges; there are filthy buildings, filthy avenues; and, slipping like shadows, advancing on tiptoe, the thieves of sewer grates arrive, releasing gigantic rats from the sewers; it is the dwarfs who act as hirsute lawyers; from a long wooden bus, other dwarfs greet the crowd: these are the wallet thieves; there are more thieves scrambling over cardboard houses; and, introducing themselves with fervent speeches are the thieves of the church, the senate, all dressed as if for a party, and suddenly a rally of striking clowns appears, carrying placards: NO LAUGHING HERE. Then beauty queens strut provocatively around monstrous fat men who toss coins at them; an elderly boxer feints at his own shadow; old shoes hang from the ceiling, and there's an enormous map of the country under a sign: PAIN RINGS OUT; a jungle scene: two men in costume, a soldier and a guerrilla, loom over the defeated—a campesino—and trample him, he's a naked man thrown to the ground: Open him up, yell the men in costume, tear that wretch to pieces!

A loudspeaker. Whose voice is it? Who is speaking? Ciruelo, who else: This way to the Invisible Circus. Step right up to the Invisible Circus. Enjoy yourselves!

The spectators advance: they are curious *bogotanos*, honest citizens, the kind who pay taxes; they came to spend a Saturday in the company of their wives and children, they've bought tickets, something good better happen, and soon, if you don't mind, something like the coupling of Christ and Mary Magdalene, and then, yes, it does, a bony actress cries out: I'm the skinniest woman in the world! and shows off her bones, her actual bony bones, those of her whole body, and she prances splendidly, squats noisily, stretches springlike to the ceiling, bends over to retrieve a hair she has dropped on the floor, and, in that mortal moment, reveals a backside as sharp as death—where had Ciruelo found her? In a hospital, laugh those in God's Laughter—frogs and toads are scattered everywhere, hundreds of toads hop in all directions, the canopy of the invisible circus bulges with toads, you can see black signs hanging from ropes like nooses, HERE WEEPS LIFE, LET NOBODY SPEAK TO HER, LET NOBODY SPEAK, LET NOBODY SPEAK.

There are two men chained back-to-back, in silence. An enormous old man, bright white with wings like an angel, clings to a horse's back and begins to bite into its neck; it's monstrous—how did they do it?—the blood splatters; the spectators hurry away from this place in revulsion, but arrive, to their misfortune, in a white hospital room: they are met point-blank by a trio of old crones, venerable, hunched over by rheumatism, and yet they are wicked, fateful, pestilent, and they steal babies, swiping them surreptitiously from their cribs, snaffling them through deceit from their mothers' arms; these are the baby thieves, selling them for a song at the market, and they are consumptive, gnarled, hateful: they leap from the stage and chase after children in the audience, pursuing them relentlessly and terrifyingly, as though it were Bogotá itself giving chase; the children scream and howl, scramble to hide under chairs, cling to their mothers' legs, and the audience laughs, cheers.

A bedroom appears, a kitchen: human heads on pillows, skulls turned into bowls, a heart in a frying pan, a tray of steaming eyes, a cranium serving as an ashtray, a necklace of young girls' lips, a belt of sewn-together nipples; it's a room lit by reddened candles, with a row of lifelike portraits, living portraits, framed, winking at us, scratching at their fleas, masturbating, cooing over their achievements, reciting them: We are humanity's murderers. I'm Henri Désiré Landru; I'm Marcel Petiot; I am the so-called Son of Sam; I'm Kemper, I killed my cat and hung its head in my bedroom; I'm Dennis Nilsen, I was too ashamed to let them arrest me in front of my dog Bleep; and I, Christopher Wilder, donated a good sum of money to saving the whales; I am Gilles de Rais, friend of Joan of Arc, a magnificent and gruesome villain; I'm Countess Báthory, and beside me reeks and resides Fickó, my foolish dwarf; I'm Doctor Herman Webster Mudgett, and I, the doctor's puppet, I tickle people till they die laughing; I'm Jack Ketch, the dwarf executioner, who sodomized sheep from the age of nine; and I'm the Nameless Killer who sold human flesh at markets; I'm the soft-spoken Vampire of Düsseldorf: one day, while walking through the park, I came across a swan, I was so powerfully affected by the bird's beauty that I leaped onto its back and ate it; and I, thirstily beside him, am the Parched One, a lascivious Russian noblewoman, my headaches only vanish upon drinking from the veins of my maidservants, I bathe in the blood of virgins to regain my youth.

The audience is stunned.

In the penultimate room, naked matrons, women in large armchairs, sitting very stiffly, their breasts sagging, all drinking coffee. They speak in soft voices about dogs, about parrots and canaries, about their favorite pets: I like tortoises, I prefer rabbits, my parakeet is called *Justlikeyou*, one day my cat told me...; they are grandmothers and housewives, surrounded by stacks of plates and bowls: it is a fact that all across this earth there are women condemned to cook day and night until they die. Suddenly, absolute silence: the women and the audience observe each other, for several minutes. Then a shocked actress shrieks: And who are all these people? What are they doing here? All of this was a mad riot that reached its peak when it became widely accepted that the final scene of the *Exhibition of Pain*, the one exhibited in the final room, about ten feet from the exit, a rape scene—one of the many presented during the exhibition, but the definitive one, the finale—was in fact genuine, the incautious woman appearing to be raped by a furious citizen dressed in a tailcoat being raped for real, her cries for help authentic. The controversy revolved around the following: had she been raped, or was she an actress pretending? And, furthermore, was it four different victims across the four Saturdays that the exhibition lasted, or just the one? But, above all else, what was the identity of the man raping her, who raped the rape victims?

Ciruelo, who else.

At this point, Bogotá's most prominent newspaper took an interest, running the story in the bottom-right corner of the front page.

A FARCE

In Bogotá, where until recently the amusing *House of Horror* had been operating, under the pretense of an *Exhibition of Pain*, misfits passing themselves off as actors from the new national theater movement gave rise to a shameful display.

After authorities received complaints from neighbors in the area, the exhibition was closed down, with those responsible—the majority of them university students—being taken before a judge. Some, and this is the most deplorable detail, were underage: high school girls from a respectable educational establishment.

Those detained from the indecent exhibition have been sentenced to seventy-two hours of incarceration, including the *Reykjavík Brothers*, acclaimed circus dwarfs, who protested their innocence to the last. Yet although this world was captured, its creator was not: his name is unconfirmed and his whereabouts remain unknown.

In the image, mothers and nuns converse with the Teusaquillo parish priest, Reverend Father Franco Bertolini.

3

The Freedom Ranch

THEY CAPTURED THE WORLD, BUT NOT ITS CREATOR.
Ipso facto, three days later he rose again. And, accompanied by
the same members of the Magma theater group, the very same
intrepid schoolgirls from Santa Teresita, as well as new converts,
he founded a *commune*, a Wellspring of Happiness, they claim
he said, an Oasis of Earthliness, a Convent of Love, a Small but
Great Sovereign Republic: *the Freedom Ranch*.

He founded it in La Miel, just a few hours from Bogotá, within
the buildings of a disused farmstead that had been famous for
its inexhaustible cows thirty years before. The farmhouse was
falling apart, and the milking parlors, corrals, and stables were
swallowed up by grass, yet right on top of these places, without
even cleaning them, the thirty-four members of the republic laid
down their mats amid droning mosquitoes, field mice, and nests
of cockroaches. In front of the farmhouse was what had once
been a vineyard, with vines that looked more like a collection of
wire shrubs; on these imagined shrubs the ranchers would hang
their clothes, pissing in the main office and shitting in the garden, vomiting in the pots of azaleas, smashing anything left to be
smashed, and, in an oval niche for a vanished Virgin, where they
could have placed a candle to illuminate the night, they instead
set up a spit for their meat, all skin, fur, teeth, bones, gases, spit-
tle, agony and resurrection.

Behind the ranch, a little less than a mile away, you could make
out the town of La Miel, its fine, white bell tower, the pale little houses with spotless green doors, the unpaved streets, swept

scrupulously each day by women dressed in black. Nobody knew what price Ciruelo paid to rent the farmstead and whether others of the republic's brotherhood shouldered any of the expenses: no, surely not. Yet, in spite of the mad disorder, the intimate mold and filth of the farmhouse, its contaminated walls, only six hundred feet away the La Miel River ran, lively, still pure—*serpent goddess* they had baptized it—and then there was the valley around it, a soft green, the dull color of uncut grass, an enormous feathery quilt, with beds of clover where the freedom ranchers would revel and sleep on sunny days, amid the smell of hay; surrounding the valley were tall and solemn mountains; and, at the valley's center, the farmhouse, which, when seen from afar, appeared to glow like the entrance to paradise.

The main road to the town wound through the hills; it was a ribbon of purple earth not too far away, and its reddish dust would be swept up by the wind and flutter down from the boughs of trees like sinister strips of gauze. Along this road, for many years, rowdy travelers had been arriving in La Miel, setting themselves up for days in the area and then departing without leaving any trace other than the remains of campfires (one of which sparked a thousand-hectare blaze), plastic bottles, split shoes, condoms, syringes, and smashed guitars; for La Miel's principal attraction, to the misfortune of its inhabitants, was the hallucinogenic mushrooms that grew abundantly at the heart of the dung of its cows, and hallucinating youngsters would come and go through the fields, all pallid, adolescent, and guileless, between sixteen and twenty-six years old; they were searching for aliens in the sky, devising the most astonishing poetry without ever writing it down, conceiving indescribable plays, composing immortal and unfinished symphonies upon staves of air; they were all so consumed by their delirious contemplations that they never had any strength left for a second round of lovemaking, and nothing united them, apart from a shared dissatisfaction with things, or so they claimed, being unable as yet to pinpoint exactly what this dissatisfaction related to, stating only that the entire world was a pile of shit.

The disturbances caused by the different gangs or mobs of visitors to La Miel are memorable; those in God's Laughter relate how one of these spiritual groups amused themselves by kicking to death a hog that had dared to grunt while they were singing; others clarify that no hog was killed, that it was merely painted blue, with little flowers on its ears and a butterfly on its back; others that they trained it, gave it marijuana to smoke, and stuffed it full of mushrooms; still others that they only got it drunk, that, in any case, the little piggy had committed suicide by throwing itself over a cliff, possessed by demons; or that they had simply taken it back to Bogotá to eat. But weren't they vegetarians? This group made an exception, recalling Darwin: the human brain had evolved thanks to the ingestion of red meat.

In any case, reports of robberies abounded: disappearances of rabbits from hutches, chickens from coops, fruit from orchards, bread from the bakery. The visitors never came off favorably; they always ended up covered in muck, had never planted a single tree, had never started a flock, never offered a helping hand, they really were miscreants, as adolescent as they were detestable. However, the natives of La Miel had no choice but to put up with these characters, because among the youngsters there was always a son of some general, a minister's grandson, the nephew of a president, a putative cardinal, some heir apparent who might well bring the curse of the army down upon them, or at the very least an investigation; so the people of La Miel simply looked on and allowed themselves to be looked at. They were resigned campesinos—but on the brink of a revolt.

On this occasion, however, everything seemed to suggest that the thirty-four members of that small but great republic had the best of intentions. For a start, they planned to stay and live in

La Miel, as they had solemnly declared in the parish church and town hall; they wanted to work for the good of their invented nation. This set them apart from the other spiritual groups, as did the plan they hoped to implement on the Ranch, their guide, the dream that the twenty-two males and twelve females had dictated during a night of collective inspiration, in the warm glow of the ancestral fire, envisioning obligations not only toward each other, but also toward the town; they wrote down and reproduced the dream on thirty-four rolls of parchment, employing intricate Gothic lettering, just like the Ten Commandments.

One of these scrolls had become a treasured possession of God's Laughter, flying from hand to hand:

FREEDOM RANCH

(Any date and any month.
From now on, time will be invented
by us, the masters of time)

COMMANDMENTS

Show unconditional respect for the Town of La Miel,
its children, its insects, its flowers and birds,
its animals.

Sow vegetables.
Construct handlooms.
Produce scarves, ruanas, skirts,
waistcoats, and slippers.

Breed sheep and goats,
chickens and messenger pigeons.

Trade produce with the campesinos.
Use of money is forbidden, only BARTER.

Daily sessions of group reading.
Reflections upon the reading.
Meditation and dance.
Abstain forever from radio and television
and other monstrosities.

Let all music be our own,
let it come from no place other than ourselves.

No prayer but poetry.

No drink but pure water from the river.
Aguardiente only to ward off the cold.

Altered states arising only from the fruits
of Mother Earth.

Rise at five in the morning. Calisthenics.
Honor the goddess Hygieia with lye soap.
Spiritual exercises.
Division of labor in accordance with abilities.

Fasting once a week.

Freedom in every respect, with no hassling anyone.

Couples to be formed at random, every night,
and for a duration of only one further night,
in case of something left unfinished
(and only if the rest agree).

Make love above all else!
All with all and happiness for all!

Total eradication of jealousy,
mockery, envy,
concealed lust,
competition,
and leadership.

Nobody is in charge of anybody,
all obey each other,
together through thick and thin!

Any ranchers failing to follow the Commandments:
shall be destroyed!

Eternal companionship!
Three cheers for Life!

(Signed, the Freedom 34)

A number of the Commandments were not adhered to: sowing of vegetables, production of scarves and ruanas, breeding of sheep and chickens, daily reading sessions, rising at five every morning, calisthenics, hygiene, fasting, and spiritual exercises, so no one ran the risk of being destroyed. The months flew by. They continued to send the same Messenger into town, an emaciated poet of the republic, purchaser of provisions: It pained me, he purportedly said, to travel those undulating streets: cold eyes watched over me, judgmentally.

And this was true: on sunny mornings, campesinos traveling along the main road would note disapprovingly that members of the republic bathed naked in the river, pairing up along its banks, issuing orgasmic expletives, tears, laughter, as though harming a sacred silence.

Things spilled over one freezing night after a torrential downpour that had lasted all day, including a hailstorm that ruined the improvised beds in the stables, twisted the wire vines, and shredded the hanging clothing. The thirty-four did not hesitate to make a bonfire using the last remaining pieces of furniture from the farmstead; and, as the fire began to languish, they fed it with books, whether poetry, shamanism, esotericism, or philosophy: they burned it all, right down to the last letter, because— as Ciruelo apparently said—*Everything must be invented anew*, a notable phrase with no amanuensis, but instead many mouths to repeat it—the old-fashioned way.

Then, beneath a sky like cut glass, bewitched around the fire, ancient dancers under the stars spun around clinging to each other's hands, wild-eyed; their dense echo rang out, tumbling down toward the town, the echo of their chants like deranged hymns, their newly minted verses, their laughter or their moans, an uproar of voices and bodies, which, heard from a distance, could have been fights to the death or pure loving embraces. Behind the tall and trembling flames, a Buddha perched on the ruins as if on a throne, Toño Ciruelo raised his arms to the sky, an ecstatic officiant, his eyes lost in a trance.

Spoke the Messenger:

"And around him we fused into one whole.

"And then, well after midnight, we followed him: filled with delirium, he had no better notion than to visit La Miel, as though a universal carnival were compelling him; he wished for the world to be as happy as we were. He raced through the streets, reaching the middle of the plaza, and, alone, our dancing spurring Ciruelo on, he put on a grotesque spectacle, yelling professions of love outside the church, with the entire town watching on, spying on us, pulsing behind their windows, not having the faintest idea what this was about, not joining in the revelry—just when we, the revelers, took it as certain that our joy was that of the entire world."

But when dawn arrived, the carnivalesque howling now extinguished, the natives of La Miel could no longer remain resigned: enraged, armed with sticks and flaming torches (just like the villagers from that black-and-white movie bent on doing away with Frankenstein), they finally corralled those still soaking up happiness, not letting up before seeing the last of them flee like rabbits across the fields on that cold gray morning. The girls were chased down by the townswomen themselves: the four they managed to capture were laid facedown and dealt one of those hidings that had them sitting in agony for months; one of the republicans almost had his ear taken off by the men of La Miel; he returned to Bogotá with half an ear, earning his nickname: Van Gogh.

There were thirty-four members of the Ranch. The twelve females all fell pregnant, incapable of naming a father with any certainty (Ciruelo had led the unions of republican love). And, of course, nobody saw Ciruelo flee, they didn't find him.

Many secrets were buried. Nobody wanted to know anything. There is talk of two schoolgirls from Santa Teresita who were confined to sanatoriums, girls who had started to believe that their faces were divided, that one face belonged to one world and the other to a different one, but that they themselves were not of this world. Another nearly died in the middle of an abortion at the hands of a midwife. The others, supported by their families, turned to specialized clinics, and then to psychologists and priests who helped them "get back on the straight and narrow." Only one gave birth to her child, they say, and she "disappeared off the map." And there's talk of a single suicide, one whose hidden delusions of the mushrooms never left her: those off-white, bitter mushrooms never relinquished their hold over her senses. They drowned her within herself.

∞

Members of the Laughter assert that the commune lasted ten months. No: it lasted six. They all agreed, however, that the small great republic fled in disarray. That, as the twenty-two males confessed: *we all wanted Luna* (Luna Sepúlveda, sixteen years old). Toño had baptized her *Luna Sepulcher, apple of discord, for whom all men die, but one is happy.*

Luna Sepúlveda recounted her distress; her two closest confidants, Esdena Bustamante and Selene Ortiz—freedom ranchers even younger than she was—listened to her incredulously: one night, someone had kidnapped her from her bed in the stable, first carrying her as though she were a feather, covering her mouth and nose until nearly asphyxiating her, then dragging her to the river and there, where her screams could not be heard, *he chewed off one of my nipples, hurt me from behind for hours, he killed me, I was dead, I never found out who it was.*

Within God's Laughter, there were a number of glaringly different opinions; one speaker believed that Ciruelo was stark raving mad—madness? I thought, if only; another pointed out that Ciruelo's intentions had actually been constructive: He tried, that person said, to separate himself from the world, himself and his followers, to create another pure, elemental one with no shackles, but those he called upon didn't measure up. That one said he'd never met Ciruelo personally, but that he'd seen him from a distance when listening to him speak on the university square, enlisting followers for his Ranch. He seemed like a hard man, he said, he knew what he was doing, he was carrying something great in his hands. He added that he'd been ready to get involved, had even traveled to La Miel (around two years ago), but it was already too late: the Ranch of Freedom was nothing but a burnt-out farmhouse in the middle of a yellow wasteland; there were abortive vegetable patches and piles of cow dung here and there with large hallucinogenic mushrooms sprouting like flowers, he said.

And listening to him, as the afternoon darkened, we recognized, with something approaching sadness, that we too would have liked to have spent at least one night on the Freedom Ranch. And then someone else stated, or revealed, as if in passing, to whomever it might interest, that Toño Ciruelo was currently holding another exhibition, this time of photography, and that, in any case, it appeared to be another Exhibition of Pain, that is to say, Toño Ciruelo was in fashion, he had people talking again, although his name wasn't in the catalog, that person said, with an irreproachable snigger, stammering over every word; he uses a pseudonym: *Pythagoras*.

We parted with a cascade of laughter.

Ciruelo could make even God laugh.

4

Inside Bogotá

I CONFIRMED IT FOR MYSELF THE NEXT DAY. IT WAS INDEED an exhibition of his photographs (I was unaware he had any such inclination), and at the Russian Cultural Institute no less: once he had assured me he would learn Russian in order to read Dostoyevsky in the original—that's how it has to be, he said, a sufferer like that must be understood even when he laughs. And he had learned Russian, you can be sure of that; he was a polyglot missing only that one language, that one tongue, that one single argot: the idiom, the dialect, the gibberish of love. Toño Ciruelo never loved anybody, and that is the single difference between some people and others.

INSIDE BOGOTÁ, announced the black poster affixed to the entrance of the institute: was this the exhibition of a dead man? A posthumous exhibition? Had Toño died in Santa Marta? Was he gunned down? Did he drown? The white letters presided over a photo of an alley like an open maw: from within its black misery, two long, pale hands emerged, as if floating, detached, just two gnarled hands that swam through the mist as if asking for bread or assistance or "a coin for God's sake, don't be an asshole!" as stated by the title of the photo. There's Ciruelo, I thought, not only because of the title but also the hands, those same giant hands of Ciruelo, desperate. But then who had taken the photo? Pythagoras? Was this a self-portrait of his hands? I didn't see Ciruelo's name on the poster, only *Pythagoras* in tiny letters.

I went in.

The flimsy catalog handed to me by an institute employee (a

black man in overalls who appeared and then disappeared) made no mention of Ciruelo, only the title of the exhibition, the titles of each of the photos, and the unexpected name of the artist: *Pythagoras*, with the caption: *Bogotano photographer born in 1960. Currently residing in Bombay.* An anonymous Colombian, I thought, catapulted to fame by saintly Russia. How had he managed to convince the institute of his pseudonym, that he lived in Bombay? This alone was an achievement, and deplorable. What was I doing here? Did I really want to talk to Ciruelo? Would I find him? I regretted coming: it was one thing to hear about Ciruelo, and quite another to hear the man himself; his friendship had represented a brief moment in my life, a flash, what was I doing here? Nevertheless, his exhibition of pain, his delirious ranch, everything concerning Ciruelo rekindled my admiration for him, why deny it?

I walked around the exhibition. The portraits were of women selling themselves on street corners, of madmen and beggars, of junk recyclers; one of those women—"Brides of Solitude" read the title—stood lifting her skirt before the camera. Ciruelo must have taken the photo on his knees; she revealed something almost like a thousand-legged spider, a furious bloodsucker; above, the woman's swollen eyes emerged: she was contemplating herself approvingly, a toothless smile, she was as bald as death, the mistress of her street full of hermits who were all jubilant at seeing her with her legs open; and then there were other brides, as young as they were toothless, smoking ravenously, walled in, their backs to the door.

There were around forty pictures in total, in all dimensions, in black and white, hanging here and there in the corridors, with me the only viewer.

Inside Bogotá.

All of the most "influential" beggars of the era were there. There was the one who wore a wooden sandwich board over his shoulders with the phrase: THE WORLD ENDS TOMORROW, I AM JESUS. I had often noticed him, wandering through crowds with the name Jesus on his back, but had never seen him ask for money. He was more of a madman, but fully worthy of his place among the everyday beggars of the capital, surrounded by pigeons on the Plaza de Bolívar, sleeping like fetuses in church entrances, pleading outside restaurants and bakeries, suffering in filthy recesses, lapping eagerly from polystyrene plates, yawning eternally, resembling ghastly apparitions; the beggars' painful servitude distinguished them from the madmen, already gone, abundantly free, displaying an almost haughty indifference: their pain was distinct; bearded, with long matted hair, far-gone eyes, and parched mouths, they could be confused for Ancient Greek philosophers; what faces, what contemplative eyes—meditative, absorbed and overly suspicious, mystical, airy, subtle and ethereal, sharp, clairvoyant, as alive as they were dead. Was this the photographer's intention, his truism? All of the portraits of madmen were titled with names of philosophers predating Christ—it is pointless to repeat them.

An emaciated madman, almost naked, sat in such a way that his body in profile—his back leaning against a corner, his skinny legs extended, long arms stretched almost to the tips of his toes—actually resembled a right triangle. The title read precisely: *The hypotenuse of the right triangle is equal to its sides.* Theory and photo signed by Pythagoras.

And this was immediately followed by a sequence of photographs of a very well-known woman: *La Botina*, another mad beggar of Bogotá, famous for her early-morning showers in the Palermo and Soledad parks. She had a secret haunt in each of these neighborhoods: around six in the morning, she would leave her bed of newspapers and undress, slowly, in the bitter cold, and shower—under invisible water, with an invisible bar of soap in her hand. She truly appeared to be washing herself with water that you could almost hear, using invisible soap, scrubbing thoroughly under her armpits, between her buttocks, scrubbing her thighs, her knees, behind her ears, completely naked in frigid Bogotá, among the trees and city birds, the work-bound citizens. Things might have appeared normal if, as well as crazy, the mad-woman hadn't been impossibly beautiful: she smiled, red with cold, and used to sing during her showers in a very fine voice. And she would dress herself as if before a mirror, dolling her-self up, painting her lips with a nonexistent lipstick that must surely be blood red, pressing the scent of real jasmine petals to her neck, and then waving goodbye to herself in the mirror and leaving to wander the streets of her life—long before she became pregnant and disappeared. But Pythagoras's opportune shots also examined the faces of each of the early risers who stood watching La Botina, all stirring within a single halo of lust; they were embarrassed Bogotanos, perhaps, but always entranced; none, however, ever left behind a coin of gratitude with which she could buy breakfast. And behind the windows too, behind drawn curtains, it was possible to make out the faces of family men peering out, savoring the undressing woman. Good photos, I thought, in spite of myself. For I would have preferred to be dis-appointed, and this was not the case.

And, forgetting myself, I peered at the other photos and suf-fered a further intimate disappointment, concerning that dark Bogotá, squalid and disturbed, falling apart. Was there nowhere in Bogotá a lover's kiss under the trees, a beautiful sunset, a friendly flirtation, a stranger's smile? No, not in Ciruelo's photos.

They were photos of cart drivers and horses: the solid, un-wieldy wooden carts called *zorras*, the gnomic cart drivers called *zorreros*, and those horses like genuine Rocinantes, also called *zorras*, and in reality nothing but equine ossuaries running upon four bones toward every cardinal point, carting discarded ma-terials from public works, heavy-duty garbage, industrial waste.

In one of those photos, an exhausted horse pulled a cart, and the man on the box seat was asleep, a bottle of aguardiente between his knees; the horse looked like it couldn't go on; the cart was loaded with sheets of lead: the slabs jutted up toward the sky like slender tombstones. This horse is going to die, I thought. In the very next photo, the horse had collapsed; it lay stretched out, expiring or snoring like its owner, because he too lay there, on the horse's belly, what a pair of models Pythagoras had found himself, I thought, and it was very possible they really were modeling for him, that they were merely posing, defeated on the ground. Had he paid the horse's owner? Had Ciruelo paid him? Was it possible? Yes, with Ciruelo anything was possible.

I walked through the corridor of horse heads, of wild horse eyes and swishing horse tails, tangled tails swatting lethal flies, of horse legs raised over puddles, and hooves sparking against stones, streaks of sweat like streamers, invisible whinnies, human hands, and whips, and then I no longer wanted to look but did: a cart was passing like a gust of wind, the horse appearing out of control, and splayed out inside the cart was the cadaver of another horse, black, skeletal, stiff legs pointing skyward, ears rigid; the two horses crossed before the viewer like a flash of life and death, the black horse a terrifying corpse with open eyes staring back at me. Why, among all the themes of this exhibition, was I unable to bear the horses' eyes, their eyes?

And I endured, to my regret, the final sequence: it was growing dark; an unfinished street stretched as gray as a concrete caterpillar, without a single flower; cracks of decomposition could be seen as if in the air; at the end of that street, a broken horse appeared to let out a whimper like an ultimatum; it had stopped, against all instructions; its back trembled, slick with sweat, its bowed head a dirty white; its whinny traveled through the air of the photo; birds cut through the air of another photo, and in another, the driver leaped from the cart, tearing at his own hair; in another he yelled up at the sky, and in another he aimed a kick at his horse's stomach, and in another, another kick with the other leg, and then many more photos: kicks, kick after kick to the horse's stomach, in photo after photo; in the last one, the bereft face of the horse turned to look at its master, regarding him like Christ, and I no longer knew what to do, a victim of the photograph.

And as if nothing could be more natural, as had to happen, at the end of the corridor, the very last portrait, the last of the madmen portrayed: Toño Ciruelo himself. I found him well-disguised as a madman—although this was hardly necessary—and slouched on top of the stone fountain in Chorro de Quevedo Square, with his threadbare overcoat, slender in his rags, you might even say powerful, smiling: *this is me.*

What was I doing here?

The entire exhibition was a bleak chiaroscuro, yet it screamed.

I was leaving the premises when I thought I heard Ciruelo's voice in the air, his bristly voice, for an instant, as if he were rebuking someone, or setting them straight, but I must have imagined it. I stopped at the half-open door. I was leaving behind the photographs by Ciruelo, or by Pythagoras, as well as his own self-portrait. I could still detect the rumble of Ciruelo's voice; and what if I bumped into him? We would walk through Bogotá as we had on so many other occasions, I would find the spirit to walk along with an old chum (I was about to write bum). During that period, my days passed by monotonously and inexplicably: I was renting a minuscule apartment in Chapinero, owed six months' rent, had split up with Clara Pozo, whom I'd lived with for two years, an eternity, and, without another voice in my bed, without a paying job (because I worked from sunup to sundown, writing), my life was as uncertain as it was difficult. Why see Ciruelo? Ah, Toño, I said aloud, whenever I see you, appalling things take place. But hadn't something just taken place? Well, there was still an ember of friendship, I confessed, in spite of my decision not to see him; let's get out of here, I thought, and pushed open the door; the sunlight dazzled me: I saw the street crammed with homeless people, I saw it so swollen with that horde of madmen and beggars (all of Bogotá calls them "disposables") it was like a market. Two carts and their drivers, or two *zorros* and their *zorreros*, had parked up on the institute sidewalk, loaded with animated passengers; emaciated prostitutes, dressed as if for a party, were dolled up, perfumed, and releasing deafening cackles; first I thought I recognized the woman who had lifted her skirt before the camera, then one of the madmen from the Plaza de Bolívar, and I understood: they'd come to see themselves portrayed, surely at Ciruelo's invitation; only Ciruelo would consider bringing along those same nutcases from his photos so they might look at and recognize themselves, and the cries of these visitors, the selfsame protagonists of *Inside Bogotá*, their bodies, their emanations, already encroaching upon the atmosphere, the beeping of a taxi unable to move due to the logjam of carts and horses, the yelling of the taxi driver, his blood boiling, hurling death threats, the almost tender protestations of the prostitutes, all of it deafened the air and ended the world.

Beside me, the black man in overalls peered out anxiously. I was stunned: one of those madmen or *zorreros* or beggars, smelling frightful, misshapen or hunched over by sickness, with a beard seeming to sprout from his very eyes, came over to me, exultant, and wanted to embrace me. I shuddered. This couldn't possibly be Ciruelo, I managed to think. I caught his hand in the breast pocket of my jacket, fingers fluttering. There's nothing to steal, I told him, and then, in a screechy voice, facing me, so I could feel his rancid breath, he said: Why don't you take off that beard so I can see you better? He must have been kidding, because my beard was incipient, nothing compared to his; he pushed me aside disdainfully and entered the institute, followed by the panhandlers who shoved past each other as if entering a cinema, amazed; I considered asking them about Ciruelo, but stopped myself: they were all drunk or high; the women swayed as though on the verge of collapse; all friends of Ciruelo's, I thought. Is this his world now? With difficulty, I pushed through the tide of bodies, the wall of foul odors, the shock of eyes, the premonition of death, those frightful visitors who would have to be dealt with by the Russian Cultural Institute—or by the black man in overalls.

I walked down the narrow street, asphyxiated, as though I could still smell, impregnated in my jacket, the beggar's fetid breath.

And in the four-cornered solitude of my apartment, while getting ready for bed and flinging the jacket far away from me, a card sprang out of my pocket; I picked it up: it was a grubby, slippery card, rectangular, with Ciruelo's name and surname printed on it. So it had been Ciruelo, I gasped, and shuddered again. That beggar was Ciruelo. I recalled him; he hadn't shared Ciruelo's stature, or was simply doubled over, pretending to be misshapen ... an actor. Again I felt those dizzying fingers in my pocket, again I saw his eyes, again I heard his voice, his screechy joke: Why don't you take off that beard so I can see you better? It was Ciruelo, how had I not recognized him?

He'll find me, I thought, he'll find me forever.

I regretted too late having started things up again.

And, before going to sleep—before never being able to sleep again—I examined the card once more, front and back: I was looking for a phone number, an address; it said only:

Antonio Ciruelo

Demolitions

5

La Oscurana

I BELIEVE HE SHOWED UP AT MY APARTMENT WITH LA OSCU-
rana in tow six or nine days after *Inside Bogotá*. He told me he
hadn't looked up my address, that he'd simply followed me the
day of the exhibition and that I'd let myself be followed: You let
yourself be followed, Eri; my shadow stalked your shadow, tread-
ing on your dark heels, like in the Cold War; I left my madmen
in Russia for you.

And then he said, triumphantly, in the same screechy voice as
the beggar who had rummaged in my pocket: A catastrophe, Eri,
it's in all the papers, I've taken over the world again.

And that's when he introduced me to the person he claimed
was his legitimate wife—that's what he told me, coloring the
word *legitimate* with secret mockery—the only woman I've been
good for, he said.

I can't remember now if La Oscurana was listening. I don't
think so. I don't think she ever listened to us.

"Tomorrow," continued Ciruelo, "we're traveling to Ecuador;
then Peru, Bolivia, in search of her Incan memory, it'll be our
honeymoon: she, the happy native, and me, the unhappy villain.
We'll be back in three months, I'll tell you all about it."

I looked at her for the first time.

I took her in.

The first memory of La Oscurana obscures everything; my
memory of her is covered in an aromatic darkness, for she
smelled of corn, grains of newly ground corn, that's what I
smelled wafting darkly from her neck toward me; it was a mist

of fear, though to write fear seems an exaggeration, yet there she stood and there was fear, her and her fear both genuinely indigenous, I don't know which ethnicity, I never inquired; her jet-black hair was in two braids, framing an oval face, a coppery complexion; her brow and cheekbones were stained or painted as though with hieroglyphs: circles and triangles tracing a red and green spiral, like a serpent; her full lips formed something resembling a pulpy fruit on the verge of splitting, the blood visible from within, they were full, yet not excessive, as if in the act of sending a kiss with just a gesture, from afar, with just a puckered expression, this extraordinary aspect was the least— or most?—spiritual thing about her, resembling the horizontal view of a woman's sex: for a shameful second I felt an urge to bite and suck them. She had black, elusive eyes, a black skirt, and a white blouse with sequins; her throat was adorned with those glittering necklaces of seeds and stones and shells from the river; she wore bamboo hoops as earrings, her body jangled as she moved—she had bracelets like rattles—her thick eyebrows almost met, and at the tip of one, very near the temple, there was a black mole. As with many indigenous women from the Andes, the shape of her eyes made her seem more like an Asian, a Japanese woman with cinnamon skin; what combination of races had created her? Without any doubt, Columbus discovered America only after it had already been discovered by some yellow-skinned explorer—centuries earlier.

She was as radiant as she was dark, youthful, healthy, neither tall nor short, and when I finally looked into her eyes, I felt that her fleeting gaze (for she instantly looked away) could make the world disappear, make you disappear, and only she would remain; she absorbed me, and I became nothing, but not in some subtle meditated way, but rather purely, like pure nature, or clairvoyance, absolute indifference or absolute detachment: she simply found herself in a world in which you did not exist.

She said not one word to me, only smiled, it was like the wind blowing past; throughout that whole day and night she never uttered a single word: she nodded, or shook her head, depending on the nature of the question, and did so with a kind of moan of an indecipherable character, I never learned what passions it guarded, whether joyous or tragic, tender or profound, and I never again saw La Oscurana, she was dead earth—according to the drama of Ciruelo, the sick man in my house.

But on that splendid morning Ciruelo was her splendid guide, death leading life. I was still unable to make sense of this new event in Ciruelo's life, this new human adventure. It's only right that I'm here with him, I told myself at the peak of an unexpected exultation, the exultationn I suffered while finding myself at La Oscurana's side that day and night. Had Ciruelo arranged this? Was it a thoroughly premeditated plan? I'll never know.

We went in search of a café on foot.

We walked through the streets of Bogotá, bare, gray, formless streets, full of potholes like traps. Ciruelo's words, the story of his life since we'd last seen each other, his own version of the Ranch, the Exhibition of Pain, drew me away from La Oscurana. I forgot about her. Today, I know I was able to disregard her only because I knew she was by my side: if, at that moment, she'd taken another path, I would have raced after her; I could not account for my body without the certainty of hers, such was the strange and lamentable nature of my first and last encounter with La Oscurana.

"Don't fall in love so quickly, Eri," said the bristly voice.

As though he were undressing me.

He said this to me as we turned a corner, whispering it in my ear, so she wouldn't catch on, so she wouldn't hear what she wasn't actually listening to, I thought.

"Where did she come from?" I managed to ask.

"This country," he said, "where else?"

Then I examined La Oscurana's features; either she wasn't listening or didn't understand us, or else she really didn't care: she wasn't even imagining us.

The café on Park Way, where Toño Ciruelo took us, was one frequented by poets, in their droves, arriving from every city in Colombia; this is indeed a nation of poets, as demonstrated by our school report cards. This time, we encountered one of the heavyweights—if only in terms of girth—of national poetry; he was not a guy I was fond of: I loathed him, and he allowed himself to be loathed; like a prodigal hog, he was sprawled out, surrounded by a court of at least ten rosy, suckling aspiring poets, and all suckled from his teats, awaiting his words of otherworldly wisdom; none of them knew me as a writer, but I knew all of them, and, sadly, neither the sucklings nor the pompous hog were true poets; regrettably, this country's authentic poets were not present that afternoon, because they certainly do exist, of course they do, and can be counted on half the fingers of a single hand; only the customary phonies sparkled. I was no longer bothered by their words, in print or through the air, but, as we walked past, as we selected our table, I heard someone say: There goes Ciruelo with La Indígena.

It was the first time I'd heard that name: *La Indígena.*

I would hear *Oscurana* from Ciruelo right there, as we took our seats, when he told me: This is my Oscurana, Eri; the region she comes from is called La Oscurana; she emerged from that land, dark as its name, in the south of this merciless country.

And he embraced her without mercy and kissed her on the mouth, or grazed her lips, because she drew her face away, as though deploring the kiss but accepting it in the end, resigned. For I was able to glimpse, in her fleeting gesture (that spirit-like furrowing of the brow), how all of us, Toño and I and the celebrated hog and his sucklings, how each and every one of us seemed to her like some filthy creature, a nightmare. Toño didn't flinch: he returned the poets' greeting with a glance, and went back to his stories, his main interest; he leaned his head across the table and spoke to me in a whisper, in his deepest deep voice; he told me who his Oscurana was. I'm still unsure if she was listening or not, or if she cared: she savored her coffee, staring at nothing, and meanwhile the poets were all dying to know what the hell Toño Ciruelo was revealing to me, but I was the only one able to hear him.

"We met," Ciruelo told me, "a lifetime ago.

"We were still children; me at school, fourteen years old, and she a new arrival, a domestic, an apprentice servant; she was trained by three more senior maidservants and an old cook, each with her own room in the big house belonging to my father, the Colombian senator; we would finally be able to flaunt having an exotic servant, a legitimate Indian, you understand? That was mamá's latest craze, shortly before she went crazy for real.

"And she would appear on the patio, in the garden, on the stairs … always. She became almost paralyzed on seeing me. I don't know if she appeared before me on purpose, or if it was I who appeared.

"In any case, when that would happen, as you know already, Eri, what urges.

"To begin with, I thought she was mute.

"As she washed the clothes, as she swept, as she scrubbed the floor, hunched over, her entire ass as if presented to the yoke, as she looked at me for just a second without uttering a word, as she walked past me, her skirt drawing that sort of bittersweet breath from inside of me, as she served me at the table, her hand reaching, her bosom above me—I idolized her, Eri, but I also despised her; one day, without knowing why, I slapped her: I discovered her behind a door in the kitchen, her dark face in the shadows, her eyes closed, she was hiding from somebody, from me, she was hiding, terrified, and I dealt her that slap that had me suffering for nights, without shedding a tear, of course: I'm still unable to discharge that fluid.

"During a family trip to the Amazon, I, the teenager, asked mamá to buy me a troupial that was for sale in its wire cage. On returning, I found her in the garden, watering flowers, and offered it to her, hopefully; without a word, she opened the cage door and the bird flew away; this rejection left me frozen; it was her slap back; it was as if we'd made our peace.

"Papá, mamá, my sister, the visitors, the entire world around us, and no one noticed I was dying.

"She would appear constantly, it could be no other way, we lived in the same house, and still ... I'd never ... you understand?

"It wasn't love at first sight, Eri, I just wanted to devour her.

"And, without knowing how, I—it was all intuition ...

"One night, I impregnated her.

"She had her door locked, but her window faced onto the patio, it was more of a ventilation skylight, open.

"I scrambled up, squeezed through; I've always suspected I was a snake in another life, and I slithered through, slid down, petrified; it wasn't sweat moistening my back but blood, I'd injured myself on the window frame, but I didn't care. I knelt down by the side of the bed as if I were praying and I touched her. I touched her for a long, agonizing while, Eri, yet still I didn't dare to graze her where it burned ... to uncover her, and, when I did ... I don't think I'll ever make another discovery like that in my life.

"She smelled of mandrake. Do you know what mandrake smells like? ... You can smell it if you bite into one.

"Her body was the root of a mandrake, offering itself, and I was a child, Eri, I'd only just begun to grow hairs like a marvel, and something else was growing even more—am I waxing lyrical? I wouldn't want to come across like you when you write—I remember that, as I slid through the window, I thought of how, on the other side, beneath the window, evil breathed—as Father Hortensio Berrío used to say: the evil with a woman's face that was calling to me; it wasn't my fault, it was the fault of the evil in women's flesh that was calling to me; she was sleeping, Eri, surely an exhausted twelve-year-old, exhausted from suffering and having to run around the house all day, serving us. But, in spite of her heavy sleep, she was calling to me, screaming, her hands and legs, her nostrils, her ears, every part of her was calling to me as though with gnashing teeth, her seven orifices. I undressed, slipped like a reptile into her bed. The tranquility of her sleep, Eri, frightened me. I smelled the hair from her head on the pillow, the warm scent of her mandrake body as if suffused into the sheets. The moonlight poured in through the window and illuminated her entirely, caused her scent to intoxicate me with whiteness, the color white; that's what I felt, the color of her scent in my nostrils, and yet the same old anxiety held me back, I suffered like a saint, I was a monk who falls into sin, no different from you and those other imbeciles from school ... At last ... my hand went straight to her loins, which trembled, jumped, spoke, gave their opinion, and, nevertheless, she slept, in spite of her simmering abyss, her frothing open mouth. I threw myself on top of her, Eri, I could see nothing but a streak, a black cave that she summoned me to enter as soon as possible, that other door, and not a whimper, Eri, not a syllable ... even my first thrust failed to wake her, or else she was pretending to sleep.

"I discovered, like all little boys, what I was missing and what she possessed, that pit in which one wants to bury oneself never to return; I entered and lashed my seed within her guts, as if I were burying myself, and I came out of her as though emerging from the earth, collapsing by her side, a dead man revived.

"I impregnated her and she allowed herself to be impregnated, despite being a child, as often happens.

"And she never made a sound.

"I said nothing either.

"When it became apparent…

"Mamá and papá made her disappear.

"It was only the one time, and I got her pregnant, Eri, I enchanted her.

"I never found out if she had the child or not; I've asked her, but she won't talk.

"If she did have that child, she did so a million light-years ago.

"After that, I didn't miss her, I forgot about her the very next day.

"I'd already discovered my reason for being, what I was born for, why I'm alive.

"I wouldn't come across her again until years later, Eri, more than ten years, nearly fifteen, if you take into account that we're approaching thirty.

"It was exactly a year ago, at a national crafts fair; she was selling ancestral instruments, ha. We somehow recognized each other. She instantly sprang back, wanted to run, but I already had her by the eyes, you understand. I said I wanted to buy an ocarina; I said I wanted to take an ocarina away with me; I said she was that ocarina; there was no one around, none of her companions was watching. I grabbed her by the hand and she allowed me to grab her, I abducted her and she allowed herself to be abducted, as though she'd been waiting for me all those years; she allowed herself to be led in silence, allowing me to bare her mandrake over and over again, and now she's my wife, Eri, I've been happy for a whole year, the only woman I've been good for; isn't that an unbeatable story, isn't it more tragic than *María*…?

Ciruelo and I contemplated her: she wasn't even looking at us: she was far away, very far away from us.

Then we heard a callous little snigger from the poets' corner, a witty barb emerging from the ice. None of them had managed to listen in on our conversation, but they should never have laughed.

6

Pummeling Poets

AFTER A CERTAIN HOUR, THE COFFEE WOULD TURN INTO aguardiente. The poets were already raising their glasses; they had wished to listen in on us, been unable to, and then one of them had chanced it with that little laugh.

"Enjoy this," Ciruelo told me, "I'm about to show you how they run like rabbits."

Why hadn't Ciruelo been sitting with the poets? I'd heard something in God's Laughter about him hanging around with poets, a kind of patron—had he distanced himself from them? Ridicule? Resentment? This time he did raise his voice, enough to be heard by those he wanted to hear, who strained their ears:

"That one with the feeble little laugh," he began, inspired, "that cyclops with one glassy eye, his head bald like a cracked egg, his neck like a bird's scruff, his nose a pear, he's missing a hand but uses a hook, wearing thick-soled shoes to appear taller, brandishing a cadaverous page in his only hand, he claims to have been a sailor, and this is true, a shark did a real number on him: for his face alone, he is already immortal and need not write a single word, but nobody cares about his face, there have been greats who were ugly but beautiful, like Aesop the fabulist, who, thanks to destiny, was a slave, a useless worker, potbellied, fat-headed, flat-nosed, stuttering, sickly, splayfooted, short-armed, cockeyed, mustachioed, a living ruin, and yet he was Aesop: his spirit elevated him. This ruin, on the other hand, is not just ruinous, he is the essence of ruin, possessing no spirit: he is slight of body, slight of soul, slight even of a self, mediocre in all the arts—though he has stuck his snout in each and rooted about—he passes for an intellectual, a critic, deciding who in this country is a poet, and the country accepts him, the country needs him, because this phony is identical to this country, he is base, he is envious.

"There, by his side, breathes a monster: he is vile, but has convinced the lowly critic he's a laudable poet, and the critic, in turn, has convinced the country of the same, the pair offering reciprocal validation, and yet they cannot save themselves, their rancor poisons them more and more against anyone who dares bring a pure poem into their circle.

"And that other one, with the face of a small devil, the first name in any national anthology that gets published—he is academic, hierarchical, and hermetic; his children and his children's children are like him, poetiliacs. He writes prologues left, right, and center, composes them for books by poets aged nine or ninety, pens them by the thousands, and his only demand: that they venerate him and agree to one of two payments: thirty gold coins or a fresh, young poetic pussy, tight and wet, virgin ass and all.

"The one farther back, with the lazy eye, inherited a farm from his hardworking grandparents and extends an invitation to spend the night and ride horses and ride damsels to every cultural administrator in existence, to translators from other countries, to publishers, to powerful critics, scholars, cultured journalists: inside such bellies does he squander his farm, and even so his work fails to progress, it reeks even more, it's shit of the purest variety.

"It's easy to make out the balloon head playing the role of the haiku poet: he has three poems; one inspired morning he wrote: *A new morn falls through Norma's dormer.* Would it not have been better for both Norma and the morn to fall *out of* this window? And the biggest heavyweight is frightening; in his lifeless pupils floats fatigue, all of the tedium, all of the horror he stores away in his rolls of fat, and what rolls of fat—he could accommodate two hundred Shakespeares, and yet he is not worth a single letter, a heavyweight but slight of invention, freely translating every universal genius in existence: he adds to their work, takes away, and is also the owner and director of a literary journal that sells and is therefore eternal, but neither he nor any of those louses accompanying him ever look beyond the ends of their own cocks.

"The youngest of the sucklings, the little calves, those brats with attractive peach fuzz, are cannon fodder for the famous fuckers who pass them around: if you allow your skull to be perforated by an immortal you will become an immortal by force, yet who is ever really immortalized? … And among all the rods, there's a sole vulva: what a face, pale by virtue of cosmetics, what a Mona Lisa smile, what a life story: the scorn suffered as a girl, forty years of enforced virginity, yet one day she chose to lean back against a post, raise her leg, and reveal the hairy crater, crying I'm a whore, this is what she writes during the foggy nights of her absolute solitude, adding insatiably that there is only one path: poetry; if I don't find poetry I'll kill myself, she cries, and that's the way it goes, you search for what you don't have; but that other one over there, with the goatee, is the garlanded one, the pinnacle, the top dog, the one and only; he's nothing but a conniving politician who has spent two hundred years publishing one sumptuous poem in alexandrines, a single poem as long as the tail of a mythical lizard, at times epic, at times lyrical, at times an ode, in quatrains or quintains, in octets, in dizains, with consonant and assonant rhymes, in oxytone and paroxytone verse, in stanzas now emphatic, now heroic, now melodic, rhythms that are iambic and trochaic and dactylic, anapestic, amphibrachic, in celebrated couplets: *A couplet have I wrought / without a moment's thought*, in linked tercets or assonated quartets, in seguidillas and redondillas, now pavanes, now sonnets, now monorhymes, and in free verse, a breathless poem stretching as long as a human intestine and dedicated to the blackest phony, the hero of the gang, the bronze statue before which he declaims, going on to declaim before other political chiefs, other sanctified thieves, telling all with his affected tongue that they are the paradigm of God's anus.

"That's what these guys are.

"A pack of celestial sons of bitches."

Now we were the ones laughing.

From where had he drawn all this hendecasyllabic information, I puzzled, all this semantic noise? Ciruelo uttered his insults, and his voice resounded like a fateful echo. La Oscurana occasionally stretched her slender hand down to her ankle and—it seemed to me—caressed it; then she brought that same hand up to the back of her neck and grazed the tiny hairs, tugged gently at her braids—was she sighing? Her toes, inside her cloth sandals painted with birds, curled up, then stretched out, and curled up again, her breast heaved, but I was unable to take my eyes off her distant face, her distant expression, her distant eyes. Where did her memory exist, where was it stranded, upon what beach? She made the ghost of a sound, though not with her mouth, a most delicate sigh through her nostrils that said "enough" without uttering the word, a sigh to which Ciruelo responded with a rueful smile: "My Oscurana is fit to burst"; and then, in his bristly voice, he said: "We're leaving, numbskulls, but not without first establishing order," and he sprang to his feet. "What are these shits laughing at," he said, and he grabbed his chair and brandished it like a weapon over everybody's heads.

"Okay, Toño," I said, "your arguments were going over well, so what's all this about?"

"It's enjoyable," he said.

"What have these people done to you? Poets or not, they're our friends, people who live for poetry and sometimes even live off it, and this exempts them from being barbarians or politicians, we should be fawning over them really, and they read, at least they read, Toño, if only their own names and poems in the newspapers, and what does it matter if they write in iambic trimeter? They aren't running around firing off shots in the mountains, they don't saw up children, chop off heads, disembowel the pregnant, they're good people, and occasionally they even succeed with one of their little verses and demonstrate God's madness, Toño, leave them be."

"It's enjoyable," he said.

"What are you talking about, you pair of faggots," ventured one of the calves.

"Let's consider," I said, "in their favor, that while it's possible for there to be good or bad novelists, there cannot be good or bad poets. Poets either are poets or they aren't, which is why we should feel sympathy for these guys."

"It's enjoyable," repeated Toño, and hurled the chair at the head of the top dog, who ducked, thank God. The chair smashed against the wall.

And they fled. The hog and the calves fled like rabbits. And why not, I said in that instant to all of them, to Ciruelo, to the poets, so as to appease them, if poets, I said, illuminated, are intrinsically cowardly, as history has shown us, then this surely owes to the fact that they appreciate the sweet honey of life in its purity, that they value the true magnitude of a young girl's kiss, a sunset, a dancer's ass, or tit, they aren't your average Joes, they're perfectly aware of the absurdity of the bludgeon or the spear, of bullets and bombs, whether homemade or atomic, of the hordes of heroes and gods who harm the only beautiful thing in this world, life itself, that every-morning orgasm, that light, that loving voice. Yet it appeared they had all stopped listening to me, or preferred not to hear: the poets were beating a disorderly retreat, all soulless, scattered, squealing like pigs, such was Toño Ciruelo's fame as a butcher; and still I persisted: What's going on, Ciruelo, leave them be, they're like us, they live for the spirit; I said this and a heavy blow to the back of my head left me seeing black and then little stars; I struggled to remain upright; my attacker was a despicable parasite—for there are better parasites—and, what baseness, he'd treacherously crashed his chair over my corpus vivendi. Annihilate them, I cried. They're scum who attack from behind! And still I had the strength to laugh, before keeling over noisily like the Trojan Hector at La Oscurana's feet; the entire world shook, centuries of silence followed my words: it was as if I'd invoked the Golem, as if I'd created a stone colossus; I noticed that the café owner himself, along with one of the waiters, was making a weak attempt to halt Ciruelo; better not to try: they were discharged with a hook and an uppercut; the poet with the Mona Lisa smile was screaming "Police!"; the one with the egg-shaped head toppled over backwards, waving his arms and legs around like a desperate tortoise; another wearing glasses called absurdly for the immediate presence of the President of the Republic—another poet—and I heard someone say "Crazy again," and, as if to corroborate this, the madman then hurled another chair toward the poetic monument that was the hog, who hadn't yet slipped away; I cheered this: that whale was nothing but diarrhea posing as a werewolf, just a pile of words; the projectile chair landed on his back but rebounded tamely off his rolls of fat; no way, it hadn't killed him, but nevertheless, my resolve fractured on hearing the pain of the poets: they were collapsing, kneeling, dragging themselves as best they could; I was horrified.

"Well?" I yelled. "These conflicts aren't for me, Ciruelo, at least let them live."

I struggled to my feet. Now I recalled the fight against the paralytics.

"Who knows," I shouted, "whether lying here shattered there isn't a legitimate poet, who knows whether fleeing desperately there isn't a future Nobel laureate!"

And it was neither a cripple nor a poet, but a devious rascal who chucked a bottle at me, and now it was I who was forced to bow in sudden reverence so as to avoid losing my senses; the youngest were retaliating, but Ciruelo took care of everything, apportioning sprightly kicks to their rosy backsides: "This is Homeric," he cried; I was a front-row spectator, becoming aware once again of the dark face of La Oscurana, angular, a sleeping panther; at no point had she been affected. Was this hand-to-hand scuffle, this battle, a familiar sight to her already? Yet, as I watched, her face hardened for a second; then it relaxed, and it even appeared she might be able to see the humorous or pathetic or poetic side to the celebrated hog's hasty retreat: she smiled as though commiserating.

And we fled Park Way.

By taxi.

"Let's go to my house, Eri. We'll celebrate our reunion." It was the voice of the magician, the miracle worker.

But I was searching for a reason to escape: No, never again, I thought.

Ciruelo was riding up front, next to the driver, the only seat where he could half stretch his frame; I was in the back, with La Oscurana; she, behaving as if I didn't exist, and I, doing the same, as if I didn't exist. It had been ages since I'd ridden in a taxi; ever on foot, just like that song about the *zapatos rotos*.

"How do you get by, Ciruelo," I asked suddenly. "Your inheritance, or did you win the lottery?"

"How much do you need?" he anticipated.

Worse than a whore, I told him the loathsome sum and said: "I'll pay you back one day."

Ciruelo laughed openly: "You'll kill yourself first."

And he extended a wad of burning bills, placed it in my hand, and I tucked the wad into my breast pocket, worse than a poet.

7

Egipto

HE DIDN'T LIVE IN BOMBAY, AS HE'D TOLD THE RUSSIANS, BUT in Egipto, a Bogotá neighborhood famous for its church: during Holy Week, the pious would often crucify themselves, nails and all, just as Christ had allowed himself to be sacrificed.

Halfway down a backstreet, a stone's throw from the Church of Our Lady of Egypt, Toño Ciruelo possessed nothing more, nothing less, than a little house on solid ground. Did he own it? Ah, an oasis; not an apartment, which is like living caged in the air, but rather a little chocolate fairy-tale house, with its inner courtyard, a mountain papaya tree, a stone laundry tub, and, around this, six cold damp rooms, each with its own ghost, ghosts from three hundred years ago; I hear them talking, said Ciruelo, they're a gang of Spanish ex-convicts who made their good life here at the expense of the Indians: today they pay penance, blessed butchers.

We entered the house and La Oscurana vanished.

The light was weak, as if from a candle; I was leaning back in a chair like an embrace, we had smoked marijuana from a clay pipe, with no effects: I was stunned; don't you have any music? I wanted to ask. Do you want Brahms? guessed Ciruelo, let's go to my study, Eri, I have to read you something of mine, to see what you think, and we entered another room; there, I did in fact hear the ghostly voices, the gruff voices of the Spanish ex-convicts, I heard them laugh gigantically and then vanish with the unleashing of a Brahms that resounded Hungarianly everywhere. We reclined like emperors on a floor of cushions; books adorned the walls; we lit cigarettes; in a corner there was a table with a burning candle and an open notebook, we were going to speak—yet, emerging from the shadow, as if becoming illuminated in sections—first an advancing thigh, then a knee, hips beneath a tunic, a glistening cheek, jet-black eyes in the blackness, light feet in painted sandals—La Oscurana appeared; she was carrying a tray with three gourd bowls, and she placed this tray on the table, took one of the bowls, walked toward me as if along a tightrope over the very top of an abyss, handed it to me silently, gave the other to Ciruelo, cupped the third with both hands, and began to sip, still standing, without waiting for us; we heard her drink, watched her like a hallucination; she drank all of it, licked her lips, and vanished again.

Then we raised our bowls to each other.

The bowl was brimming with some inexplicable drink.

It tastes to me of glory, said Ciruelo, of that Glory whose entire body is like fire, of her sex like a bat's wings that you lick absurdly as though you'd been bewitched since before birth, within the fibers of your memory.

I laughed, stupefied, and looked at him—what drink was this?—but maybe Ciruelo didn't exist; for the first time the giant was not master of his own ears. Eri, he said, I love you. And, I'm going to read to you, hold on, and with that he fell asleep—right there, right where he lay between the cushions, as soundly as stone.

Impossible to believe it. Was he pretending to sleep? I shook him by the shoulders, nothing; he even had his mouth open.

And, like that, the seconds, minutes, hours passed.

I searched the house. What was I seeking?

Who?

There she was, behind a half-closed door, through a backlit veil, very far away, lying on her side in an enormous bed, turned toward me on one elbow; her eyes watched me, this time unblinkingly. I assumed she was probably naked beneath the shadows, I assumed she was waiting for me. So this is her world, I thought.

"You put Ciruelo to sleep, didn't you?" I asked.

She didn't answer.

"Why won't you talk?"

She didn't answer.

"Who are you?"

Nothing.

"What's your name?"

Nothing.

"It's better not to speak, is that it?"

She didn't speak.

"But it's also worse," I said.

Did she smile? It was like a shadow across her lips. Across the lips I had wished to bite, to suck, that morning. But they were lips of stone.

I looked up at the ceiling: large spiderwebs hung everywhere.

"Did Toño put you up to this?"

She didn't speak.

Was it fear? Was it her fear? Or was the fear mine?

"I swear you'll say something to me, sooner or later."

I took a step, pushed the door.

She stayed there. Waiting for me.

Yet, behind the steady gaze, behind those shining eyes, there was only emptiness. A white emptiness. As after staring at the sun: blind.

I turned around.

At the center of the freezing courtyard, surrounded by the old rooms with open doors, I pressed my hands together as if praying and looked up: not a single star. Far away, behind a door, I saw the large shadow of Toño, defeated, and, behind the next door, that other shadow among shadows, petrified, her eyes were still there, unblinking.

I left Toño Ciruelo's home.

And twenty years would have to pass, his twenty invisible years, before I would see him again, here, in my home, sleeping identically, like a stone. Dead?

8

The Teeth

DEAD.

Toño Ciruelo was dead.

"I won't be dying today," he'd said upon waking, as I came over to say good morning, and he'd said this with genuine astonishment: "I'm no longer dying, Eri. Get me a cup of coffee and I'll be off." Seated, the ruana over his knees, he wasn't sweating or trembling, and his inquisitive eyes prowled each corner of the apartment as if discovering it for the first time. I saw he'd recovered his Arhuaca bag; he had it slung over his shoulder, ready to leave at any moment, impatient, happy.

"I don't imagine they'll carry on searching for me at this point, Eri. They'll think I've run off to Calcutta, just like in that song about the Pinzón brothers from school, you remember?"

> *The brothers Pinzón*
> *were some Spanish sailors*
> *who sailed with Columbus*
> *a grand old buccaneer*
> *and they set sail for Calcutta*
> *in search of distant whores.*

But he ceased his humming and grasped my arm, urgently:

"And if I do die, Eri, it's easy: you just return my corpse to the street at midnight, shut the door, and go to sleep, you'll see how nobody comes asking for me, nobody wants to hear about a dead man ever again."

He let go of my arm and then immediately grabbed hold of me again:

"In any case, be careful. Don't betray any connection to me. Leave me in the street without anyone noticing: I'm not thinking of the police so much as the nuns … and the others; don't let the others or the nuns find out, Eri, don't let them discover I died in your building, because they'll snuff you out, just like that; they'll think you're my successor, and you will be, without doubt, you are the potential executor of my memoirs, of my posthumous depravity, but enough, Eri, don't pull that face, nobody's going to die, this is just in case, relax."

And he released my arm. Suddenly, he waved both hands as if he were swatting flies.

"It's true that my life was a tomb," he said, "but I won't demand you write my epitaph: *Here lies another.*"

And he began to laugh exaggeratedly. Again, I became distracted, dazed, watching that hand on which the absent index finger glared. How had he lost it? I would never dare ask him; I thought that it appeared to have been severed by a bite.

Then Ciruelo asked if I had any music. He requested I put on the Revolutionary Étude, by Chopin. I owned that Étude, but had sold my record player a year earlier.

"You always screw up, Eri, you never have what's required, how is it you haven't killed yourself already? If I'm going to die, I'd like to do so in the arms of Chopin, in the arms of that tenebrous Étude. What revolution? It's pure death, the consumptive was dying, and voilà, but if we can't listen to it that means I won't be dying, period."

Yes. That morning, I too had believed Toño Ciruelo wasn't going to die—in spite of his curious recommendation in case of death. He stuck out both his arms, flapped them, stretched, even dared to smoke a cigarette with his coffee.

"Eri, it's incredible: I feel hungry."

I told him there was rice with chicken in the fridge.

"I'd have to clean my teeth, and then stick them back in."

And he took out his teeth, tops and bottoms, two rosy sets of dentures that he slammed down on the side table. He sat staring at me, unblinking, and then opened his mouth—that enormous piehole like a dark pit, even more toothless during his horrible burst of laughter. The only real teeth that had survived were two long, yellow canines, like those of a movie vampire.

"See?" he yelled. "You see how they forced me into decrepitude? I'll tell you right now. Right now, I'll reveal where you can find those who did this to me."

He waved the dentures furiously before my eyes, like a terrifying trophy. I couldn't understand, was he still hallucinating?

"Do you want me to tell you where to find them?"

"Who?"

"The dentists."

"Where?" I asked reluctantly.

"At my house," he said. "Under the stone laundry tub."

And again, he unleashed his laughter in my face. I felt ashamed of him, of the universe, I became terrified: I wish you'd explode, I thought, I wish you'd vanish from my life forever.

But he wasn't hallucinating and launched like a train into his tale.

"They were two trainee orthodontists," he said, "two gorgeous young tooth-yankers, with tight little asses and pink tongues; the taller one was living proof of the saying: *hair on the lip, juicy clit*; the other one cried out for help but also cried out, more, more, I want more, ha, it's a long story, Eri, and I'm ashamed to confess the defenseless position I found myself in: I lay in a dirty bed in a run-down hospital, I'd suffered an accident and was left in their hands, those four rosy hands armed with instruments resembling drills and pliers, torture devices.

"My front teeth and molars must have decayed years ago, dedicated as I was to the chewing of hallucinogens; my gums were loose and rotten, I knew that, aware of my disintegration, but it wasn't that big a deal, Eri, there must have been a solution, a treatment, to save most of the pieces, or put in those implants, pins, screws, what do I know—but I had an accident and the adolescent dentists pruned me, harvested me, ter-mi-na-ted me.

"I'd been run over by a Volkswagen full of nuns. There were four nuns, all sitting there chatting with God at sixty miles per hour, and they plowed into me; they were those very same nuns who would become my future friends, my confidantes, my consolers, my poisoning girlfriends. Accustomed to carrying saints, they carried my unconscious body to a miraculously nearby hospital, dropping me more than once according to the hospital guard: "Those nuns probably bashed your head in worse than the Volkswagen," he said. The doctors operated on me in six different places, including my crushed testicles; they removed my heart and put it back, they sent me to sleep, and that's precisely when the tooth-yankers appeared: they wanted to practice on a little lab rat, me, so they could graduate with honors. Little friends of the doctors; little voices; a little perfume; a little caution; little whores. They had their way with me, as they do with any vagrant in this country, from removing the eyes to the kidneys or liver; with me, it was my teeth they swiped, they stripped me of my chompers, except for these two canines, who knows why."

And he continued by showing me his grotesque canines.

"It's a long story, Eri; but the fact is, there they are, in my house, chatting away beneath the stone laundry tub. They are resting to one side of La Oscurana: those three keep each other company nine feet underground, perfect fertilizer for the courtyard, next to the papaya tree."

"So you're still living in Egipto, Toño," was all I could think to say, dumbfounded.

"Right there, Eri. You've got a good memory. Thank God no one knows where I live, except for you, the chosen one."

Ah, that bristly, perfidious, and yet melancholy voice, recalling its crimes! Not for nothing would he die a few hours later, and we would never know whether it was from poison or heart failure or just because.

Toño Ciruelo, dead.

Impossible not to recognize the change, that inevitable station arrived at by someone who has just died: his face was no longer his face, yet it was; or else it was something neutral, a solemn stain that bore no relation to the person who had animated it, but which murkily, remotely, called him to mind. Grief for Ciruelo? Never. Only fear, that same vague and permanent fear he'd inspired in me since I first met him, and sympathy: lying there now, so sober, so modest, so austere, *him*. Such toppled strength. And a sort of cold silence, outside, inside, made me die like he had: it was his rigid body, beside me, transferring its coldness. In the long run, Ciruelo had determined what was most substantial in my life: death. Having known the maker of deaths since childhood made him more than a friend, it made him death in the flesh and blood, dazzling light and all; one by one, I recalled his final words, in a red swirl, and my mind stumbled over his face, here and there, laughing or reviling the world, and, though I could hear his cavernous voice, the surrounding silence was cold, I felt I *had* silence, that I was the cold silence, the cold silence in every object, in my bones, the cold silence in my liver and in my heart, I felt that I too had died.

The entire evening darkened. Absurdly, I thought about the Friday afternoon of Jesus's crucifixion, which Ciruelo had so often satirized: *They gave him urine to drink*, he would say ebulliently, while urinating next to churches on nights dulled by alcohol.

And night fell. Since Toño's death, time had become extraordinary in its disconnectedness. I consulted the calendar: he'd died on a Sunday evening, January third—no Friday crucifixion for Toño—and he'd died in my home, died by my side; a nice mess you've left me with, I said to his inanimate body, now they'll say I killed you.

I won't be dying today, he'd said that morning, and now, as if to contradict his rigid corpse, he was repeating it: I won't be dying today. And that morning, he'd asked me for a bowl of water, in which he had washed his dentures and cleaned them with his nails, shamelessly; they were genuinely filthy, with scraps of food fossilized in the gaps between the teeth—like clumps of sand; scraps, I believed, of flesh and bone; then he daubed the back of the dentures with a bluish paste he took from his trousers and stuck them in, jubilant; he appeared to grow twenty years younger; his voice changed; this time the guffaw was natural, not that of a mummy; he ate the frozen rice with chicken, refusing to have it warmed up: he swallowed it down true to his own style, in three bites; it was my rice with chicken for the entire week, yet it disappeared in seconds, and he even scraped the bottom of the bowl with the spoon, a spoon he then licked with an obscene gesture.

He asked for more coffee and then repeated like a joke the business about the two brutish beasts, who, he said, had stripped him clean of his chompers, without any warning, they demolished me, Eri, they deboned me, despoiled me, deveined me, and fashioned me these false teeth I was only able to use after a year of torment: I thought I'd never be able to eat again, except for compotes and pap like a baby, or chicken broth, until I dissolved and disappeared, I couldn't forgive them, Eri, I shouldn't, how could I forgive those monster dentists, even more monstrous than me? I tailed them, invited them to a tearoom—by way of humble thanks—I flattered them, I begged for their sympathy, and they felt sorry for me, Eri, became my friends, my lovers, I beguiled them, and then it was too late for them: you can now visit them in Egipto, if you like, and if not then don't go, it's your loss.

He asked again for coffee, and then, in spite of the strong coffee, his voice and spirits began to flag: he accepted that he should leave my home that night.

"As a precaution," he said, "though I know all too well they'll continue searching for me day and night, the others and the nuns, because they're frightening too, Eri.

"One of them, Reverend Mother Consuelo Kopp de Brigard, of the most distinguished Bogotá lineage, and for that reason the convent's superior, writhes around in bed like a perfect whore, and, just like any whore, she's cruel and vindictive; nevertheless, she assisted me during the difficult days; I helped her to sate her most exalted instincts: she had the body and face of the Madonna, she was the only beauty at the novitiate, so mystical she was all flesh, and I so carnal I was all mysticism; and what nuns: at the very end they poisoned me, not as a form of justice, but because I stopped offering them my merchandise. Jesus! I was screwing sixteen nuns a day in the audacious medieval fashion: I would disguise myself as a gardener, and what flowers I watered, more like thistles; one of them, the first time I tore open her blouse, had a pair . . . like fried eggs: she was a dwarf with the face of a Pekinese but you should have heard her howl, the biting, the kicking, as if she were doing it for a thousand saints; another one was plump and rosy, the best cook among them, not in the kitchen but in the sack, one slip and she'd devour your little sausage raw; one was missing a cheek, but got along fine with just the other three; this one had a single tit, that one had a missing eye, another was lame, noseless, and still another was bald and stark raving mad: she'd been driving the Volkswagen that ran me over; another was a sleepwalker, another immortal, the renowned and celebrated Old Nun: she confessed to me that she loathed Sister Consuelo Kopp de Brigard and had dreamed of bringing judgment down upon her with blows of a crucifix, asking jokingly whether it wouldn't be even better to use the point of a knife; she subtly let slip she knew a place where a chest filled with golden chalices was hidden, and it sounded like an assignment, Eri, but I'm no one's hit man.

"That Old Nun suffered from the torment of envy—which is the same as saying unsatisfied vengeance. I learned that years before (this revealed to me by one of the novices I slept with), Father Jacques Hérault, a missionary accustomed to the feminine amusements of the cloisters, had a tryst with the ravishing Madonna de Brigard while passing through Bogotá, and that the Old Nun, overpowered by an absurd love (the innocent reverend had simply complimented the anisette cookies she'd prepared for him, calling them confections from the hands of a saint), never forgave her young superior after discovering her at midnight adopting a very spiritual position by the altar, the one place no one ever expected to discover anybody, embracing the legs of the crucified Christ, her habit around her neck, as the sweet missionary, whose mere face resembled a French kiss, exorcised her from behind like an amorous sage.

"The Old Nun's thirst for revenge could at least be taken out on the novice who'd told me that story, as I later read about in the newspapers: haven't you heard about the Old Nun who abducted an initiate, took her back to her cell, sliced her up like a puzzle, and kept her in a suitcase under her bunk until she began to smell? A scandalous crime in Bogotá, a city as accustomed to crime as daily bread; the newspapers all echoed each other; and on the television: Would the old woman be judged according to civilian law or the law of God? She was judged by the Pope, God's representative: he turned her into a little sheep and put her out to pasture in a convent in Cundinamarca, that's what they're like, Eri, my nuns—why didn't I watch my back?—all of them sick, resentful, truly ugly; although above all else, Eri, ugliness helps us to imagine, it washes our hands so we can do as we please; hateful but loving, they were an oasis in my life, they hid me while the others searched for me, they tended my wounds, I was the martyr they'd always longed to adore, the leper they dreamed of licking, they combed my long hair and swore they were combing Christ, swearing the same as they dressed me, and especially as they undressed me, why did they conspire against me? Ah, bless them, each one a treacherous Judas."

And, despite drinking a fourth and fifth cup of coffee, Ciruelo told me he felt tired, a strange tiredness, Eri, how strangely tired I feel. And he begged me not to wake him, saying he would have "another siesta," and, sure enough, he threw himself down on the couch to sleep: and how was I to know it would be *that* siesta.

9

A Hundred-Page Notebook

AND THERE I WAS, BESIDE A CORPSE, THE CORPSE OF TOÑO Ciruelo. The corpse of my friend, I repeated to myself—without either the word friend or the word corpse seeming real to me yet. And not a single tear.

It was after midnight already, and I switched off the living-room lights. I followed Toño Ciruelo's instructions to the letter, his terrible instructions, worse than a tragicomedy. I opened the door to my home, stuck my neck out, scanned in all directions: nobody. I dragged his corpse (which wasn't just heavy but burned me) and left it in the middle of the street, and yet I hesitated on recognizing the shoulder bag full of secrets; within, it must contain the hundred-page notebook, the key to his life, the cipher, his twenty invisible years, but I didn't retrieve it, I didn't touch the bag, I left it there, slung across the shoulder of its abominable owner: Never again, Toño Ciruelo! I yelled to myself.

And I leaped back inside my home like a murderer and shut the door in shock: had I been seen dumping the body? I fled to the study, to my bastion-like chair, my desk of books and papers, and an unknown fatigue, which prevented me from thinking, sank my head onto my folded arms, beneath the lamplight. I believe I slept for six or ten minutes that were as deep as centuries, and then woke with a start, as though I'd been slapped on the head; indeed, someone had slapped my head, and I believe—or am certain—I felt the presence of Ciruelo beside me, or interpreted his memory as something physical, his hand with its missing finger summoning my attention in his own way: that cold slap on the head. I'm not sure what I said, what I yelled, but on opening my eyes I could make out, on a corner of the desk, on top of my books and papers, Toño Ciruelo's notebook: it was the first thing I saw.

"So you've left me your notebook," I exclaimed, "your posthumous gift, Ciruelo, your posthumous depravity, as you put it."

It was a gift like a fatal shudder—to read that notebook, to keep it with me forever—I placed my hand on its cold cover, dragged it before my eyes, but was unable to read a single line. And how could I, if I had only recently left your corpse, I thought, delivered you, returned you—as you put it—to the street, to the mercy of the solitude of the dead, that ever-unknown solitude; as though I myself had murdered you, I thought.

It wasn't fear: I was unable to read simply because I was certain that Ciruelo's corpse was still in the street, somber, curled up, outside my closed door. But I didn't peer out to corroborate this. There were some dregs of aguardiente left in the bottle; I drank this down like water, but was unable to master the trembling in my hands. How much time passed? Was it getting light? I tried again to read the first line and could barely make out: *now the story begins.*

I slammed the notebook shut as though I'd just received an electric shock, and lamented having chucked Toño Ciruelo's corpse away like garbage. How could I? What had I become? You were grandstanding when you suggested I do it, Ciruelo, you're a lie on two legs, a delirium, a simulacrum, a utopia. Am I going to cry? Wouldn't it be better to bring it back in here with me, call the "authorities," accept the risks, tell the plain and simple truth: he was a school friend who showed up to die in my home, give him a Christian burial, him, Toño Ciruelo, write his epitaph and let life move on, sing, dance, even if "the others"—his others—would "snuff me out."

I switched off the lamp, was left in the dark: it wasn't getting light.

I went straight over to the living-room window facing the street and, during that brief journey, heard sounds, strange sounds coming from outside, like groaning. I half drew back the curtains: thieves were removing the shoes from Antonio Ciruelo's corpse.

Within moments he became a naked corpse in the night.

They were the shadows of two thieves. I could make them out vaguely under the lamplight, they must have been nearly kids, as young as they were amateurish: they'd only just noticed the shoulder bag and appeared to be arguing over its contents; shadow hands gripped the wallet, tugged at it; I heard Ciruelo's keys fall onto the sidewalk, the keys to his house, three or four of them bound by a heavy copper ring. The sound was like a terrifying signal in the night. As if that reverberating sound had woken Ciruelo, had shaken his slumber, pinched his cadaver, infused him with breath, I sensed his corpse stretch like someone beginning to wake for good. Or was it just my imagination? The mist? The night? The weak light from the streetlamp? Were those simply the reflexive movements, the spasms, the gases, the tremblings of cartilage usually experienced by corpses? No: the corpse raised an arm, a hand scratched its forehead; the hairs stood up on the back of my neck; you're alive, I cried internally, or aloud, and I rebuked him as if he were standing next to me: Did you faint? Catalepsy? Another of your melodramas at my expense? The corpse took a deep breath, its chest throbbed, slowly, broadly; it was astonishing: the thieves still hadn't noticed, they never would; having come to an agreement, they were examining the contents of the wallet beneath the glow of the streetlamp, and had begun sharing the money, but that's when the argument flared up again, there was a struggle, I could hear the insults, motherfucker, do you want this little blade in your guts, faggot? He's alive, he's alive, I wanted to shout to them, wanted to warn those same thieves; too late: like a flash of lightning, Ciruelo's pale-white corpse sprang up between the thieves, calling to mind a ballet dancer. There was no chance of defense: the corpse had them gripped by the throats, hoisted them like dolls, shook them in the air before smashing their heads down on the concrete curb.

There they remained, rigid.

I'd already drawn back the curtains completely: I thought that, in the glow of the streetlamp, from the street, Ciruelo would be able to see my horrified expression; it wouldn't be long before he noticed me peering out, a shocked damsel in her palace. I was unable to move, though I was disposed to run to the door and open it for Ciruelo. I didn't because, petrified, I saw Ciruelo coming over to my window, his keys, wallet, clothes, and shoes under his arm, slowly, inexorably, I saw him inch toward me, a naked corpse before my eyes: would he smash the window? Would he pulverize me? He just smiled, mute, triumphant. Had he pretended to be dead? It was so totally Ciruelo to be more than capable of reducing the palpitation in each of his veins. Had he pretended to be dead to see if I could carry out his astute assignment, returning his body to the street? Had he pretended, just to see if I was that big of a coward? Ciruelo was fully capable of stopping his heartbeat, he had killed so often that he would know just what it was like to die, what it was like to be a stiff. His face on the other side terrified me: he pressed it to the windowpane, squashing his nose against the glass; his mouth, deformed, but continuing to smile mutely; then he withdrew his face and poured his full gaze into my eyes.

It was as if he were waiting for me to apologize.

"When are you going to come visit me, Eri?" the bristly voice asked; I didn't hear it from the street, I heard it coming from hell, and then his eternal laughter, odious, vile: I'm leaving you my notebook, Eri, so you can learn.

And he vanished, naked in the night. The grisly proof of his presence was the two rigid bodies of the thieves outside my apartment.

Then I returned to my desk and switched on the lamp. This time I did feel able to read. And I felt, furthermore, though it shames me to acknowledge it, happiness, jubilation, giddiness, pleasure at Toño Ciruelo's being alive, an absurd pride, a swagger that Toño Ciruelo lived, and would live no matter what at the very end of it all. I felt satisfaction, the bitter vanity that Toño Ciruelo had forced death to flee—to scamper off on its bony heels. What would become of him? Villainous men like him tend to live happily into old age, surrounded by gold and grandchildren, while only the just get sick, suffer, and die.

now the story begins

IT WAS THE FIRST PHRASE OF TOÑO CIRUELO'S NOTEBOOK, ON the first page, and the first I read without reading on. It didn't begin with a capital letter, it didn't really seem like the beginning of a story but rather the continuation, the final strand; and, in the gutter of the notebook, I discovered the remnants of three torn-out pages, just before it: an oddity, then, befitting Toño Ciruelo's notebook, because the notebook's contents were odd, a brief succession of unfinished stories—with nothing to connect them, apart from Ciruelo himself.

Only in the first pages does he appear to strive to offer some sort of coherence, to seek an explanation for himself or a clarification of the causes that have made him who he is. And he does this, it seems to me, with the intention of imitating my style, which he knew very well, yet ridiculing it. Then come those untethered scenes, terse and vulgar, written in his own voice, which must have been composed over intervals of years and which are the greatest oddity, unlinked words that somehow became linked together and ultimately capsized me, causing a rapture that was between disgust and bedazzlement due to that shameful succession of unconnected crimes, who knows whether real or chimerical. And then the final oddity: more than half the notebook, seventy of the hundred pages that comprise it, dissolves into insults. Nothing but insults. In his notebook, Ciruelo launches an exhausting barrage like that of a raging madman who has recently lost his mind, a string of uncontested offenses against everyone and everything, against the world, institutions and governments, races and creeds, against sculptures and paintings, sonatas and symphonies, against the most exalted moments in human history, against its monuments, against even animals and vegetables, against the stones, against planets and satellites, *fucking moon don't shine so brightly!* Insults from which not even I, of course, was spared: *and I hope you get trampled on by fame, Eri, that terrible mother with sour milk, I hope glory shoves its pustulous finger up your asshole until it reaches your heart, you bastard, Eri, and then forgets you.* Hollow and pedestrian insults, one after another; a litany of grievances, offenses, outrages, and blasphemies that, although never repeating themselves, offered a good account of the time he must have spent suffering or laughing while composing them, and which, in addition to confirming his repugnance for humanity, I might dare to claim lay bare his sadness, his exhaustion, his solitude; there would be no point in reproducing them here. Between the first pages and these later ones, months or years may have passed, it was like a diary without rhyme or reason, without dates or locations, without its author even once displaying the slightest interest in himself or his potential reader—should either of them one day read it and wish to discover who he was.

I read the notebook in three days; I didn't leave my home while reading it, and required three days not so much because of its length, but because I often had to turn back, to read over and confirm to myself that what I'd read was true. I didn't know if it was fiction, I wanted to believe that it was: Ciruelo was prone to invention, as he'd demonstrated in episodes of our shared life. It was equally possible that this was a factual testimony, from beginning to end, but I will withhold my opinion; let each reader forge their own; I will leave Toño Ciruelo in your hands and wash mine in the meantime, although I should note that, in the end, I always hoped that what I'd read must simply be another one of Ciruelo's inventions, intended to ridicule the world—or himself.

Or me, why not.

Throughout the text, there were words here and there I found impossible to decipher, and which I have marked with asterisks (***), as well as other isolated ones: solitary headings, in capital letters, like warnings, like calls or cries for attention, without, I believe, it ever having been Ciruelo's intention to provide sub-headings. VILE DISCOURSE, for example. All of those capital letters floated in among a load of very dark drawings of women's faces and sexes, decorated with cartoon eyes and thighs and belly buttons that the editor of this book, as generally happens, refused to reproduce—not so much considering them sinful or depraved, he told me, but rather devoid of quality.

Only when the fragmented stories begin does Ciruelo's style become his own, pared down and dry, with no literary pretensions—which raises him, I feel, to the heights of an indifferent realism, intimate, essential, but always in chaos. Ciruelo almost never pinpoints the location of events; things could be happening here or there. To begin reading the notebook at the end would be the same as in the middle. I kept it with me on the nightstand and would occasionally open it and read, here, there. Why had he included those loose pages and the brief collection of scenes like an appendix? Ciruelo had been right: I learned much from his notebook; among other things, I learned that I had never lived, and that he had; in his own wicked way, he had lived. And while those precarious pages may seem all that can plausibly be recovered, I am still unsure if I am making a mistake revealing them, I am still uncertain if my own recollections aren't just another mistake, and whether, for that very reason, neither of our two presences, Ciruelo's or my own, deserve to see the light of day.

I have made no corrections, additions, or deletions: I have explained already why I omitted the compilation of insults, although, there are further insults on the pages that follow.

Vile Discourse

NOW THE STORY BEGINS, I SAID, MY FACE IN HER FACE, BUT she didn't appreciate the gravity of my words, Eri, my ultimatum-maxim, she simply laughed and said, so begin, I'm trembling with fear; I'd already put my hand around her neck and I burst out laughing like her, and that's how she died, laughing, she was my most refined killing, the perfect one, her face as if frozen in happiness, oh, oh, ha, oh, during that bloody Sunday afternoon, I should have declared that death the killing of the seventh bull: motionless, the matador raised his sword and the bull sank to its knees and died without the point ever touching it, it was magic, the crowds all smiling; she asked: What did the bull die of? and I replied: It was already dead, and on hearing this, a premonition of her own death, she, who didn't suspect that she was already dead, pressed her body even closer to mine, telling me how all that scent-of-blood stuff, all that torero "dressed as if naked" had got her "fired up," she said, and I snuffed her out, Eri, my thirtieth snuffed-out girlfriend, oh, oh, ha, oh, but it wasn't easy achieving such exquisite heights, it was centuries of pain, you knew me already when I began to suffer, and I write "suffering" with barbarous justification, it wasn't easy accepting myself, allowing who I really was to live inside me, and allowing the death of the self who'd struggled to survive; my name is Antonio Ciruelo, I tell my future girlfriends, I am Count Toño de Scythe, kneeling before you, I left the tomb thirty years ago, one April day; I was born in my country, I tell them; if I'd been born in another country, if I'd had other parents, surely I'd be otherwise, but I'm my parents' son, I'm from my country, I cannot be otherwise, I am who I am, a man of my country, of my century, the son of my parents, and I slice them at the neck, they don't even flinch, they look at me as if it were a game, it's how they like it, and they yell swine—as though they truly wanted me to be one. Oh, oh, ha, oh.

The causes? Only the devil and our ancestors know them. I must certainly display a significant reduction in prefrontal gray matter and dysfunctions in my subcortical regions, oh, oh, ha, but I'm a cultural phenomenon, they made me at school. One time, a Doctor Salta used sodium pentothal on me to obtain my confession, and I told him I was the friar who'd been riding the flying cow at the time, there was another holy inquisitor who wanted to *** and another ***, but I would flee, I'd take some little pills to turn myself invisible, the doctors would feel my head and were unable to discover anything abnormal—except for its Greek design. Using the *** Test, they showed that I possessed an uncommon intelligence—a hybrid of an Einstein and a cat—and that I displayed accentuated regressive tendencies, concealment of thought, affect dominated by primary drives, that is to say, a typical epileptic personality, oh, oh, ha, what a *** commotion; they made me do word associations, so I said what I wanted and wanted what I said, a beatific martyr, I had a whale of a time, they discovered I behave the same when presented with any type of word, that I possess an insuperable reptile brain, Eri, an incapacity to form what might be described as intimate relationships through the limbic system—like the bond formed between women and their children—that is to say: the reptile, me, lacks the affect typical of a normal mammal, you; but, they asked me, what does a quadruple-murderer dream about? Oh, oh, ha, oh, I-dream-a-bout-my-ma-má, I'm coming apart; at thirty years old, you're still too young: midway down your path in life, according to the one with the laurel wreath on his head; at this point in my life I finally acknowledged that, though it was possible for me to seduce any woman I desired (I had seduced them since childhood), that was not my pleasure. Neither the approach, the sparring, the flirtation, the sweet kiss on meeting, the briny kiss on parting, nor the common and soporific "act," or the stages of pleasure and disenchantment, the relationship, the everyday stupidity, oh, ha, all of these did absolutely nothing for me.

My path was the abyss.

My pleasure was a taboo: the lethal surprise, the *swift* pain (I am not cruel, I believe), immediate asphyxiation, and witnessing it, oh, playing God, if not giving life then at least giving death, oh, oh, oh, the eyes of the dead women, Eri, their tender hearts, it wasn't easy to give myself free rein, I would crash up against fear; it's true that I'd already had the misadventure with my Oscurana—what a tragedy! The only woman I was ever good for— and it's also true that there'd been other fits of a family nature, which I will refrain from mentioning because they aren't worth the breath, unfortunate mishaps in which I was also the victim of bad luck, but ... now it was different, Eri, this time it was all mine; I considered each step, I was going to do it, and, nevertheless, I became upset. "No," I thought, "it isn't possible for this to happen to me, a paragon of virtue, a product of generations," and then I'd instantly reply to myself, telling myself—like the classic Bandido— that I had more than enough justifications to abhor nature: Who gave nature the right to deprive me of what it has given others? It seems to have gone around gathering all of humanity's flaws and used them to construct me; well then, from now on I will swear a mortal hatred toward it as well, I'll destroy its most beautiful creations, I'll achieve my desires by force, I'll tear up all around me that prevents my becoming master, absolute lord ... and then I could hear the other one inside me, the sarcastic cripple, his prophetic voice rebuking me: For your iron heart and viper's smile, for your deadly schemes, for your hypocritical soul, for your seductive deception and false sensitivity, for the pleasure you find in the pain of others, for your fraternity with Cain, I come to condemn you to be your own hell.

I listened, Eri, to those voices: both excoriated me.

I began to follow, to pursue *** along the avenues, haunting parks and villages, immersing myself in markets and circuses, waiting outside the doors of cinemas, and with each woman I imagined the exact moment when I would snatch her away without anybody seeing, or what I'd say to lead her off, how I'd win her over—which is to say how I'd conquer her. I imagined every step required to have my chosen one follow me, on infinite occasions, surmising, devising, fantasizing over the details, the pros and cons, and one day I stopped imagining and got down to work, but without ever concluding the conquest; I was amiable, I introduced myself, "I don't normally do this," I'd say, "forgive me, I'd just like to be friends." Forgive me—I asked their forgiveness from the start! And they accepted me, Eri, without any need to overpower them, without any assistance from hypnosis. But on reaching the definitive moment—in a park, for example, on a Sunday, my favorite day, when solitary women wait in every direction as if they'd sprouted on street corners—I ... I'd back out, I wasn't able to *make death*, Eri, as I used to say, as I described it, it was as if I were frightened of myself, as if I provoked terror in myself, and I'd flee. They ended up alone, in the distance, intrigued by that well-mannered guy who had suddenly bolted off.

I wasn't fleeing from them, Eri, how pathetic. I was fleeing from myself.

At this very moment, I'm still fleeing as I write. One day, I'll no longer be able to flee, I won't want to. I won't answer to Reason.

I'm dead.

∞

It wasn't days or weeks, but years spent in constant pursuit: that's what I lived for, what I lived off, it was my only air, "practicing crimes" as I would say, because that's what I called "that time"—and I demonstrated to myself that I could win out, that I could emerge unscathed from each of those projects, that for me consummation was impossible; but I suffered on account of that same victory, I sought my own defeat, I wished to do what I wanted, I'd go back and study the details in each and every one of their eventualities, I calculated, inferred, followed the plan, put it into practice, peered into the abyss, the kiss of death, the near scream, and always, in the end, I would flee from myself.

I'd return home, useless, ruined, at the peak of an unspeakable anguish, lie on the bed exhausted, destroyed, and for hours go over every minute detail of the pursuit, every gesture of the chosen one, the color of her hands, her eyes, her outfit, her way of walking, what had she smelled like? I squirmed in the midst of the most absurd pain, wishing to sleep and never wake.

For years I agonized like this, in the most savage solitude.

But there came a day when I was able to cast off the wicked Toño Ciruelo, the false one, the one baptized in church, the one who'd *** in ***, and unearth the authentic Toño Ciruelo struggling to prevail. Yes, finally there came a day when I could leave myself with but a single occupant: Me. Complete.

And I'll tell you how I made my mind up. What helped me— or who.

A murderer, Eri, whom I learned about in the newspapers.

I followed his trail. I did the work of a police officer, me!

I determined the area in which he "worked" based on newspaper reports, vague stories that told of a trickle of missing girls. I was in his thrall. I visited the region where I expected him to be, Him, that monstrosity, that ogre, that leviathan, that bogeyman, an aberration of this country, an error of humanity, a lapse of the soul, a social abortion, that behemoth, that ghoul, that freak, that wolf of a man: none of these terms can describe him, an adequate name has yet to be conceived.

Why was I drawn to him? I imagined, invented, a final hope, how naive; I thought: he'll terrify me so much I'll become terrified of myself, I'll despise him so much I'll despise myself, he'll disgust me so much I'll be disgusted with myself, his very poison will cure me. I promised and repeated to myself that this was the only way to forever elude my purpose, that I would finally put an end to my yearnings to make death for pleasure; those yearnings were annihilating me; I was a skeleton of myself, which is why I set out in search of the ghoul; perhaps seeing him would dissuade me from carrying on, I'd be shamed by the simple fact of finding myself looking for him. I would even do the very thing this country's authorities are unable to do, bring him to justice.

A hero, Eri, me!

I would arrive at each location to find he'd already abandoned it. He left behind his trail of corpses, his invisible cemetery—because, despite being everywhere and murdering, nobody ever saw him, nobody wanted to see him. And I won't claim to be any less a criminal because I've never killed a child, I'm the same, or worse, but that *** never arose in me, may God and the devil absolve me. And his crimes excited me: with enviable chutzpah, he left a small corpse buried in the garden of the police station, in the Fundo district of San Javier. In Palos Verdes, San Fernando, a woman with a coffee cart unmasked him: her missing daughter had been with him last; she herself had seen them talking and she'd done nothing because she was busy serving coffee to three workmen. When she turned to look, her daughter had vanished. He was detained as a suspect, locked up for exactly twenty minutes. After this thorough investigation, they let him go. In this country, justice collaborates with the monsters, and why not? It's in the hands of monsters.

A reality in my favor.

This will be the final night, I wrote in my notebook—tomorrow I'll return home and forget myself forever.

I was surrounded by the desert. I'd noticed a small hut in the middle of a sugarcane field. Night was falling. He had to be inside: Him; there was a full moon, the wind had been blowing hard until then. Suddenly nothing could be heard but my heart. I approached in the shadow of the stalks, just one more shadow. I put my ear to the mud wall, kneeling; in the dead of night I could hear his moaning, it was horrifying, his terrified weeping: it sounded like the weeping of a child ... I discovered a chink in the wall and peered through: the moonlight revealed his shadow huddled over a body, embracing it as though they were both asleep, the sobbing coming as if from a dream, was he crying in his sleep? Was he repentant?

With just one of my hands, I could have crushed him. Yet I didn't. My mentor, my double. His evil impelled me toward my own. I found nothing to hold against him, I couldn't, I wasn't able to, I refused; leaving him, I returned, even more sickly than before. I had merely learned: feel no shame, get rid of ***, let nothing and no one *** ... I'd been with ***. He hadn't looked at me, hadn't needed to speak to me; I'll never forget him, buried away in that hut: he was weeping with sickening joy.

Since then, my notebook has become a record of *** events, Eri, ***, other pursuits.

Oh, to live in a boarding house. Things would be easy. To force myself, transform myself into a social creature, to laugh. What a fine guy. If I dispensed money liberally things would be even easier. I should become a boarder. I would truly slip into the cage with the little birdies. I would start to exist genuinely with myself—so long as I existed alongside my future girlfriends. If I didn't exist with them, I didn't exist. I kill, therefore I am. I shall defeat them in the strangest ways. Nothing sweet. More of a blood-red-crimson-almost-blue-like-the-walls.

And thus, and only thus, will I be able to say—with him, like him—that the total degeneration of my spirit has begun.

That there is no human guilt.

That both abnormality and sin arise from the same soul. That the laws of the soul are so unknown to science, so obscure, so indeterminate and mysterious, that, as yet, there can be neither physicians nor final judges.

That writer from St. Petersburg is right, but he's missing something.

There's always something missing.

This Is Here

THE THREE SICK WOMEN IN THE HOSPITAL TALK ABOUT their stomachs, all night long they have talked about their stomachs, and they cough, perpetually. They are attended by a young nurse, who does everything from cleaning their asses and necks to giving injections and other forms of jabbing; she's a white creature dressed in white and the source of a *** scent that's enough to ***, her blood screams to be sampled, her eyes demand it of me on looking away, timidly, from mine; it's this city's fault, Eri, you breathe in a vaginal air (you'd write feminine, ethereal-womanly, etcetera); why labor, no writer can be Mozart.

She must have discovered my hidden side. She didn't just faint, she wet herself. Me, soaked in her yellow dampness. A short while earlier she'd believed herself a budding girlfriend, she confided her worry that if we made love without protection she could end up pregnant.

He's a manual laborer, I go to his little shack in the mud with roosters, cats, a white sheep—blackened with grime. I select his eldest daughter, a scrawny green-eyed thing. "I'll pay her a good wage," I say, "send her to visit you every month." He hands her over to me, and I receive her.

Now with this dog I feel more alone.

My spirit is invaded by a strange intelligence, foreign.

I go to the maternity hospital. There are dozens of recently pumped mothers; milk and blood are in the air. Consumed by their newborn children, their faces all reflect the same spent happiness. The pregnant women smell mostly of blood and milk, it's something acrid but sweet in your nostrils that makes you sneeze. I take the biggest whore. Her sex a smudge like a moon, a pink abyss at its center.

Two female apprentices discussing their hidden ***, one complained of sleeping too much, the other of not sleeping; you should sleep together, I told them. I grazed one with my fingernails, the other screamed; a delicious chase. Then, both were laid out, naked not so much outside as within.

She had a pink ribbon around her waist, with a gold bow, as though the whole of her were a present. She appeared before me as if rained down from the sky. "Tell *** I say goodbye, I beg you," she said, on being returned to heaven. Back in the village I asked for the person she'd named. No one knew.

Would you like me to mimic Socrates and say: do not forget, Crito, to pay for the maid I devoured in the bakery? But who, you asked, would wander through the fields with a rooster in a basket? Who said that all humans carry, innately, the capacity for crime? Who assured us that there is no crime of which we do not deem ourselves capable?

My "associates," Eri. Listen to their names: Lothario Gómez. El Negro Martín de Porres. Mondongo. Tic-Tac. Anemic. Carmenzo the Dawn Duck. Urn Wall. There was another they called Double-Edge, and Moon Psalm. Also, the Shadow, and Monday Walter. Hook and Sofrito. Pandemic and Saint Paul. Isauro Vega. They were all introduced to me by Ancízar. Two were indigenous-looking: El Candela and Yucabrava. Salchichita was a black man. Nicknames—or names I gave them?—but names before men. A ferocious brotherhood. Triumphant beasts. Together through thick and thin, sharing out gold and corpses. I invented my own prophecies.

I left their light dresses there, very near the bodies, scattered flowers.

"Speak," Socrates instructed me, "so that I may see you." And I heard another bodiless voice that told me: Stop, there's still time. I nipped her beneath the plantain tree. "A last request," she asked me. "The last." Then: "That it not hurt." Just like a wedding night. A sacrament. A marriage vow.

The horses we'd happened upon were sick, coughing, an orangey foam coated their lips; long tears furrowed down from their eyes; they didn't whinny, just mewed like suffering cats. Our girlfriends also cried out in the mist; we struggled to distinguish between them.

Back at the restaurant I could observe him at my leisure: what a horrible face, what a repulsive expression. Was I identical? Was this me?

I give off coldness. The women around me scream and flee without knowing exactly why, they regard me strangely and then flee. In the deepest depths of their viscera, they know I want to devour them.

A beautiful landscape: yellow guayacan trees. Beside their trunks, the unclothed body of the young Australian woman, browning in the sun. She glows, shivers, turns over like a hand beckoning to me. I learned at the hotel that she had come, alone, "to discover the Amazon."

All these guests listen to me, captivated.

When crossing on corners, I noticed that men and women would hold their hands to their noses, stumbling, nauseated by the smell I gave off—swamp flower, rose of hell, but a flower nonetheless; I ran like the wind, and they were never able to catch me.

Another dog: large, black, bloodthirsty. Dangerous dogs seek out dangerous masters. I didn't give him a name, I called him "dog" and he understood. We lasted a year together. I fed him other dogs.

All across this valley the cries of birds ring out, the purring of insects, a crackle in the air. Beneath its heat I possessed a number of them, in my own way—they were plump and ruddy, pious cooks from the convent.

Sing to me, God, for I have given you that grace, and forgive me for I know not what I do.

On the day I die, another will be born.

I spent a good year working as a thanatologist, that is: a makeup artist for corpses. I was also a priest and a music teacher. I taught languages. I sold sweet *obleas*. I was a photographer of my crimes. I cured the sick. I was a thief entering his own home through the roof.

The sugar mill, its smell of hot *panela*; around it, melting bees; it was a Sunday for making death, men and women from the countryside were in a perpetual slumber, drowsy, mindless, simply living themselves to death.

Her mother, after inspecting all the passengers, chose me and sat her by my side, asking that I watch over her.

A clever cross-eyed student. I opened her Edgar Allan Poe book at random and read aloud the sentence that appeared: *Men usually grow base by degrees.*

I created my own happiness during that Festival, when the whole town sneezes en masse. People were left overturned, stiff, naked, my mark on their skin. With my stiletto blade I could pierce a breastplate and perforate a heart, I was immaculate, delicate, my fingers, my teeth, my tongue, my entire body involved.

Time can pass quickly or slowly. It depends on her.

La Pescada, with the profile of a fish, her skin seemingly covered in scales, squirts out children like eggs; she saved me from dying without ever realizing it.

The scent of the intimate flesh of the pair of them.

CITIES WITHOUT HEAVENS

The cockroach was trying to tell me something with its tiny legs, as though asking me to follow. I followed it along the most twisted recesses, through dark and perfidious thoughts to the deepest reaches of my heart.

After dinner in the dining area, full of noisy foreigners, she said she was going to bed. She raised her arms, stretching, parted her knees—which had been pressed together tightly—and stood up with a sigh. I imagined her sex like a throbbing piece of cheese. "I'll walk you to your room," I said. "That's very kind," she replied, "it's awfully late and I'll be safer if I'm with someone." As we crossed the dark grove, she told me all the warnings her embassy had issued in relation to the disappearances. "They frighten me," she said. "It's far worse," I said. "In this country foreigners aren't just kidnapped, they're also roasted, carved up and eaten; they say the meat of a foreigner is far more tender, it tastes better." Her blue eyes opened wide and she said: "You've got a real sense of humor." When she tried to scream, I put my hand over her mouth. Then I threw her over my shoulder and ran. It was that simple.

We sailed around the island. The sea became utterly black, a color I never imagined possible. A gull passing overhead dropped its shit, the greenish splotch landing in the center of her protruding navel. "I'm in for some luck," she laughed, more innocent than the gull that shat on her. I found her sacrum immediately. For an instant, it hurts to play God.

Down below, on the sunny patio, other women sat their prodigious backsides on the wooden benches. I should have killed myself. I slept naked, sprawled on the floor among pieces of flesh for an entire week.

She covered her face with her hands, but didn't stop peering at me through the gaps between her fingers. Her body was trembling in such a manner that she appeared to be clapping with her butt cheeks; it sounded identical to an applause, which I put a stop to with the firmest of smacks; the red shape of my hand appeared swiftly against her pale skin.

I had everyone intrigued by that sound, that peculiar sound in the night. It was me. Below seethed the quagmire. There was scum on the water. Poppies all around. Something like the hooting of an owl could be heard. Surprised at myself, I fell asleep: I didn't make death. I dreamed I was a simple man, lacking vices.

They found her eyes among the guadua shoots.

The nuns assured me they perceived God's design in all this, for they could read, written in red ink on the palm of my hand: *I've been to heaven.*

Gina Regio, a hardened prostitute from Catatumbo, used to tell how she'd met a man with three testicles. Another man had the most perfect pair of pink tits she'd ever seen. The first was called Marinito Santángel, and the second was an indigenous man from La Sierra: Nombre-de-Dios. Gina Regio, experienced, wise, original: she slept with two enormous white dogs. With both, she would say, she'd made the love of loves. For that reason, and that reason alone, I absolved her: she sprang from her bed into the corridor, so quickly that the specters watching over her were unable to hide. Her dogs followed her. Sleep fell over the house.

To sleep with a beloved corpse.

She suffers from joy. She explains to me that mites *swim* in household dust, in grass, tree pollen, in hair from cats and dogs, bird feathers, eggs, milk. In summary, I reply, we're bright-eyed and bushy-tailed mites! She likes being provoked; she crosses her legs, and her modesty, of course, is an act. I confess that I dream in black and white; she says she dreams in color. She snaps at me, throws her phone against the wall: she's so simple, she's complicated. There's an ever-present frown on her face. She spits at me. I pin her down, flushed, buxom, among her flock of mites.

When we come face-to-face in the fray, she kisses me hard, hungrily, with her own kind of love, she kisses me, nothing more, nothing less. Her uncontaminated soul grazes my hair as it rises and disappears.

"So are you going to kill yourself for her?" I told her I asked her suitor, "Do it, kid, go ahead." I said the suitor leaned over the balcony, and all I had to do was lift him by the legs and toss him. She listened, avidly. "It's not true," she said, "it can't be." But she tingled with excitement—with much shame over her pleasure.

FRIGHTS

I too was given power by a god to say how much I suffer.

I saw the blind woman going past; I took her by the arm, without any hesitation. "Thank you," she said, "but there's really no need, I've already crossed the avenue." For the first time, a gorgeous blind woman. I didn't let her go.

We'd built up trust already. He gave me an Antioquian machete—a spare. We were drinking beer in an empty lot when we saw the girl go past, on her way to school. Then he blurted out, in his hoarse, cloying voice, "Damn I'd lay her out and open her up and lick that slit and swallow her." He had his eyes fixed on her as though bathing her in red.

The student stole two small books from my bag, *The Autobiography of Benvenuto Cellini* and a volume by Bernardo Bazin: *Magic Skills and Magic Spells*. He should never have done that.

The little girls were listening to me, attentive. I told them about the mother who'd begun to swell and swell even more until a small boy armed with a pin came along and bang!—he deflated her.

Take therefore no thought for the morrow. (Matt. 6:34)

A year of silence. Only in dreams do I see myself with people. Only in dreams do I speak.

I found the door: *Dance Hall*. As in a henhouse, when the crafty fox attacks and spreads panic among the hens who see him, flapping their wings and raising clouds of dust, until finally one falls between the teeth of the fox, who escapes quickly without releasing that neck, so the diaphanous *** stopped their practice to observe me, dumbstruck: who knows what face I must have been wearing. I put them at ease by saying I was the Academy's new guard and that outside, at the entrance, there was someone asking urgently for Eugenia Ángel: she came forward daintily, without hesitating, her rouged face glistening, a youthful scent, of underarms, her sweaty body barely hidden beneath the tiny costume, and she left the hall, filled with grim forebodings; I followed, at the ready, solicitous, right behind her.

I dug a hole in the ground and buried her there, alive, standing, head poking out, food for the buzzards.

REGRETS

The dead man is still alive, I told them, revealing myself.

I listened to Nancy's testimony: Everyone wants to sleep with me, and why not? I want to sleep with them too, I give it to everyone, I'm fourteen years old—as if years were centuries. I told her that in classical Greece they'd raised statues to the most distinguished whores beside the most valiant warriors, that she'd have been one of those. Really? she asked, someone like me made into a statue? Yes, yes, I told her.

And I wrote on the town's main wall, using a thick brush and red paint: *Nadia Hurtado, you know who I am, I'm here, I'm coming for you.*

I had to put on the stiff's clothes—with great difficulty. They were tight on me.

She was drowning, a hundred feet from me. I swam out to her, grabbed her by the hair, pulled her up onto the riverbank. She dragged herself on her knees, far from the water, as far as she could get. Then she collapsed, facedown. She was heaving up water. Thank you, she said, and coughed some more, desperate, and even more so when she sensed I'd begun to take possession of her body, that I was worse, far worse, than the water.

A slender, fragile *** with long brown hair fell in love with me, pouncing on my mouth and kissing me copiously, as if purifying me. And she even tried to defend herself; she managed to leap to her feet and race off across the llano, barefoot, her muslin gown in tatters; it appeared she was singing, that she would take to the air as she fled, yet she fell back down.

I've seen that doves eat carrion too.

The color of death is not black or red, but a transparent white.

The prisons cannot cope, you would need to make a prison of this entire country.

Loneliness has an unpleasant odor.

I checked their names in the guestbook: Martha Hackman, Julie Ray, James Chandler, Jim Peters, Paul Andrew, Donna Hunter, Claire Small, Kathleen Schama, and Simona Wilson. Laura Gil's little hotel is what we call *pispo*: full of tiny details, small flowers, antiques. Tomorrow, the picturesque group of tourists will visit the "cloud forest." My dog and I will escort them.

I just met with La Negra Clara. She oozes sex from all her pores. Her gaze is steady, peaceful, like that of a cow; her spongy sex throbs, her solitary sex, all alone, her sex that smells of freshly ground coffee; the forested region of her sex; though, come to think of it, isn't her sex something frightful? Then La Negra Clara assures me she's a spirit seer.

After making death I would convince myself I was dreaming. That from one moment to the next I would awaken. That what had taken place was impossible. I was convinced of this, yet I did not wake, and I continue dreaming.

I, putrescent.

Father Anselmo boasts about his parish garden. Acacias and eucalyptus trees surround us; the long green limbs bow down to brush the tops of our heads. They warn him of my presence, yet he fails to notice.

ASCETICISM

We are alone, my mortality and I.

Apocalypse: *Time should be no longer.*

Baltasar Morón, a biblical campesino: he lives with his six daughters.

Would you like me to tell you what it tastes like, Eri? Or would you prefer to one day try it with me? Nobody receives a dinner invitation like this overnight. It tastes of ash, as though you were biting into a clump of earth.

To better understand this country, this phrase from little Sir Fred Hoyle: *Things are the way they are because they were the way they were.* And Juvenal: *No man becomes a villain all at once.*

They called her La Tiempa. I never found out why.

My business is abject. It's what I call Crossing to the Other Side.

I descended to Avernus. A sad chat with my parents. They thanked me for shortening their way. My sister appeared, uninvited. I promised to do the same for myself.

Whistling, I spent that whole day whistling like a laborer who has finished work.

We danced, and I embraced her for a long, long time. Suddenly, clairvoyant, she told me that she felt as if she were being embraced by a bat, that its black, sticky wings were adhering to her back, covering her, asphyxiating her.

La Tiempa appeared again to warn me that the three roughnecks were already waiting for me downstairs. Then you'd better go, I told her, there's going to be a good old ***. She didn't leave, but hid behind the door to see what would happen. She was killed by a stray knife.

She said, absurdly, at the end: *Wake me up when I'm dead.*

Adel Johnson, the veterinarian at her zoo. Expert in orangutans. Owner of a monkey called *Darwin*. She released two great farts at the instant of the blow. *Darwin* watched us in silence.

She was still calling for her mamá when I banished her.

It was years, Eri, of studying deaths; years of enlivening children's parties.

The spurt of her blood in my face, warm. And, nevertheless, the day continues.

There is no longer any silence, nor birds. Only this noise within, this cry of disgust. I carry the smell of all the bodies inside me.

Beneath my face, her kind of feminine growl summoning me.

Three months without talking. I think my voice got lost somewhere. Yesterday I strained to hear my own voice and all that came out was a squawk.

Love for me would be to kill you with my hands.

When I began talking again, my voice was still different, other, as if another had taken control of me. Never again will I hear my own voice.

There's nothing to steal here, he told me. He was sitting in the middle of the living room, hands on his knees; he was old, ninety; he seemed grateful that someone was keeping him company, even if it was a thief. He said he was heating up some coffee, and would I like a cup.

"So what?" I say. "There's a small creature inside of me who only feeds on dead women."

I shouldn't have *** her. It was the excitement; it recalled the best times of her life, for she said, gratefully: "I certainly wasn't expecting this at my age." It was her swan song and her final breath.

I, wretched.

She had a set of small pearly whites, pointy, implacable, which severed my index finger at the root with a single bite, a single yank, her strength arising from horror; I think she must have dislocated her jaw, for I was unable to make her drop my finger, she herself was attempting to open her mouth to spit it out, but couldn't, her jaw stayed locked shut, the disgust reddening her face; she began to choke with my finger lodged in her throat, her own repulsion obstructing her, I assumed she was pleading for help, but I just tended to my wound, using her own kerchief as a bandage; I was astonished by the changing color of her face, from green to purple, then a pale black; she tried to run but only managed a step.

There are animals that display a human condition, hyenas, for example, or those dark scavenger birds, those harbingers, who tend to follow lions in the jungle and take advantage of the remnants of the hunt; others feed off the backs of whales, pecking at them, and still others, like mosquitoes and bats, fasten themselves to the legs of horses and oxen in the night and suck on them while they sleep.

ULULATION

Her blonde head was in my lap. I read her fairy tales. Her mother desired me. Her father watched me nervously. Both ended up offering me their blessing. In the end, I limited myself to burying my nose in what was pink and hairless, a scent like white lilies.

I can't remember what I said to her in passing, me, spiritual, it must have been something endearing: her little vagina definitely felt a jolt on hearing me, for she went bright red like a tomato ready to be cut.

CONDEMNATION

It was a desert of salt, Eri, I was going to die, I fell to my knees, a gust of sand toppled me over. I was saved from this final submission by the voice of a young girl speaking in dialect: a girl with a goat by her side. The girl was dark, the goat white. What was she asking? I don't know. I followed her, on all fours, through the burning desert. She led me to fresh water, to a settlement of happy Indians, who surrounded me. I think I was delirious enough to ask if they planned to make me into stew. They lay me on a bed of wool, under a canopy, and gave me food and drink. I believed I was dying. I heard church bells, how extraordinary. Life returned. I thanked them. I left along the same salt path, well shielded by a hat they'd placed on my head. Far from the village, in a shady nook, I came across them again: the dark girl and the white goat. The girl didn't speak. I plundered her there. I believe we both screamed from fright. There, I was Him, a tormented soul. I was controlled by fate, I too would succumb. The girl went rigid in the sand, her petrified eyes watching me; the goat sniffed her ear—as though whispering something to her. Either I became a martyr or her ghost poisoned me—from one moment to the next my insides began to ache, all my bones began to creak. I don't believe myself old enough for such a tragedy, I'm not even fifty, but it's not just my bones, after that, I suffered from a malignant sleep, a vile sleep that isn't rest but a condemnation from that single ghost, a shameful sleep in which I disgust myself, I rot, and prepare to die, what a horrible experience, what soullessness, what unmelodious music, what sons of bitches,

(And here follow Toño Ciruelo's insults, the seventy pages of insults in his grubby notebook.)

The End

I AM IGNORANT OF THE WHEREABOUTS OF TOÑO CIRUELO.
After reading the manuscript for the first time, I finally went
out into the street: the bodies of the thieves had disappeared.
I asked myself if it had been real—not so much the thieves as
Ciruelo himself, beginning with his arrival in my home, sick or
faking it, claiming to have killed La Oscurana.

His notebook remained by my side for a while. Then I came
to abhor reading it. For years, I kept the notebook out of sight; I
don't know why I didn't destroy it. But I did something similar:
I hid it until I forgot where it was hidden: aversion? Sadness? I
was never able to say for sure.

I traveled frequently, working on my own things. Whenever
a memory of Ciruelo returned unexpectedly in my life, I would
bury it.

The day I moved from my home, one of the movers asked what
he should do with the notebook he'd found in the freezer of the
fridge, under the ice trays—like a piece of rotten meat, I thought.
It had been damaged by the humidity, but was still legible. I read
it. The invincible demon possessed me once again. Then I raced
over to the Egipto neighborhood, in search of Toño Ciruelo, but
I could no longer find his house. In its place, they had put up, or
were putting up, a sinister apartment block—yet another of those
Bogotá buildings that remain perpetually under construction.

New Directions Paperbooks—a partial listing

Siegfried Lenz, The German Lesson
Alexander Lernet-Holenia, Count Luna
Denise Levertov, Selected Poems
Li Po, Selected Poems
Clarice Lispector, The Hour of the Star
  The Passion According to G. H.
Federico García Lorca, Selected Poems*
Nathaniel Mackey, Splay Anthem
Xavier de Maistre, Voyage Around My Room
Stéphane Mallarmé, Selected Poetry and Prose*
Javier Marías, Your Face Tomorrow (3 volumes)
Adam Mars-Jones, Box Hill
Bernadette Mayer, Midwinter Day
Carson McCullers, The Member of the Wedding
Fernando Melchor, Hurricane Season
Thomas Merton, New Seeds of Contemplation
  The Way of Chuang Tzu
Henri Michaux, A Barbarian in Asia
Dunya Mikhail, The Beekeeper
Henry Miller, The Colossus of Maroussi
  Big Sur & the Oranges of Hieronymus Bosch
Yukio Mishima, Confessions of a Mask
  Death in Midsummer
Eugenio Montale, Selected Poems*
Vladimir Nabokov, Laughter in the Dark
  Nikolai Gogol
Pablo Neruda, The Captain's Verses*
  Love Poems*
Charles Olson, Selected Writings
George Oppen, New Collected Poems
Wilfred Owen, Collected Poems
Hiroko Oyamada, The Hole
José Emilio Pacheco, Battles in the Desert
Michael Palmer, Little Elegies for Sister Satan
Nicanor Parra, Antipoems*
Boris Pasternak, Safe Conduct
Octavio Paz, Poems of Octavio Paz
Victor Pelevin, Omon Ra
Georges Perec, Ellis Island
Alejandra Pizarnik
  Extracting the Stone of Madness
Ezra Pound, The Cantos
  New Selected Poems and Translations
Raymond Queneau, Exercises in Style
Qian Zhongshu, Fortress Besieged
Herbert Read, The Green Child
Kenneth Rexroth, Selected Poems
Keith Ridgway, A Shock

Rainer Maria Rilke
  Poems from the Book of Hours
Arthur Rimbaud, Illuminations*
  A Season in Hell and The Drunken Boat*
Evelio Rosero, The Armies
Fran Ross, Oreo
Joseph Roth, The Emperor's Tomb
Raymond Roussel, Locus Solus
Ihara Saikaku, The Life of an Amorous Woman
Nathalie Sarraute, Tropisms
Jean-Paul Sartre, Nausea
Judith Schalansky, An Inventory of Losses
Delmore Schwartz
  In Dreams Begin Responsibilities
W. G. Sebald, The Emigrants
  The Rings of Saturn
Anne Serre, The Governesses
Patti Smith, Woolgathering
Stevie Smith, Best Poems
  Novel on Yellow Paper
Gary Snyder, Turtle Island
Dag Solstad, Professor Andersen's Night
Muriel Spark, The Driver's Seat
Maria Stepanova, In Memory of Memory
Wislawa Szymborska, How to Start Writing
Antonio Tabucchi, Pereira Maintains
Junichiro Tanizaki, The Maids
Yoko Tawada, The Emissary
  Memoirs of a Polar Bear
Dylan Thomas, A Child's Christmas in Wales
  Collected Poems
Tomas Tranströmer, The Great Enigma
Leonid Tsypkin, Summer in Baden-Baden
Tu Fu, Selected Poems
Paul Valéry, Selected Writings
Enrique Vila-Matas, Bartleby & Co.
Elio Vittorini, Conversations in Sicily
Rosmarie Waldrop, The Nick of Time
Robert Walser, The Assistant
  The Tanners
Eliot Weinberger, An Elemental Thing
  The Ghosts of Birds
Nathanael West, The Day of the Locust
  Miss Lonelyhearts
Tennessee Williams, The Glass Menagerie
  A Streetcar Named Desire
William Carlos Williams, Selected Poems
Louis Zukofsky, "A"

*BILINGUAL EDITION

For a complete listing, request a free catalog from New Directions, 80 8th Avenue, New York, NY 10011
or visit us online at ndbooks.com